ALSO BY KATIE RUGGLE

Fish
out of
Water

KATIE RUGGLE

sourcebooks
casablanca

Published by Sourcebooks Casablanca, an imprint of Sourcebooks
P.O. Box 4410, Naperville, Illinois 60567-4410
(630) 961-3900
sourcebooks.com

Cataloging-in-Publication Data is on file with the Library of Congress.

Printed and bound in the United States of America.
VP 10 9 8 7 6 5 4 3 2 1

For all my wonderfully patient readers

ONE

"Welcome to the Yodel Inn," said the stocky middle-age Black man. "Where there are *no dull* moments."

Dahlia tore her gaze away from her phone, blinking at him. She'd futilely hoped for a response from her sister, but only Dahlia's twenty-plus frantic outgoing texts filled the screen, the last of which was undelivered due to no cell service. After a night of no sleep, a delayed morning flight, and *hours* of wandering around the mountains looking for the teeny-tiny town of Howling Falls, she knew she wasn't at her sharpest, but the odd emphasis gave her pause. "I'm sorry. Did I miss a pun?"

He grimaced. "Yodel, no dull? Supposedly it rhymes."

"Oh!" Now she felt bad she hadn't caught it immediately. Normally, she was a huge word-play fan, but it'd been a stressful twentyish or so hours. "It does rhyme—clever!" She tried to make up for her initial lack of enthusiasm, but he still looked mopey.

"I wanted 'Welcome to Yodel Inn, where yo-delight is our delight,' but I was outvoted."

"I do like yours better," she said, finally taking a moment to glance around the small motel office. It looked like a tiny fake log cabin, but it actually *smelled* like freshly cut pine, which made her wonder if it wasn't fake or if they just used a really authentic air freshener. The pun-master and front desk clerk was wearing a red plaid flannel shirt with a name tag proclaiming his name was Bob, and the whole scene made her feel like she'd wandered onto the set of a maple syrup commercial.

"Thank you." Bob looked a little brighter at her approbation. "Do you have a reservation?"

"I don't," she said. "I'm Dahlia Weathersby. My sister, Rose Weathersby, is staying here?" She couldn't help the lift of her voice that turned an optimistic statement into a question. The Yodel Inn and Tavern was the only lodging in Howling Falls, but relief still flooded over her when the man nodded.

"Yes, she checked in early this week. Would you like a room close to hers?"

Although Dahlia would rather make sure her sister was alive and well and then immediately return to her life in California, she knew she'd need to stay at least one night. The sun had been sinking behind the mountains when she'd finally spotted the "Welcome to Howling Falls" sign. Even if her most optimistic dreams came true and she found Rose chilling in her room at the Yodel Inn, Dahlia would still need a place to sleep, and her sister was a horrible bed hog. Pulling out her driver's license and a credit card, she slid them across the counter. "Yes, please. Just tonight for now."

He entered her information, ran her card, and then grabbed

a key marked with a nineteen off a nail on the wall. She noted that the only missing keys were two, six, and seventeen.

"Which room is Rose in?" she asked, even though she figured she could take an educated guess.

He paused. "Didn't she tell you?"

"She's not answering her cell," Dahlia explained, feeling a sickly dip in her stomach saying the words out loud.

"Well, I don't think I should give you that information," he said slowly. "I take our guests' privacy very seriously."

Maybe you shouldn't keep all the room keys behind the desk for anyone to see then? "She sent me an emergency text yesterday, and I haven't heard from her since."

Bob looked alarmed. "Emergency text?"

"Our private code that we only use in emergencies. 'Tell Mom hi.'"

"Tell Mom hi," Bob repeated slowly.

Practically smelling the skepticism radiating off the man, she repeated, "We only use that in drastic situations."

"What if she just wanted you to tell your mom hello?"

"She wouldn't," Dahlia insisted. "It's our secret code."

"Secret code." He was sounding less and less convinced. "Sure she's not just out of cell range somewhere?"

Dahlia knew it *was* highly likely that Rose was fine, just out of cell range or distracted by new people and places. It wouldn't be the first time her sister had forgotten to check in with Dahlia for days or even weeks. The emergency code couldn't be ignored, however. That brief final text was the only reason she was here arguing with flannel-wearing Bob at the Yodel Inn in Howling

Falls, Colorado, instead of doing a million other things at home in California where she belonged.

A wiry white woman who looked to be pushing seventy entered the office and immediately moved behind the desk to join Bob. She was also wearing red plaid flannel, because that seemed to be the town's uniform—or at least the inn's.

"Would you mind calling Rose's room?" Dahlia asked.

Although he narrowed his eyes in suspicion, he did as she asked while the older woman looked on with obvious curiosity. Dahlia was disappointed but not surprised when he hung up with a shake of his head. "No answer."

"Any chance we can take a look in her room? Make sure she's okay?"

His horrified expression told her that the answer was no. There was zero chance he was going to let her into her sister's room. "Absolutely not. Like I said, I take my guests' privacy very seriously."

"Have you seen her today?" she asked.

"I don't keep track of my guests," he said with an offended huff. "That would be a gross invasion of their privacy."

"Rose? That pretty blond girl in Room Seventeen?" The other hotel employee piped up, making Bob groan. "I haven't seen her for a few days. She's probably off exploring the mountains. She looks like a real nature-lover, that one."

"Becky," Bob huffed. "Don't be giving out guest information."

"Did you talk to her?" Dahlia asked, hope surging. "Do you know where she might've gone?"

Becky shook her head. "But I saw her heading over to the

tavern side a few evenings ago, so you'll want to have a chat with the bartender. Oh, and Glenn too. He's always over there, drinking beer and gossiping. Maybe she talked to them."

"Such a breach of ethics," Bob muttered.

"Thank you," Dahlia said to Becky gratefully, ignoring Bob's grumbling. It wasn't much information to go on, but at least it was a lead. *Someone* in this town had to know where Rose was. It was just a matter of finding the person who could lead her to her sister—her healthy, happy, completely unharmed sister. She had to believe that was true, since the alternative was unthinkable.

———

One side of the Yodel Tavern was connected to the motel, and the other shared a wall with a...*taxidermy shop*?

"That's my place," the fiftyish white man at the bar told her proudly, giving her his business card. "Glenn's Taxidermy. I'm Glenn."

"But why next to a bar?" she asked, pocketing his card, even though she wasn't quite sure why she'd ever need taxidermy services. However if she ever *did* need something—or someone—stuffed in a lifelike fashion, now she knew she could call on Glenn. "There doesn't seem to be much potential for crossover business."

"You'd be surprised," the bartender muttered.

Dahlia blinked, tempted to ask, but her squeamishness outweighed her curiosity, and she let the subject drop. "I'm Dahlia."

"Dulce." The bartender nodded as she continued to slice the lemons and limes on her cutting board.

They were the only three people in the bar, probably because it was still early in the evening. Or possibly because the town of Howling Falls was so *tiny* that Glenn and Dulce very likely made up a large percentage of the local population.

"My sister's supposed to be staying here too, but she hasn't responded to any of my texts since yesterday, and she's not in her room." Earlier Dahlia had even peered through the crack between the drapes into Number 17 but hadn't spotted Rose. Now she pulled up a picture of her sister on her phone and showed the other two. "Have you seen her?"

"Sure," Glenn said, and Dulce nodded. "She was in here a few days ago. Tuesday?"

"Must've been Monday," Dulce corrected. "I was off Tuesday."

"What time?" Dahlia asked, her heart giving a hop of excitement.

Glenn tilted his dark head in thought. "Just after four. I had a meeting with my accountant at four thirty, and it was right before that."

"Did she talk to you? Maybe mention what she'd been doing? Or where she was planning on going?"

Her hope deflated when Glenn shook his head. "Nah, she just swung through like she was checking out the place, but she didn't stay long enough to chat."

"She didn't talk to anyone?" Dahlia asked, disappointed.

"Just Winston," Dulce said.

"Winston?"

"Winston Dane." Glenn winced as he said the name, which sent Dahlia from hope to concern.

"Why'd you say his name like that?" she asked. "Is he awful? Dangerous?"

"Nooo?" The way Glenn stretched out the word doubtfully made Dahlia's worry double. "Just…unfriendly. He's the local hermit. Doesn't care for people much. He wouldn't commit *murder* or anything like that. I don't think. I mean, I couldn't swear on my *life* that he doesn't have a stack of corpses in his basement, but it's doubtful. Sort of doubtful."

Anxious prickles coursed down Dahlia's spine. One of the last people who'd talked to her sister before her disappearance was a people-hating, possibly corpse-collecting hermit. What trouble had Rose stumbled into?

The front door opened, making Dahlia jump. A uniformed cop entered, heading toward their small huddle at the bar. Even though the Silver County Sheriff Department had dismissed her concerns when she'd contacted them last night, Dahlia was tempted to ask this police officer for help. She had a sympathetic face.

"Hey, Dulce," the cop, whose name tag read "Officer H. Bitts," said when she reached the bar. Her dark hair was pulled back into a severe bun, and her makeup-free brown skin was flawless. "I just picked up Mike Tippley's golden retriever on Front Street again. Mike's house is locked up tight, and his car's gone, so I set the dog up with food and water at the shelter."

Dulce sighed. "Thanks, Hayley. That Bailey is an escape artist. I'm working here late tonight, but I'll call Mike, let him know he can pick up Bailey in the morning."

The cop nodded and turned away, giving Dahlia a quick once-over. "Nice outfit," she said.

After a surprised moment, Dahlia smiled broadly. Before her flight that morning, she'd just thrown on some favorite jeans—for emotional support—with a chunky red sweater and tartan scarf, but the unexpected compliment gave her a much-needed boost. "Thank you. You have gorgeous pores."

Officer Bitts blinked. "Thank you?"

"I do makeovers professionally," Dahlia explained. "My clients would kill for skin like yours."

"Okay." Bitts still looked uncertain as she turned toward the door.

"Wait! I'm looking for my sister," Dahlia blurted out, unlocking her phone's screen again and holding it out so the cop could see Rose's picture. "Rose Weathersby. I haven't heard from her since she texted me our emergency code last night."

Bitts glanced at the phone screen. "Emergency code?"

"Tell Mom hi." Dahlia grimaced when the cop's expression flattened to professional blandness. "It's our sister code, asking for help, like when a blind date goes wrong, or my model bailed at the last minute…" She let her voice trail off when she saw the skepticism peeking out of the cop's neutral expression.

"I haven't seen her," Bitts said. "Have you filed a missing-person report?"

"Yes, last night, with the sheriff's department, but they seemed…unconvinced that she was actually missing. I didn't know Howling Falls had a police department."

"It's small. No need to file another report with us, since we'll get a copy from the sheriff. I'll keep an eye out for her."

Forcing a smile, Dahlia held back her torrent of worried frustration and just said, "Okay. Thank you."

"Good luck," Bitts said before heading to the exit.

Dahlia watched her leave and then turned back to Glenn and Dulce, who were watching her with sympathetic expressions. "Do you think the antisocial hermit did something to Rose?" she blurted.

"I'm sure he didn't," Glenn said, although his doubtful expression blocked any comfort his words might've provided. "He wouldn't... I mean, he *probably* wouldn't, although who knows, since they always say serial killers are the quiet ones..." His voice trailed off with a flinch when he saw Dulce's ferocious scowl directed at him. "Excuse me, ladies. I should go check on something." He pushed off his barstool and hurried toward the taxidermy shop door.

Once he disappeared inside, Dulce said, "Winston didn't do anything to your sister. He's a sweetheart."

Dahlia turned to the bartender, some of her worry washing away at the conviction in Dulce's voice. "He's not a people-hating, corpse-collecting grump after all?"

"Well..." Dulce grimaced. "I wouldn't say he's *not* a grump, and he's not exactly *social*, but it's a definite no on the corpses. I can't imagine him hurting anyone. He just really likes his privacy."

"Okay," Dahlia said slowly. "So is this just a guess, or do you know him better than Glenn? Because I got the impression from him that this Winston Dane is part Jeffrey Dahmer and part chupacabra."

Dulce snorted. "Glenn's a drama queen. I'd take everything he—and most of the gossipy locals—says with a serious grain of salt." She leaned over the bar and lowered her voice. "Don't tell anyone, because Winston wanted to stay anonymous, but he made a *huge* donation to the Howling Falls animal shelter. He's the only reason this town even *has* a shelter. Besides, you only have to read one of his books to know that guy's a cream-filled doughnut inside."

Dahlia leaned closer. "Books?"

"Hang on." Dulce came out from behind the bar and crossed to the bookshelf in the corner. She scanned the small collection before pulling out a well-read paperback. Returning to the bar, she handed the book to Dahlia.

"Dane Winters?" The author's name rang a bell. "Oh! I've read some of his books before. Your scary hermit writes cozy mysteries?"

Dulce nodded. "Cozy mysteries with a bumbling, romantic hero even."

"Right." Dahlia smiled as the plot of the books came back to her. "Mr. Rupert Wattlethorpe."

Dulce smirked at her. "See what I mean?"

Scanning the back of the book—on which the author bio was suspiciously absent—Dahlia slowly nodded. "I do, although I still want to talk to your not-so-scary local hermit about what my sister might've told him. Do you have his cell number?"

"No. No one does that I know of."

"How about his address?"

Dulce snorted. "Yeah, but it won't do you much good. He basically lives on a secured compound, and even if you could get to his front door, I doubt he'd answer it."

Resting her chin in her hand, Dahlia gave the bartender an innocent smile. "Oh, I'll figure something out."

———

Picking a padlock with a bobby pin and a lip pencil was harder than Dahlia thought it'd be—which was saying something. She hadn't expected it to be *easy*, but she was slightly irritated at everyone involved in making the movie *Deadly Beauty II*, since the heroine had indeed picked her lock in just seconds. Granted, she hadn't used a Barbara Whitmore Lip Trick in Iconic Rose sharpened to a wicked point, but Dahlia couldn't imagine another instrument making things any easier.

Except maybe a key. Yes, a key would be nice.

With a huff, she put her sadly mutilated lip pencil back into her compartmentalized travel makeup bag, peering at her other options in the dim moonlight. *Lip tint, eyeliner, serum, moisturizer...* She made a face. No one could've predicted that her search for her missing sister would mean sneaking into some local hermit's lair, but not even *considering* the possibility she might need better breaking-and-entering tools when she was packing for this adventure felt like a lack of planning on her part. Sure, she'd look good while failing to pick this lock, but a glamorous fail was still a fail.

Then the slightest bulge in a tiny pocket of her compartmentalized bag caught her eye, and she yanked out her point-tip tweezers. "Hello, beautiful. I'd forgotten about you," she crooned in barely audible celebration. Crouching so she was at face level with the lock, she woke up her phone again. The directions she'd found on the internet filled the screen, and she smiled victoriously as she balanced the phone on her leg above her knee.

"I know, random internet lock-picking instructor person," Dahlia muttered under her breath, "that you said raking the lock is inelegant, but as this is possibly a life-or-death matter, I'm shooting for expediency here. For once in my life—fine, maybe twice—I'm taking the inelegant-but-easy route." That said, even the so-called easy method of picking a lock wasn't really *easy* for her, and it took another several minutes of struggling with her tweezers and bobby pin before the padlock clicked and dropped open.

She stared at the opened lock for several seconds before a satisfied smile curled her mouth. She'd actually *done* it. She, Dahlia May Weathersby, had picked a lock with just the contents of her—admittedly well-stocked—makeup bag and an internet tutorial. Returning her improvised tools to their proper compartments and zipping up the bag, she grabbed her phone and stood, wincing as blood rushed back into her sleeping feet.

"Note to self," she whispered at a barely there volume, "next time you pick a lock while breaking into some weird mountain man's property, don't crouch. Kneel."

With that decided, she removed the padlock and unwove the chain as quietly as she could manage. The eerie silence of the mountain night made every clink of metal against metal sound like an air-horn blast, but she told herself she was being paranoid. She couldn't see a house, which meant the mountain guy couldn't see her…hopefully.

Unless he's hiding behind that pine tree over there, her extremely unhelpful brain offered, but she shut down that nonsense immediately. "Knock it off." Despite her words, her growl was almost soundless, just in case someone *was* lurking close by. "Quit trying to psych yourself out."

Just because this guy had all—well, most of—the residents of the tiny mountain town of Howling Falls, Colorado, terrified of him, just because he lived in the middle of nowhere, just because there was nothing around but snow and dark cliffs and trees and moonlight shadows shaped like monsters and wailing wind and a brutal-looking fence topped with razor wire didn't mean that she should fear for her life. Mr. Winston Dane, Hermit, surely was a rational person who would be happy to talk to her about whether or not he'd played a role in her sister's disappearance.

Dahlia shivered. "Okay, that's enough thinking."

She did her best to shut off her brain as she slipped through the opening in the gate. She mentally debated ease of exit over disguising the fact that the gate was unlocked—just because she couldn't see any cameras didn't mean they weren't there—and decided to rewrap the chain but leave the paddock open. She doubted her ability to pick a lock a second time, especially if she was in a rush.

Turning back to the thick stand of trees, she blew out a breath and straightened her shoulders. "The things I do for you, Rosie-Toes."

She started walking on what she couldn't really call a driveway, since it wasn't even gravel, much less paved with comfortingly civilized asphalt. It was more two strips of dirt about six feet apart, worn down by driving a car—no, not a car, she mentally revised, but a pickup, one of those loud, jacked-up monsters—back and forth until the two grooves were formed. Snow dusted the ground, but she was grateful she didn't have to trudge through drifts up to her knees. Her black boots were, relatively speaking, practical, chosen for breaking and entering, but they weren't anything real mountaineers would wear or anything. Even just a few inches of snow would've made things very uncomfortable for her.

The moon was almost full, just slightly rounder on one side than the other, but as the trees thickened, their branches stretching above the driveway to form a natural tunnel, things got dark. After tripping over a protruding rock for the third time, Dahlia chose comfort over caution and pulled out her phone again. Turning on the flashlight app, she directed the illumination to the ground right in front of her. The edge of the light caught on a sign, and she paused, turning her makeshift flashlight so she could read it. No Trespassing.

There were no threats, no murderous implications, but the sign still felt ominous. Reminding herself that she was doing this for Rose, Dahlia braced herself and walked on. The eeriest part of the walk, she decided, wasn't the dark shadows turning the trees on either side of her into yawning caves where serial killers were bound to be hiding. Instead, it was the silence. Except for the continual groan of the wind and creaking branches, there was…nothing. No traffic, no other humans, no buzz of electronics, no life noises at all. That lack of background sounds was strangely terrifying.

Dahlia bit back a laugh. *I'm confronting a hermit in his potentially heavily armed hideout, and* that's *what I find terrifying? The quiet of nature?*

It wasn't just the silence beneath the drone of the wind that made her uneasy, though. It was the complete lack of civilization. In the city, she was surrounded by people at all times. There, one shout would bring at least *some* of them running if she ever needed help. Out here, it was just her and one scary-ass mountain man. She could scream her lungs out, and no one would ever hear.

"Enough of that," she muttered, needing to stop freaking herself out immediately. She focused on the track ahead, tilting her phone to send the light farther in front of her. All she could see was more snow-dusted driveway and infinite trees. This driveway—as pathetic as it was—apparently continued for *miles.*

Rose, she reminded herself. *My sister needs me. Maybe. Probably. Or she might be perfectly fine, like that time she decided on the spur of the moment to fly to New-freaking-Zealand and forgot to let me know for three days, or that* other *time, when she spent two weeks at that monastery in Iowa with no cell signal or internet so she could learn how to make elderberry wine. Quite possibly, I'm risking my life for no reason. Maybe Rose's 911 text wasn't an emergency after all.* Despite these optimistic thoughts, just the slight possibility that her sister *was* in trouble was enough to keep Dahlia in sister-rescue mode. With a silent sigh, she trudged on.

Her fingers were starting to ache with cold, so she switched the phone to her left hand, shaking out her right and jamming it into her jacket pocket to warm up. As the light bobbled with the motion, she saw a reflected gleam and came to an abrupt halt.

Was that an eye? Every predatory animal she'd ever heard of living in Colorado—bears, mountain lions, coyotes, wolves… *Wait, are there wolves here?*—flashed through her mind in a second. Aiming the flashlight with a shaking hand, she slowly focused the beam back on the spot where she'd noticed the reflected light.

There! To her utter relief, it wasn't the light bouncing off the homicidal eyeball of a carnivorous beast. It was simply a piece of shiny trash that'd ended up on the ground. Maybe Mr. Weird Hermit himself had tossed his gum wrapper out of his truck window.

That didn't seem quite right, however. Dahlia cocked her head and moved closer to study the object. It almost looked as if it was suspended off the ground. Crouching down, she peered at what was definitely a wire—as thick as a guitar string—stretched across the entire width of the driveway, about six inches off the ground.

"Are you a trip wire, Mr. Shiny?" Dahlia asked under her breath, using the light from her phone to follow the path of the wire. Straightening her legs but staying bent over, she moved to the side of the driveway and between two evergreens, expecting to find the end of the wire tied around a sapling or something similar.

Instead, there was a disconcertingly sleek arrangement of wire and pulleys that looked completely out of place next to the rough trunks and scrubby brush surrounding them. With the light, Dahlia tracked the wire's progress as it moved through the system and up to the dark canopy over the driveway. She turned her phone to the branches above her and had to grin at the sheer campiness of what she found.

"An enormous *net*, Mr. Weird Hermit?" she whispered, trying very hard not to laugh out loud. "Someone's been watching too many Scooby-Doo reruns. Or has a Spider-Man obsession."

Still internally snickering, Dahlia stepped over the wire with exaggerated care. Now that she'd seen the trap, it would be extra humiliating to be caught in a huge net like some cartoon villain just because she'd been careless and caught the wire with the toe of her boot. To make doubly sure, she stayed to the far side of the path, at the very edge of the net suspended above her, and hurried to put that particular trap behind her.

After just a few rushing steps, however, she forced herself to slow, sweeping the light from side to side over the driveway, looking for any sign of another trap. She thought of all those rocks she'd tripped over before she'd decided to use her flashlight app and cringed. It was sheer luck she hadn't triggered something and had sharpened spears flying at her or a giant mace swinging toward her head or stumbled into some other Temple of Doom-like...well, *doom*.

Shaking off her distraction, she focused on the ground in front of her. Every so often, she'd shift the light to the trees lining the drive, but she hated those moments. The light from her phone barely penetrated into the gloom, and it just activated her already overstimulated imagination.

She paused, running the light across the driveway in front of her. It was hard to tell because of the dusting of snow blowing across the space, but it looked like the two tire tracks jogged to the left slightly before returning to the center. For the paths to be worn as smoothly as they were, Mr. Weird Hermit would've had to have taken the same tiny detour every day for months— even years—so it wasn't just that he'd gotten distracted texting one time and swerved slightly off-center. No, this would've had to have been a pattern, and a pattern meant there was a reason.

Moving a little closer—but not too close—Dahlia swept the area with light, searching for anything that didn't belong. Now that she was looking for it, the slight impression jumped out to her quickly, the straight line not fitting the natural surroundings. It would've blended just fine into a sidewalk or building or any other non-natural structure, but here in the curve and waves of the organic world, it looked as obvious as a flashing light.

Once she'd spotted the first straight line barely marking the dirt, it was easy to follow it to the corner, until the entire large square was marked out in her mind. It would've been easier to hide if all the leaves and loose dirt hadn't been blown off, leaving a smoothly swept surface. Even the bit of snow didn't help hide it, instead settling against or in the tiny cracks delineating the square. It was smack in the center of the driveway, so anyone driving straight down the middle would run two tires right over it.

As Dahlia gave the almost-hidden square a wide berth, her imagination ran wild, and the temptation to examine it more closely almost got the best of her. Was it something as innocuous as a sensor, alerting Mr. Weird Hermit that someone was approaching? Or was it something more fun—like a trapdoor that'd drop trespassers into a spike-lined pit?

Okay, maybe not so much fun for the trespasser, Dahlia acknowledged, giving the square a final glance before she pushed forward. She couldn't help the *tiniest* feeling of smugness for sneaking past not only one but *two* of Mr. Weird Hermit's traps. Immediately, she gave herself a mental slap, because getting cocky was how she'd trip her way into whatever came next.

Forcing herself to stay alert, even though this was the longest driveway in the history of driveways, Dahlia pressed on. The flashlight on her cell phone started to dim, and she paused to stare at it, debating whether to preserve the little charge that remained in the battery or use the light for as long as possible. The thought of being stuck in the middle of nowhere with Mr. Weird Hermit and his apparent hatred of trespassers without the ability to even make a 911 call made her turn off the flashlight app and darken her screen.

Once her eyes had adjusted to the small bit of moonlight filtering through the bare tree branches, she started forward again, even more cautiously in the limited light. She made it around a bend in the drive and came to an abrupt stop at the sight in front of her.

The claustrophobic press of forest fell away, and a ten-foot concrete fence rose seemingly from nowhere. It was startling to come upon it, so out of place. Dahlia had expected an Unabomber-type shack, or possibly a single-wide trailer, or—in the best-case scenario—an adorable log cabin with woodsmoke curling from the chimney. This tall, solid fence, so smooth it gleamed in the moonlight, was just...weird.

"You do call him Mr. Weird Hermit for a reason," she reminded herself very quietly as she approached the fence, angling away from the wrought-iron gate. Although she couldn't see any obvious cameras, she had to assume they were there. In fact, he'd probably been watching her progress this entire time, but she still didn't want to be obnoxious about it. There was no reason to throw the fact that she'd outsmarted his traps and made it to...well, this patently unscalable, very tall wall of a fence.

The trees ended a good fifteen feet from the fence, and so did their helpful shadows, so she felt exposed as she moved across the open space. The lack of close by trees was also unfortunate in that there were no helpful overhanging branches that she could use to get over the wall. Once she was right next to it, she sighed. This was going to be tricky.

The painted concrete surface was as smooth as it had appeared from a distance, about twice as tall as she was without any handy toe- and fingerholds. She moved closer to the single gate, hoping for a gap she could slip through if she turned sideways and sucked in, but the wrought-iron bars were so close together that even a Chihuahua would have trouble squeezing through.

Can't go through, so I guess I'm going over. She grimly eyed the wrought-iron spikes at the top of the gate as she moved closer to the hinges, hoping they'd give her a little bit of a foothold. Tossing the strap of her bag over one of the spikes so it hung high off the ground, she backed away, trying to distract herself from the sheer impossibility of what she was about to attempt by planning the lecture she was going to give Rose when she was found safe and sound in some mountain hippie commune, unable to charge her phone because all the community electricity was needed for the grow lamps in the pot greenhouse. Or maybe Rose had decided to become a Rocky Mountain version of Dian Fossey, and she was holed up in a cave with a pacifist family of bears and *no* electricity, about to bed down for their winter hibernation.

Honestly, considering her sister, neither would surprise her. But on the small chance Rose was actually in trouble, Dahlia had to at least *try* channeling her inner parkourist.

She sprinted forward and jumped at the gate, grabbing two vertical bars close to the top. Lifting her feet higher, she pressed them against the bars, her left one finding the tiniest bump of a hinge she could use as a foothold. Releasing her right hand, she grabbed both sides of her bag strap, using it like a rope to help haul herself up as her feet slipped and scrabbled against the bars. The material creaked but held.

"Thank you, Lavinia Holt," she managed to gasp as her left hand grabbed the top horizontal bar between two vicious spikes. "For designing bags that are...not only cruelty-free... but...also...durable." Her right hand grasped the top bar as well, and she pulled her body up high enough that she got her left foot onto the top of the fence. After an awkward twisting scramble, she managed to shift around to the other side of the spikes. Yanking up the bag's strap so it was clear of the spike, she clutched it in her sweaty fist along with the top bar as her feet dangled. Squeezing her eyes closed, she sent a tiny prayer to the patron saint of breaking-and-entering fashionistas, released her hold on the fence, and let herself drop.

Her feet hit the ground with a jarring *thump* before she fell backward. Opening her eyes, she mentally checked herself for any major injuries, but all her parts seemed to be intact.

"Ha!" she exclaimed before remembering where she was and the importance of being quiet.

Standing on shaky legs, she tugged down her top layers and brushed off her butt before looking around. Prior to scaling the gate, she'd just been able to see a few trees scattered around before everything disappeared into the darkness, but from her new vantage point, she could make out a dark shape big enough to be a dwelling of some sort.

Blowing out a bracing breath, she slung her bag over her shoulder and turned toward what, with her luck, was probably Mr. Weird Hermit's torture barn and antique doll emporium.

Although she kept half an eye out for any traps, she marched toward the structure with more speed than was probably wise. The problem was that Dahlia was pretty much over the weird hermit's nonsense. Her muscles were sore and still trembling, her carefully chosen outfit was a definite mess, and the clock was ticking. The longer Rose was missing, the more likely it was that she was seriously hurt or even...

Nope. Dahlia firmly cut off those fatalistic thoughts. Her brain was not allowed to go there. Instead, she focused on the building in front of her, a black shape silhouetted against a not-quite-as-dark sky, and forced her legs to keep walking. *Almost there.* She was so close to completing her quest. All she had to do in this portion of her find-Rose adventure was defeat the big bad—well, perhaps not *defeat*, but more just have a chat with—and then she could move up a level, hopefully to the one that Rose was on.

She walked—fine, *stomped*—closer to the structure, near enough to see that it was indeed a house. The details became clearer the closer she got, and her determined thoughts were whisked straight out of her brain when she saw that there was a man standing on the porch.

No, not a man. A giant. A mountain. A *monolith.*

The guy was tall. And broad. And, judging by the scowl she could finally see once she reached the base of the porch steps, he was *pissed.*

TWO

Resisting the urge to take a cautious step back, Dahlia instead climbed the steps. Every one of her instincts was shrieking that she should run away from this man, but she couldn't. Not now, not after she'd made it up the endless booby-trapped driveway and over that wall. Not when Rose's safety was paramount. What was Dahlia's fear in comparison to that? Absolutely nothing, she decided. After all, he probably only looked so big and intimidating because he was on the porch, five steps up from where Dahlia stood on the ground. Once she was next to him, he'd very probably seem especially average.

She still wanted to turn tail and run off into the night.

The other thing that stopped her from fleeing like the chickenest of chickens was that to escape, she'd have to climb that wall again. If she actually had a conversation with the weird hermit and she was her most-annoying self, he'd likely open the gate and kick her out himself, just to get her gone. After all, everything on his property made it obvious that the man liked his bubble of solitude.

"Hi," she said, her voice sounding too loud after so much repressed quiet. "Are you Winston Dane?"

She reached the top of the steps and realized that the man was still ridiculously tall. It hadn't been just a trick of perspective. The guy was a giant, close to six and a half feet, she'd guess. To make matters worse, his arms were folded across his chest, which made his muscles pop in a very intimidating way. His full beard didn't hide the sharp slice of his cheekbones or the sparks of absolute fury spitting from his eyes. A scar followed the line of his left eyebrow and continued to his ear, and a smaller groove ran through his top lip, twisting it into a slight sneer—or possibly he'd constantly sneered his entire life, so his face had gotten stuck like that, and the scar was incidental. The overall impression he made was of rampaging hotness with enough flaws to be interesting, but it was hard to pay attention to that when he was so obviously and intensely angry.

Since he hadn't said a word—hopefully not because his serial killer nickname was something like Silent Slicer or Winnie the Quiet Disemboweler—she filled the conversational gap. "I'm Dahlia Weathersby. Does your pit of doom have spikes on the bottom?"

That didn't get quite the reaction she was hoping for, but a touch of confusion did bring his furious eyebrows a little closer together. "What?"

Oh, his voice is nice. Although it was true—he had a deep bass rumble that Dahlia could feel vibrating in all sorts of interesting places—she still elbowed that thought back as she explained, "Under that trapdoor in your endless driveway. If I'd fallen through, would I have landed in a pit lined with sharp spikes? I'm dying to know what's under there—although not *literally* dying to know, obviously, or else I would've jumped up and down until I was dropped in." When he just continued to stare at her, she watched his face for any telltale twitch. "Orrrr…a pile of venomous snakes?" When his expression didn't change, she tried again. "Maybe water then? An underground pool with alligators? I know! Piranhas!"

"Who *are* you?"

"I told you. Dahlia Weathersby." She gave up on satisfying her morbid curiosity and focused on the reason she'd risked the spike pit in the first place. "You know my sister, Rose."

She watched his face even more intently this time. This, after all, was why she bothered taking her life into her hands and broke into the property of a weird hermit in the middle of Nowhere, Colorado, in the first place. Her close scrutiny didn't help, however, since his expression of great irritation with a hint of bafflement didn't change. Either the guy had a fantastic poker face, or he had no idea who Rose even was.

"Rose? I don't know a Rose."

She examined him for several long moments. Her gut was pretty sure he was telling the truth, but he could just be an excellent liar. Her instincts were fairly reliable, but not infallible, after all. "You've never met her?"

One burly shoulder rose slightly in a shrug. "Not that I remember."

Her eyes narrowed. She had two witnesses who'd clearly seen him talking with Rose. She hadn't picked a lock and dodged

multiple booby traps just to be turned away by feigned igno-
rance. Unless he'd just never gotten her name? "She's twenty-six,
tall, blond, pale as a ghost, blue eyes, looks like she could be in
an ad for ethically sourced, organic Icelandic yogurt made from
free-range goat milk?"

He paused, his unscarred eyebrow doing a quirky little hop.
"She's your sister?"

The doubt in his voice wasn't anything she hadn't heard
before when people found out about their family connection.
With Dahlia's olive skin, almost black hair that threatened to
bounce back into curls forty-five minutes after being straightened to within an inch of its life, and dark-brown eyes—not to
mention her unimpressively average height—she was used to
people asking if she was adopted. "Half sister. I look more like
my mom. So?" When he just stared at her, she made a hurry-up
circle with her hand. "Have you met her?"

"Yes."

Relief flooded her. Despite the eyewitnesses, a part of her
had started to wonder if the lock-picking and spike-lined-pit
dodging had been in vain. "That's what the bartender at Yodel
Inn and Tavern said. Also, the taxidermist confirmed it."

"The…taxidermist. Glenn?"

"Dark hair and potbelly?" When he grunted in the affirmative, she nodded. "He was having a drink at the bar when
you and Rose were talking Monday afternoon *and* again when
I was questioning Dulce earlier tonight. I got the impression
he doesn't stray far from that barstool." Winston didn't reply,
not even with a bounce of his eyebrow, and Dahlia realized

that she hadn't actually asked a question. "So what did you talk about?"

"We didn't."

She sighed. "Really? You're going to lie about it now? We just confirmed three seconds ago that two people saw you talking with Rose."

"It's true. We didn't talk," he insisted mulishly. "*She* did."

Dahlia let her head drop back with a groan. "Why are the hot ones always so pedantic?" Before he could posit a theory on why this was always, always true, she asked, "What did *Rose* talk about then?" She put an extra emphasis on her sister's name to stress how ridiculous the man was being. She hadn't survived multiple booby traps and a fall from a very low height just to go around in conversational circles.

His frown deepened, but she was pretty sure it was a sign of him thinking, rather than increased irritation. "Howling Falls."

"What about the town?"

"No, the actual falls," he clarified.

Hope raised its head. This was the first potential lead since Dulce the bartender and Glenn the taxidermist had pointed her in Winston Dane's direction. "Did she go see the falls? Did something happen there?"

"Not to my knowledge." The line between his brows linked up with the end of his scar, making an interesting furrow that wasn't *un*attractive.

Focus, Dahlia.

"But she was *planning* to go to the falls?"

"Yeah."

She waited for him to continue, but that was apparently all he was going to say without further prompting. Holding in a frustrated sigh, she offered that prompt. "When?"

"The next morning. Tuesday." That timeline fit, since Rose had mentioned starting a new adventure in her second-to-last text to Dahlia on Tuesday morning. "The hike to the falls takes a few days, so she's probably not missing, just out of cell range."

"No, she sent me a text late Wednesday—yesterday—asking for help."

That eyebrow jumped again. "What'd it say?"

"'Tell Mom hi.'"

His frown grew even more ferocious. "You think *that's* a cry for help?"

His doubt was slightly annoying, but she reminded herself that Winston Dane was a stranger who didn't know her or Rose or anything about their messed-up family situation. *Lucky guy.* "That's our code for 911. My mom died having me, and Rose's mom's a…" She paused, debating how much to share with this guy. According to her gut—and Dulce the bartender—the chance he'd had something to do with Rose's disappearance was low, but it was still possible, plus time was a consideration. "Rose's mom likes both of us to call her by her first name, Kelli." *Although we sometimes call her other, not-so-nice names, but only behind her back, since we aren't rude bitches. Unlike Kelli.* "So neither of us has anyone in our life we call 'mom'."

"I've used our emergency text a few times in less-than-life-threatening situations—once when I was on a blind date and the guy was flashing all sorts of red flags, and another time when

I was on the *Cara and Corbin in the Morning* show and my model canceled at the last second, so I needed Rose to fill in." When the furrow between his eyebrows got deeper, she figured he needed some backstory on that last example. "You see, Cara's a sweetheart, but Corbin's always been a bit of a…umm, let's say a *challenge*, and he would've thrown a complete fit about my 'lack of professionalism' if he knew I was model-less, so I sent Rose that stealthy nine-one-one text, and she came right away." Dahlia sucked in a much-needed breath of air. "Rose hadn't ever used it before, though, until last night."

Winston still looked mostly surly and annoyed, but Dahlia was pretty sure she saw the tiniest glimmer of curious interest at this. "Nothing else? Location? Details?"

"No." It was a huge relief to have someone believe her about the emergency text. The Silver County Sheriff Department had blown off her frantic call yesterday evening, which was why she'd jumped on the first flight to Colorado this morning, and Officer Bitts had been sympathetic but skeptical at the bar. "Silence. I tried tracking her phone a bunch of times, but it's off…or dead." She immediately regretted saying the D-word when terrifying worst-case possibilities started trying to shove themselves to the front of her brain. She pushed them back—just like she'd been doing since Rose's text yesterday—and forced herself to calm, although there was nothing she could do about the tremor that rippled through her body. *It's because it's freaking cold here*, she lied to herself.

Winston sighed, sounding as resigned and exhausted as if it'd been *his* sister who'd disappeared and *he* was the one attempting to interrogate a close-mouthed, pedantic hermit in his ridiculously well-trapped compound. "Come in."

Not expecting that invitation, Dahlia blinked at his back as he unlatched the door and held it open for a long enough time that his resigned expression shifted back to irritation.

"Uhh… Okay then. Guess I'm going inside." She jerked into motion, stepping through the doorway even while wondering if walking willingly into his house was a stupid thing to do—stupid enough to put her in the same category as the first person to die in the opening five minutes of a horror movie. The audience would definitely be screaming at her right now, but really, she figured, what was the difference between standing on his front porch versus his living room? It was still only the two of them, and he was a whopping pile of muscles while she was impressed with herself when she managed to get to the gym three times in one week. Despite this unarguable logic, however, she still felt an uneasy tightening in her belly as she stepped inside.

Then he flipped a light switch, illuminating the interior. She looked around, and the unexpectedly sweet feel of his home startled any apprehension right out of her. It was stupid, of course, since she knew very well that there was no reason a dismembering sociopath couldn't have a talent for decorating, but she'd walked in expecting either clichéd woodsy bourgeois with tan leather and dead animals, or clichéd modern bachelor with *black* leather and chrome—with a non-zero chance of going full-on weird hermit, with partially assembled bombs and lots of monitors. She'd gotten none of these. Instead, the place was huge helpings of *cute*, so much so that the sight of it left her off guard and defenseless.

They'd entered into the lofted main room, and the varnished pine of the beams and floor glowed gold in the warm artificial light. The dark-blue couch had a cream-colored throw draped casually over it, and both looked so incredibly soft she had to resist curling up and taking a nap, even though she'd been moderately scared for her life only seconds ago. The matching pair of armchairs wouldn't have been out of place in a sweet grandma's living room, as long as said grandma had a thing for lounging in comfort. The furniture that wasn't upholstered somehow managed to appear both whimsical and natural, as if it had grown out of the shiny wooden floor, twisting itself into the cutest possible form which also served to function as a dining table or bookshelf.

Unable to believe that this was the home of a weird, booby-trap-creating hermit, she shot him a sideways glance. "Did you do the decorating?" she asked. Maybe he'd bought the entire place furnished and accessorized from an artsy, cozy bohemian so that he could focus on digging spike-lined pits and the like.

To her surprise, his grunt was affirmative, and his slight air of defensiveness made her believe it. As if to prove himself further, he crossed the room and plopped down in the corner of the dreamy couch, his flannel shirt and wool-socked feet fitting into the decorating scheme with shocking ease. In fact, his large presence made the couch even *more* tempting, which Dahlia wouldn't have believed possible.

It bothered her to keep her boots on before crossing the

gleaming floor, but there was still a chance she might have to book it out of there at a moment's notice, so she left them on with a grimace. She wandered the room, reading some of the titles in his extensive book collection. There was quite a range of genres, which—as someone who also read anything and everything that caught her interest—made her reluctantly like him even more.

"Sit," he ordered.

She studied him for another long moment before deciding it wouldn't hurt to do as he'd commanded.

"Sorry about not taking off my shoes," she said as she lowered herself onto one of the gorgeous green armchairs. "I really do have manners, but better to be rude than have to run through the forest in socks, I suppose."

That eyebrow of his bumped up. "Why would you have to do that?"

"Run through the woods in socks?" she clarified. At his chin lift of a nod, she shrugged. "Since I'm keeping my boots on, I *won't* have to. Now, what *exactly* did Rose say to you?"

He blinked, and for a second, Dahlia thought he might press the issue, but then he answered her most recent question instead. "Just what I said. She was going to Howling Falls."

"Going to Howling Falls the falls, yes, but there was more. I know this because Rose is a chatterer," she told him firmly. "She has extensive conversations about apple production with strangers at the grocery store and can talk for hours with the person in front of her in line at the DMV about the history of the internal combustion engine. I know you're a more…reserved type, but there might be a hint of what happened to her in her one-sided conversation, so if you could be just a *hair* more loquacious for once, I'd really appreciate it." She sat back and waited for his eyebrow to lower and for him to start talking.

To her surprise, he did exactly what she asked. "I went to the bar Monday around four looking for Alex Vickory."

"Who's that?" Dahlia scooted forward to perch on the front of her too-comfortable chair. It'd be disastrously easy to sink back into its cushy softness and let Winston's rumbly voice vibrate her to sleep—something she hadn't done since she'd gotten Rose's last text yesterday.

He gave a jerky wave, as if dismissing Alex Vickory's importance. "She owns a small-engine repair shop. I needed a part for my chain saw, but she'd closed up early because her brother was in town, according to the sign on the door. I checked Yodel's, but they weren't there."

Despite everything, Dahlia felt a laugh rise in her chest, and she choked it down with mixed results. "If they had been, you were going to drag this poor woman away from her drink and her brother and force her to open up her shop and find the part you needed?"

He looked at her blankly, as if the answer was obvious. "Yes."

"Rude. Why not just come back the next day?"

"She might've still been out." His tone implied that Dahlia's suggestion was completely unreasonable. "Your sister ran into me as I was about to leave."

She frowned. "She just randomly stopped to talk to you?"

"No, she *ran into* me." He thumped his hand against his chest as if to demonstrate.

"Physically? Like crashed into you?" Dahlia's first instinct was to laugh, since that was so like Rose to have her head caught up in the clouds and not see this enormous, hulking bulldozer of a man planted right in her path, but then she wanted to cry, since that was so like Rose.

"Yeah." His answer pulled her out of her sentimental struggle, and she was grateful, because getting weepy about her sister who was quite definitely *just fine* was a waste of time. "She fell backward, but I caught her before she hit the ground."

"That was very meet-cute of you two." If tears of worry were unhelpful, the tiny zap of what felt disconcertingly like envy was even more useless, so Dahlia pretended like that tiny blip hadn't happened.

It was his turn to side-eye her.

"Never mind," she said again, annoyed with herself for sidetracking him. It was hard enough to keep him talking without tossing in whatever nonsense that'd been. "What'd she say?"

"She apologized, asked if I was okay." His tone conveyed the contempt that silly question deserved, and Dahlia held back another amused snort. It would be like a bunny hurting a big-ass bull by hopping into its leg. "Didn't give me any time to answer. Just said she was visiting from California, loved the town, said it was adorable."

"She's not wrong." As distracted as Dahlia had been, even she could see that the little mountain town was objectively adorable.

His grunt sounded skeptical, but he didn't comment before continuing. "Said she came here specifically to hike to Howling Falls. Told me it was the third-tallest waterfall in Colorado at two hundred and forty-two feet." From the slight condescension in his tone, he'd already known that.

Holding back an eye roll, she gestured for him to keep talking.

"She was going to leave early the next morning." The furrow connected to his eyebrow scar deepened, indicating he was thinking. "She was excited." He lifted his hands in a shrug. "That's it."

"Isn't this the wrong time of year?" Even as she asked the question, Dahlia already knew the answer. Her sister was never one to do things the easy way.

"Said she came during the off season to avoid the crowds."

"Did she say whether she was going to do the hike by herself?" Dahlia asked, frowning in thought. "Or if she'd met any of the townspeople in particular?"

His negative head shake apparently covered both questions.

"Did she seem to know anyone at Yodel's?" When he gave her a blank look, she elaborated. "Anyone greet her, especially by name? Call out to her when she came in? Give her a glance full of secret meaning and private messages?"

"No."

Disappointed, Dahlia sank back in her chair and was immediately enveloped by its squishy, cloudlike cushiness. She knew she needed to sit up straight or she might never get up again, but she gave herself a minute to indulge in its comfort before resuming her search for Rose. "Okay," she said slowly as her thoughts worked themselves into some type of order. "She was going to hike to the falls Tuesday morning, probably by herself, although we don't know that for sure. I got her text asking for help Wednesday afternoon."

As an infinite number of catastrophic scenarios flashed through her mind—Rose getting lost, tumbling off a cliff, falling into the water and plummeting over the side of Colorado's third-tallest waterfall to fall two hundred and forty-two feet—Dahlia knew what her next step would be. She also knew she was extraordinarily unqualified to take that step. Although she loved her urban home in California and adored her job, she suddenly wished she had a whole different set of skills. Why hadn't she taken a wilderness-survival course or two, just in case her sister disappeared in the mountains and Dahlia had to find and rescue her?

With a defeated huff of laughter, she refocused on the flannel-wearing mountain of a man across from her. Her gaze must've given away at least part of her developing thoughts, because his expression turned a bit hunted. "How would you rate your search-and-rescue skills?" she asked innocently.

"No."

"No isn't on a zero to ten scale," she scolded lightly as she sat forward again. It might've been her imagination, but she was pretty sure Winston pressed back against the couch just the tiniest bit, as if everything inside him was screaming to run away. She smiled, wanting to reassure him, but she must've failed since he only looked more wary. "Would you consider yourself an intermediate or advanced hiker? How about tracking? Can you do that thing where you look for bent twigs and partial footprints so you can follow someone's trail?"

"No."

She cocked her head, studying him closely. "No to which question?"

"All of them." He shoved to his feet and started pacing.

Dahlia pressed her lips together to hold back a smile. Apparently, his need to flee was getting the better of him. *Perfect.* "Hmm… Somehow I don't believe you. Someone who builds hidden spike pits in his driveway would tend toward the survival-y type skills, wouldn't they?"

He sent her an irritated glare, but his heavy frowns and sharp looks seemed to be losing their power to scare her. "It's not a spike pit."

"It's not?" She wiggled a little closer to the front of her chair, excited to finally learn what was under that hidden trapdoor. "Piranhas then?"

"No," he huffed. "Not an underground tank filled with piranhas—or alligators," he quickly added before she could take another guess. "Or sharks with laser beams attached to their heads."

She laughed at the movie reference, and he lost another few dozen stone-cold killer points. "Ah…venomous snakes then."

"Of course not venomous snakes." He shot her an incredulous look. "Who jumps right to the venomous snakes?"

Slightly offended, she huffed, "I didn't jump *right* to venomous snakes. I went to spikes, then piranhas, then alligators, and *then* venomous snakes. It was a circuitous path."

"You forgot sharks."

"Sharks was *your* idea," she reminded him. "A ridiculous one."

He stared at her. "Nothing."

"What?"

"There's *nothing* in the pit," he said slowly, as if making sure she understood each word. It was a little condescending of him, honestly. "It's barely a pit. Its purpose is to disable a vehicle or trap an intruder on foot until I can make it out there to question them. I don't want to actually hurt anyone."

"How would it trap someone if it's barely a pit?" she asked.

"For someone on foot, the door springs back and latches. And it's deep enough to hang up a vehicle if one or two tires drop into it. Not ideal, since the driver and any passengers are still mobile, but at least they can't use the vehicle to ram the gate." To her surprise, he actually explained. "When the door's latched, it can only be opened from the outside. When it opens, a sensor is tripped, and a message is sent to me." He tapped his smartwatch. "Same with the net."

"The net's awesome—very old-school cartoon villain. Do you really get that many unauthorized visitors that you have to have booby traps, plural?" she asked, fascinated enough by him that she allowed herself to get sidetracked.

"Everyone *else* is smart enough to stay away," he said with a meaningful glare.

"Since you have all the motion-sensors and cameras," Dahlia asked, "aren't the pits and nets just overkill...and a bit weird?"

"No." He looked the tiniest bit sulky. "They're not weird. They're...fun."

"For you, maybe." She didn't admit that it *had* been kind of fun outsmarting the cartoony traps. "Don't you just have to go out all the time to free angry squirrels and raccoons and the like?"

"No. Most of the time the deterrent devices aren't active," he said impatiently. "You triggered a motion-sensor alarm at the exterior gate. Since it took you an hour to pick the lock, I had plenty of time to remotely activate the traps."

"Since I managed to evade all of your very tricky booby traps," she said, bringing the conversation back around to where she needed it to be, "do I get a prize? Maybe you offer one favor of my choice?"

He snorted, pausing his pacing to prop his ham-like fists on his hips and glare at her more directly. "No. This isn't a fairy tale, and you're not Hercules."

"You're muddling your fairy tales and Roman mythology," she informed him kindly. "Although I'm very impressed with the twelve labors reference."

His only response was a glower.

"Okay, how about this." She hadn't wanted to go in this direction, but he was leaving her no other choice. "You help me find Rose, and I won't reveal your location to your rabid fans."

That shocked him. She could tell because his expression went blank and he blinked once before responding. "I don't have fans."

A little disappointed that he hadn't even asked about her inventive scheme, she decided to explain it to him anyway. "Sure you don't, Mr. Winston Dane, secret mystery writer and star of the docuseries *City Survival*."

Instead of a blink that time, she got a complete arm crossing, which was a little distracting, since no one's arms should be that thick. "That was years ago. No one cares about me anymore. And I wasn't the star. I was only interviewed a couple of times."

"People most certainly do still care about you. A *lot*." She smiled at Winston. "You should search your own name online sometime. Do you know that one clip of you glaring at the camera and growling 'I'm always watching' became a meme?"

From his grimace, he was well aware. "I was talking about being aware of my surroundings."

"I know. I watched the whole interview." She'd been mesmerized, unable to look away, but she didn't mention that part. "People were *obsessed* with you—still are. You're the reason a boring docuseries about urban safety became a cult classic. When you dropped out of sight a few years ago, your fans didn't forget. In fact, people became *more* obsessed with you. They started reporting every possible Winston Dane sighting, like a real-life version of *Where's Hot Waldo*. If they get any hint of where you live or, you know, your exact geographic coordinates, your stans will descend upon this compound by the *thousands,* treating your front gate and fence and booby traps like a fun challenge, knowing that the prize at the end is…"

"*No.*"

"Yesss." She drew out the word, feeling like a super-fashionable super-villain. "It'll be like *The Bachelor* meets geocaching. Calling all Winston Dane fans! See those muscles? That sexy glower? That lumberjack beard? He's all yours—plus the fun of mastering an obstacle course! Haven't you always wanted to learn how to pick a lock?"

"You're evil."

"Nah, not really." Dahlia gave him an impish smile. "I just really love my sister. So what time tomorrow morning do you want to start our hike, adventure buddy?"

———

Now that Winston had agreed—albeit grudgingly—to be her wilderness guide, Dahlia knew she should skedaddle before he changed his mind. Pushing her exhausted body off the heavenly cloud of a chair was one of the hardest things she'd ever done, but somehow she managed to stand. "So I'll see you at the Yodel Inn tomorrow first thing. Guess now I'll just..." Like the world's dorkiest dork, she pointed both thumbs toward the door.

Although she thought her imminent exit would put him in a better mood, Winston's scowl deepened. "You can't."

Is this the part where things get creepy? she wondered, sidling a couple of steps closer to the door. She probably should've expected that blackmailing the weird hermit into helping her would have less-than-fun consequences. "I...can't?"

With a look of exaggerated patience that banished her twinge of unease for some reason, he gestured toward the window.

"Oh." Big drops of rain were splatting against the pane. "No problem. A little rain won't kill me." She winced as the patter turned into a downpour. "Wow, that's a lot of rain. And wind. And... Is that hail?"

"Yes."

The walk back to her rental car was going to suck. She

peeked sideways at him, judging her chances. "Any possibility of getting a ride down your driveway of doom?"

His sigh was so deep it sounded as if it started all the way from the bottoms of his feet. "No."

"Oh." *Fair. I did just blackmail him, after all.* Her gaze landed on the window again as the hail turned from a tiny *ping-ping-ping* to a rapid rattling. Just the sound made her skin sting in anticipation.

"You shouldn't be driving in this." His next sigh sounded more like a groan. "You'll have to stay here."

"Stay?" Despite the absolutely horrendous weather, the thought of not returning to her hotel room hadn't occurred to her. "Like…a sleepover?"

He shot her an unreadable look. "This is just going to get worse as the temperature drops and the roads get icy." Crossing the room with what Dahlia could only call a stomp, he swung open a door and waved an arm as if gesturing her inside.

She approached cautiously, still considering the possibility—as faint as it was—that he might lock her inside. If he did, he was the most reluctant kidnapper she'd ever met—not that she'd ever knowingly met any kidnappers. Since she didn't have a control group to judge typical kidnapper behavior, she couldn't really say for certain whether his actions fit the mold or not.

The moment she stepped into the room, all of her concerns became inconsequential. Even if she were held for ransom, she wouldn't mind it if she got to stay in this wonderful room. It was all warm colors and soft fabrics, with a bed that practically begged her to curl up in the covers and sleep for a week. It was obviously a guest room, lacking the life clutter that most people's bedrooms contained, but it held a warm, welcoming feel that most guest bedrooms lacked.

"Now I know how Gretel felt," she said, unable to resist running her hand over the soft burgundy blanket folded over the foot of the bed.

"What?" Winston asked from where he still hovered in the doorway.

"When she spotted that candy house in the woods." Dahlia admired the many pillows piled on the bed. "There was no way she could've resisted taking a bite."

Winston cleared his throat, sounding like he was choking a bit. "You hungry?"

With a laugh, Dahlia said, "I wasn't hinting about food when I mentioned the candy house."

He just twitched a shoulder and waited.

"Not really." She placed a hand over her worry-knotted stomach.

His brows drew together in a ferocious frown. "When'd you eat last?"

She had to think about it. The whole day had been a rushed blur of traveling and stressing about Rose. Food hadn't been a priority. "I had coffee this morning."

"Coffee doesn't count."

"Oh! I had a packet of that pretzel mix on the plane."

After giving her a flat stare, he turned around and marched away. "Come on," he ordered when she didn't immediately follow him.

Curious, she left the adorable bedroom and trailed after

him to the kitchen. "You don't have to feed me," she protested. "You're already letting me stay after I ambushed you in your secret lair."

"You didn't ambush me." He sounded almost offended as he grabbed a mixing bowl from a cupboard. "I knew you were coming since you spent forever picking the lock."

"Hey." She tried to mimic his scowl. "That was my first lock-picking experience. I'm sure I had a decent time compared to other novices."

He just grunted and let the bag of flour hit the counter with a little more force than necessary.

Giving up on trying to stop him from feeding her, she leaned against the counter in a spot out of his way. She couldn't seem to stop staring at him. There was something about Winston Dane that fascinated her, making it almost impossible to look away. "What are you making?" she asked, mostly because sitting silently and ogling him seemed creepier than ogling him while having a conversation. "Can I help?"

"Pancakes. And no. Just sit there."

Holding back an amused sound at his less-than-polite way of declining her help, she repeated, "Pancakes."

He paused in the middle of cracking an egg to look at her. "Don't you like them?"

"Of course I like pancakes," she assured him. "Who doesn't like pancakes?"

Apparently satisfied with her answer, he finished breaking his current egg and grabbed another.

Finding herself drifting back in silent-staring mode, she

continued. "I just haven't had them in years. I'm not sure why. Pancakes are excellent, especially for dinner. There something about eating breakfast foods for non-breakfast meals that makes me feel like a rebel."

His right eyebrow jumped at that, and he *might've* almost smiled.

Despite her plan to keep the conversation going—single-handedly, if necessary—she found herself lulled into a weirdly peaceful silence as he mixed up the batter and heated the griddle. He glanced at her a few times, until he finally asked, "What?"

"What what?"

"You're quiet," he explained. "And you're looking at me strangely."

Leaning her chin on her hand, Dahlia decided to be honest. There was something about the warm, bright kitchen with the rain and hail lashing at the windows that created a feeling of cozy intimacy, tempting her to spill all her secrets to this stranger who didn't feel like a stranger. "I don't think anyone has ever cooked for me before."

He paused, considering her. "Never?"

She thought back all the way to her earliest memories. "Not unless they've been paid for it. Never just to be nice."

He poured perfectly round circles of batter, concentrating just a little too hard on his task. "I'm not nice."

"Mmmhmm."

"I'm not."

Dahlia batted her lashes at his downturned head even though he couldn't see her. "Of course you're not nice. A nice person would've insisted I stay over after barging uninvited into their home and blackmailing them, just so I wouldn't have to walk and/or drive in bad weather. And a nice person would've cooked pancakes for me." She paused. "Hang on…"

Since he couldn't argue that he wasn't nice when he was in the actual process of doing nice things, he just made a grumbly noise and continued making pancakes for her.

As they cooked, he sliced up a banana and some strawberries, placing them on the breakfast bar in front of her, along with a bottle of maple syrup and some butter. "Juice?" he asked, pulling a glass from the cupboard. "Milk?"

"Just water, please." She watched as he filled the glass from the dispenser on the fridge and handed it to her. "Aren't you eating with me?"

"Already ate," he said, as if he wasn't a giant machine of a man who could probably ingest calories all day long and still need more. Flipping pancakes onto a plate, he added a fork and set it in front of her.

She glanced down and then froze at the sight. Her eyes stung with tears for some strange reason. Telling herself she was just tired and overwrought, she blinked them away. Still, her emotions stuck in her throat, making it impossible to say anything.

Instead, she picked up the perfectly heart-shaped pancake that topped the stack of round ones and held it up in front of her mouth to hide the beginning of a delighted smile, meeting Winston's gaze over the top. Clearing her throat, she managed to say, "Oh no. He's not nice at all."

"An accident. The batter got away from me."

"Mmmhmm."

Making defensive grumbling noises, Winston started

cleaning up with more rattling and thumping than Dahlia figured was really necessary. She took a bite of the heart-shaped pancake and decided it was the best thing she'd ever tasted.

———

Dahlia sat sideways in the window seat of Winston's guest bedroom, staring out at the still-raging storm. *Is Rose out there in this mess, or is she tucked away somewhere warm and safe?*

A knock made her jump and turn her head to see Winston hovering in the open doorway, a stack of blankets in his arms.

Standing, she moved toward him. "What're all those?" she asked curiously, gesturing to his armload of fabric.

"Blankets," he said, as if it was obvious, which it kind of was, but Dahlia was still confused.

"But there are at least four on the bed already?" she said, her voice turning up at the end in question. "How many blankets will I need tonight? Do you turn off the heat in your house or something?"

"What?" It was his turn to sound confused as he set the blankets on the foot of her bed. "Of course not. Why would I turn off the heat?"

"I don't know." She waved at the tall stack. "That's a *lot* of blankets. Are we planning to make a fort?"

"A *fort*? Of course not." He was looking at her like she was the strange one. "You're from California. You're not used to this climate. I don't want you to be cold."

Just like the unexpectedly heart-shaped pancake, his consideration knocked her emotional feet out from under her. "Oh. Thank you."

He grunted what she assumed was something in the realm of "you're welcome."

Dahlia still felt off-balance, so she offered, "We'd still have enough for a blanket fort, if you want to make one."

"No fort."

"You sure?" The teasing allowed her to find her footing again. "I make a mean blanket fort, if I do say so myself."

"No." He paused. "Need more pillows?"

"Um…that's okay." She did a quick count. "I think these *eleven* pillows should be adequate."

Tipping his chin up in a brief nod, he turned to go but paused. "There's one of my T-shirts on top," he said, gesturing to the stack of blankets he'd just delivered. "Figured you'd need something to sleep in."

"Thank you." Just like that, she was ready to tear up again. Something about this man and his unexpected sweetness and sincerity threw her for a loop. "That was nice of you."

"Not nice," he positively growled before stomping out the bedroom door, barely pausing to pull the door shut behind him with a firm *snap*.

Picking up the borrowed T-shirt, she couldn't resist sniffing it, a little disappointed that all she could detect was the slightest whiff of laundry detergent. She pretended like she hadn't wanted it to smell like vanilla cupcakes—just like Winston Dane.

Clutching the T-shirt against her chest, she looked down at the towering stack of blankets. "And he says he's not nice," she murmured, unable to hold back a smile.

THREE

Despite the ridiculously comfortable bed, Dahlia spent a restless night coming up with various sorts of danger her sister could be in. Midway through imagining Rose surrounded by dozens of rattlesnakes, she managed to doze off. Despite her late night, Dahlia was wide awake before dawn. Luckily, Winston was up at an impressively early hour, and he insisted on making her oatmeal before driving her back to her rental car. Dahlia returned to the Yodel Inn to shower and dress in one of her mountain-chic outfits—cream cashmere turtleneck sweater, chocolate-brown leggings, low-heeled faux-riding boots, and fleece-lined leather jacket. She even had time before Winston's arrival to make up her face in her best fresh outdoorsy look, as well as have a fairly unproductive chat with the Yodel Inn's front desk clerk.

When Winston pounded on her door soon after she returned to her room, he wasn't about to charge off to the falls immediately. Instead, he insisted on searching her sister's room at the Yodel Inn. Reluctantly, Dahlia had to admit it was a good idea. She did believe, however, that Winston suggested it just to give himself more time to try to weasel out of their hike. From his extra-cranky expression, he hadn't come up with any ideas on how to escape her evil plan.

"Bob—he's the front desk guy—" she started, only to be interrupted by Winston's muttering.

"I know Bob."

Holding in an eye roll at his grouchy tone, she continued as if he hadn't said anything. "Bob said that Rose booked the room for two weeks, which eliminates the possibility that Howling Falls—the town—wasn't doing it for her so she just picked up and left."

His right eyebrow twitched. "That was a possibility?"

"Not really, because of the emergency text, but it's still good to know she was planning on coming back here." Her stomach gave a worried twinge, a sensation that'd been all too common since she'd gotten her sister's last message. "I tried to get him to let me in her room again this morning, but he refused—said he's a stickler for privacy and basically threatened to call the cops if I kept pushing." She gave a huff. "Since this place has old-school keys, I can just pick the lock."

His heavy sigh sounded as if it came from the very depths of his soul. "What room?"

"Seventeen."

Without another word, he turned and marched along the front of the motel. Dahlia scampered after him. Instead of irritation at his high-handed takeover of the situation, she felt an interesting lightness. She was used to dealing with everything herself—flat tires, clogged toilets, the discontinuation of her favorite color of lip tint—so having someone else be in charge was…sort of nice? As much as Dahlia liked having control of her own life, dealing with all the little blips and bobbles and bumps was exhausting. She'd never had the chance to dump a problem into someone else's lap and take a big step back, brushing imaginary dust off her hands, so this experience was a revelation.

She really, really liked having help.

"Maybe I should hire an assistant," she mused, still rolling this sensation around in her mind, feeling it out. Unless Winston Dane was applying, she really didn't want anyone else hanging around her all the time. Even though they'd just met a day ago, she felt comfortable around him, like she could show her true self and he'd accept her completely. Something about him made her feel safe.

His grunt made her smile, but it dropped away in amazement as they arrived in front of the door to room seventeen and Winston pulled out a little leather case containing lock-picking tools.

"You have a kit for this?" she asked, impressed and also envious. How much quicker would picking the lock on his fence have gone if she'd had actual tools, rather than trying to force one of her favorite lip pencils to be something it wasn't. "Poor Iconic Rose Barbara Whitmore Lip Trick never even had a chance."

Winston slowly turned his head to stare at her. "None of those words made any sense."

She nodded. "I know. It wasn't fair of me."

"Still not making any sense."

She stared back, Winston's pretty hazel eyes making her lose the conversational thread for a moment. Forcing herself to look away, she gestured toward the very specific tools he had in his hands. "Well? Show me how to do this properly."

He glanced down, looking mildly surprised, as if he'd forgotten what he held. Then he grimaced as he pulled out two of the silver tools. "Why would I teach you how to break into my place *faster*?"

"Aren't you on the side of efficiency?"

"Not when it helps get you inside my home," he grumbled, but the words didn't hold his usual angry force. Instead, he seemed almost resigned, which was excellent. She was wearing down his resistance even more quickly than she'd expected. She tucked her hands in her pockets in order to keep from gleefully rubbing them together, since that was a total giveaway super-villain move. He shot her a sideways glance as he slipped a tool into the lock. "No comment? That's new."

She offered him an innocent smile, which widened when he gave a surly grunt in response. Her amusement disappeared, pushed aside by indignation, when he popped in a second tool, fiddled around for just a few seconds, and the lock clicked open. "Seriously?" she huffed, her envy and grudging admiration warring for supremacy. "You make it look easy."

"It is easy." The slight self-satisfied smirk on his face was more attractive than it had any right to be. Normally, smug wasn't a good look for anybody, but he made it work somehow.

"Good job," she said approvingly, and his expression turned suspicious. Throwing him off his game made her quite pleased with herself, which brightened her mood even more. "Let's go look for clues."

"No." Despite the negative, he walked into Rose's motel room with the confidence of someone who'd just paid for it.

"Isn't that why we're here?" she asked, following him in and relocking the door behind her before she looked around. The motel room was a mirror image to the one she was staying in, both cleaner and cuter than she'd expected from a place that was the only lodging option within fifty mountainous miles. "Clue-hunting?"

"We're not saying the word 'clue.'"

"Um...random, but if it's important to you, I guess I can try," she said doubtfully. "Personally, I hate 'nasal' and 'glut,' so I understand avoiding words that feel gross in your ears."

When he didn't respond, she interrupted her scan of the room to peer at him. He was staring at her with more bafflement than irritation, which was a new look for him. "You're so strange."

She snorted as she moved toward the open suitcase sitting on one of the beds. "Coming from a weird hermit, that's quite a compliment."

"I'm not a hermit," he grumbled, although she noticed he didn't try to deny the "weird" part.

"Sure, you are." She rifled through the suitcase, trying not to cringe at Rose's clothes. Dahlia understood dressing for function, but there was no excuse for picking things that were uncomfortable and just plain ugly for ugly's sake. She held up a pair of stiff cargo pants that were an unfortunate color that blended the worst of brown, gray, and green. Dahlia had gifted Rose several adorable pairs of cargo pants—fitted, yet still comfortable, in soft fabrics and warm colors of chocolate and velveteen-rabbit gray. She was pretty sure they'd never left Rose's closet. Instead, her sister wore those cheap, rough, unflattering abominations for some reason. "You have the beard, the flannel, and the inhospitable compound. It's the mountain hermit trifecta." After checking the pockets—empty—Dahlia dropped the hideous pants with a shudder, and then picked them up to fold them properly. Even ugly clothes deserved respectful handling.

Winston made grumbly noises as he searched the bathroom. "I go to town."

"That's nice," Dahlia answered absently as she folded the last T-shirt and replaced it in Rose's suitcase. She hadn't found anything useful among her sister's clothes, so she moved to check the dresser.

"A real hermit wouldn't leave their property," he continued. Apparently, she'd struck a nerve.

"Mostly staying home, avoiding people, and doing all your shopping online doesn't make someone a hermit." The dresser was empty except for the Bible in the top drawer, so she moved to the tiny closet.

Winston propped a shoulder in the bathroom doorway and crossed his arms as he scowled at her. "That's the *definition* of a hermit."

"Nope. That's just a normal person. If my job didn't require that I work with people in-person, that'd be me most of the time. Being a hermit is more of an energy."

"I have hermit...*energy*?"

"Definitely. Nothing wrong with that. You should own it." The closet was empty except for a few hangers and one of Rose's jackets—a stiff canvas thing with such a boxy shape it wouldn't be a good look on *anyone*—draped over a hook on the inside of one of the doors. She checked the pockets, not very hopeful of finding anything useful, since anything useful would be with Rose. Just as that pessimistic thought crossed her mind, her fingers brushed against the smooth surface of paper. "Oop! A clue!" She gave Winston a guilty look. "Sorry. Glut. Nasal. Now we're even. I'll do better. But look! A cl—potentially useful piece of possible evidence!" She pulled out a folded square of paper and waved it toward Winston.

He didn't seem to share her excitement. "What is it?"

Unfolding the square, she gave a delighted *whoop*. She couldn't have asked for anything better. "A map." At his doubtful look, she waved it at him again, this time open so he could see that she wasn't making it up. "Seriously. She left us a map. How perfect is this?"

He snatched it out of the air mid-wave and flattened it out on the top of the dresser. Dahlia scooted in next to him to get a look at the paper, since she'd been too busy celebrating to actually examine the thing.

"Looks like she got it from the front desk," she said, tracing a curving line of highlighter from a starred spot to a black, handwritten X. "Someone marked up this map to Howling Falls Falls for her."

Winston grunted what sounded like agreement but then paused. "Only one."

"One what?" she asked absently, studying the paper in front of them. Since maps weren't her forte, most of the squiggles and lines made no sense to her. Good thing she'd convinced Winston to join her on their find-Rose quest.

"One falls. It's just Howling Falls, not Falls Falls."

"Then how can we distinguish between the town of Howling Falls and Howling Falls Falls?"

"Just—hmm." He interrupted himself with a sound she couldn't interpret.

"What is it?" she asked.

"This isn't one of the routes to the falls."

"It's not?" She frowned at the map as if it'd betrayed her. "But it says Howling Falls right here. Unless that's the town? See, if the mapmaker had used the double falls, there wouldn't be this confusion."

"There is no confusion." He said it with such gritted-teeth confidence that she would've believed him if she hadn't been, at that very moment, confused. "It shows both routes to the falls, but this highlighted trail goes away from it. See here? This starts at the falls and leads west." His forefinger traced a line that ran from a starred point on the map to an X. "Not sure what that X is indicating. There's nothing special there that I know about."

They studied the map in silence for a few seconds before she asked, "How long would this take an experienced but occasionally clumsy hiker?"

"One and a half, two days, depending on which route she took. If she followed this highlighted path from the falls to this X, it'd probably be an extra four, five hours. Hard to tell since it's just drawn in, though."

"One way?" Dahlia asked, frowning at the map. It looked much shorter on paper. "Or one day out to the falls and one back?" She decided to focus on his more optimistic estimate.

"Just to there." He jabbed the star on the paper with a forefinger. "Three or four days total, depending on how much time she plans to spend at the falls. If she went to whatever this is…" He followed the drawn line with his finger again and shrugged.

"Even if she just went to the falls, she definitely lingered." Looking at the map with new eyes, she grimaced, feeling discouraged. There were all sorts of things that could've happened to Rose, especially if she'd taken the weird sketched-in path or wandered off the trail. They could search for her for months—or even *years*—and never find a trace of her. Quickly pulling the hand brake on her negative thoughts, Dahlia focused on a circled spot on the map. "Isn't that this motel?"

Winston leaned a little closer to the map before saying, "Yeah. Close by, at least. Circle covers half a block."

"Bet Bob drew this for her then." She cocked her head to the side and eyed Winston as a thought occurred to her. "Why would he want her taking this weird trail? How well do you know Bob? Is he the type of guy who'd keep women who look like yogurt models in his basement?"

"He doesn't have a basement," Winston said, as if that fact removed all possibility of Bob being a kidnapper and/or serial killer.

"In his attic then." Dahlia barely contained an eye roll at Winston's lack of imagination. "Or his garden shed."

Stubbornly, Winston gave his head a sharp shake. "Bob lives in a trailer."

"Even better." She was warming to her theory. "Out in the middle of nowhere—"

"In the Flower View Trailer Park."

"Oh." Although that took most of the wind out of her sails, she still had one last play. "Maybe this X is his remote cabin that he inherited from his actual hermit of a great-grandmother?"

"No."

"How can you know that for *sure*?" she asked, because he had a tendency to say "no" with a certainty she wasn't convinced was always completely merited.

"No one'd live in the Flower View Trailer Park unless they absolutely had no other option."

Dahlia blew out a long breath, reluctantly letting go of the idea of Bob as the convenient villain as she refolded the map and stuffed it in her jacket pocket. "Fine."

Before she could posit any other theories, there was the thump of knuckles hitting the door and then the jingle of keys.

"Bob!" Dahlia growled almost soundlessly as she grabbed Winston's hand and bolted for the bathroom. She thought that she'd have to drag him after her, but he seemed to understand the urgency and followed her closely, even soundlessly closing the bathroom door behind them.

Her intention had just been to find a place to hide until Bob saw that they hadn't, in fact, broken into the very room he'd just refused them access to, but Winston had other ideas, skirting around her and kneeling on the floor next to the toilet. She watched as he lifted a section of floor, revealing a crawl space used to access the plumbing.

He waved at her impatiently, and—refusing to think about the rats, spiders, and other small, bitey things that almost surely lived in that dark, cobwebbed space—she dove for the hole, scrambling in and to the side so that Winston could squeeze his large self in next to her. He closed the access panel in the floor above them, just as the front door groaned open and thumped against the wall.

Lying on her front in the dirt, Dahlia froze, not wanting to make a sound that might give them away. She had no doubt that Bob would follow through with his threat of calling the police, and then that nice Officer Bitts would arrest both of them, which would be awkward and embarrassing and eat up tons of Rose-finding time. The ground was lumpy under her, and she refused to speculate on what certain prominent bumps may be, since she was heavily invested in retaining her sanity. The press of Winston against her side was the only thing keeping her calm, the warm pressure of his shoulder and hip incredibly grounding. She was strangely tempted to take his hand, but she was worried that even the rustle of that tiny movement would give away their presence.

The floor above them creaked under the front desk clerk's weight, each step getting louder and closer as Bob crossed the hotel room, entered the bathroom, and stopped almost directly above them. Unable to take the suspense without a little physical moral support, Dahlia hooked her pinkie finger around Winston's. That small touch bolstered her courage, but she still held her breath as Bob continued standing there.

They were just inches away from detection, and Dahlia's muscles tightened with the strain of holding still. She would've thought not moving was easy, but her contrary body struggled with every second of enforced stillness. Her legs needed to twitch, her toes were cramping, and her stomach churned with anxiety. The adrenaline coursing through her didn't help, since it was urging her to either run away or throw a punch, and it didn't care for Option C: Just stay *still* for a freaking second.

Although she'd been hoping for Bob to move, when he finally did, she startled. He stepped toward the shower and then the curtain rings clattered against the rod, making Dahlia very glad that they weren't currently crouched in the tub. She made a mental note to compliment Winston later on his next-level hide-and-seek skills.

Maybe it was her imagination, but Bob's retreating footsteps as he left the bathroom sounded a bit more defeated and less triumphant than his march in. Dahlia forced herself to stay still, just in case it was a bluff on Bob's part, only allowing her excitement to show in a squeeze of Winston's pinkie finger. To her shock, he squeezed back.

Endless minutes later—although in actuality, it was probably less than five—Winston pulled his hand from hers and started army crawling away. Dahlia had figured that they'd leave the way they'd arrived—through the bathroom floor—but apparently her partner in crime had a different plan. With a mental shrug, she army crawled after him. At least he was going first, so his big body could clear a path through the cobwebs and bug corpses.

During her anxiety-filled wait under the bathroom, Dahlia's eyes must've adjusted to the dim light, because she could see general forms—enough to know when to duck her head to avoid whacking it against a hanging waste pipe. She could also see Winston's hulking shape in front of her, which was more reassuring than it ought to have been, but she wasn't about to start analyzing why that was. First, they needed to get out of this very gross crawl space.

After what felt like an endless slog—but was probably just another five minutes—Dahlia's abs and deltoids were burning. She decided to add crawl-space escape to her wrought-iron-gate-climbing exercise program. It'd be a full-body burglary-preparation workout. The gym clientele would go nuts for it.

The space suddenly filled with light, and Dahlia flinched, afraid that Bob had discovered them after all. Once she blinked several times and the glare faded to a glow that was still bright but at least not blinding, she realized that it wasn't Bob who'd lit up the place, but Winston. He'd opened a section of insulation and siding that closed in the crawl space. She wasn't sure if he'd opened an existing access door or just knocked down a chunk of wall to make his own, but either way, they were almost out.

As she wiggled after him, she made the mistake of looking around. Thinking she caught the glow of beady animal eyes, she launched herself through the opening, sucking in a gasp of air as if they'd been underwater rather than just under a motel floor.

Rolling to her back, Dahlia caught her breath and enjoyed the warmth of the sun on her face and the lack of visible spiders. "Excellent work, Winston."

"Thanks." There was a wealth of sarcasm in that single word, which just increased her admiration for the man.

She sat up and looked around. It appeared that they'd emerged in the back of the motel, hidden from any witnesses to their escape by the building and a line of scrubby evergreen trees in the other direction. Winston was already replacing their improvised exit door, and she hurried to help. They managed to get it mostly wedged back into place. It was a bit too rough of a patch to pass close inspection, but it wouldn't be noticed by a casual glance either.

Dahlia dusted off her hands. "Let's go talk to Bob."

His eyebrow had an opinion on that plan. "Might want to get the spiders out of your hair first."

Her immediate reaction was to slap at her head until either she knocked herself unconscious or every possible spider was dead, but Winston caught her hand before she could get in more than a couple of good whacks.

"Spider*webs*," he corrected, a bit late in her opinion. "Stop that."

Then, to her absolute, jaw-literally-dropping shock, he ran a careful hand over her hair, brushing away any remaining cobwebs that clung to her. For one of the first times in her entire life, she was speechless. She had no words—none at all. Instead of saying anything, she just stood there as he removed any trace of her crawl-space adventure, and then…

Tidied her hair? *What is happening right now?*

Still in a state of bewilderment, she turned obediently when he nudged her shoulder so he could brush off her clothes as well. Once he was done, he gave her a final once-over and a short nod. "Better."

He turned to go, but she caught his hand to stop him. "Hang on," she said. "You're still looking a little rough." She reached up to brush cobwebs and dust and what could be a bug corpse—but she refused to look at close enough to confirm—out of his short hair and beard. When she moved to the nape of his neck, he shivered, and she held back a wicked grin.

Throw me off my game by being nice, will you, she thought with a mental smirk. *Now it's your turn to be discombobulated.*

She was more thorough than necessary, turning each flick of her fingers into a sneaky caress. It quickly morphed from revenge to fascinated study as she explored the hard contours of his body. His multiple layers of clothes disguised his true form, but she could feel enough through the fabric to make it difficult to stop. She lingered long enough to start feeling like a perv, however, so she reluctantly gave his pant leg a final swipe along his calf—*how can a calf muscle, of all things, be sexy?* she wondered—before straightening up and giving him a final once-over like he'd given her.

"Good?" he asked when her once-over turned into a thrice-over.

"Very good." The words came out in a sort of growly purr, a

sound she hadn't even realized she could produce. Clearing her throat, she tried again. "Shall we go talk to Bob?"

He dipped his chin in agreement, but instead of charging ahead, he fell in next to her, and she tried very hard not to give him any side-eye. She knew this new awareness was all on her side. It was just that she was a sucker for a cinnamon roll, and Winston Dane wasn't just a cinnamon roll—he was a *stealth* cinnamon roll, hiding his squishy sweetness behind a scowl and some booby traps.

Focus, her inner voice reminded her, and she knew it was right. Winston was a distraction. If she'd been in Howling Falls on vacation, she could've maybe indulged in some of that sweet cinnamon-roll goodness, but Rose's life was likely on the line.

Her newly forming crush needed to wait, especially since he was going to be her wilderness guide—albeit grudgingly. Dahlia needed to stuff her inconvenient feelings deep down inside, which she knew she could do. She'd had plenty of practice, after all.

FOUR

SOMEHOW, THEY MANAGED TO GET to the motel office before Bob returned. Dahlia leaned against the front desk, affecting a look of boredom as the clerk stormed in not even thirty seconds after them. Bob came to an abrupt halt at the sight of them, but he collected himself quickly when Dahlia gave him a politely inquiring look.

"I'm not letting you in that room," Bob said, hurrying around to the other side of the desk, as if the bulky piece of furniture gave him some protection. Dahlia couldn't blame him. She imagined a scowling Winston could be terrifying to someone who hadn't seen him gently tidying her hair.

"Oh, we totally understand that," Dahlia soothed, as if she hadn't berated the man for exactly that not even an hour earlier. "We just forgot to ask a question."

"What is it now?" Even though Bob still sounded grumpy, he also seemed a bit frazzled, and she wondered if he was feeling guilty for erroneously thinking they'd stoop to breaking into Rose's room.

Her smile widening at the thought, Dahlia pulled out the folded paper they'd found when they had indeed broken into her sister's room and held it up for Bob to see. "Did you mark up this Howling Falls Falls map for Rose?"

He squinted at it but refused to come closer where he could see it better. "No, that's not from here. Our maps are different." He gestured toward a small rack holding a half-dozen brochures sitting on top of the reception desk. Dahlia tucked Rose's map away before examining the motel's options, which were indeed antique tan instead of white, glossy instead of matte, and in a completely different format.

Replacing the motel's map, Dahlia asked, "Where do you think she got this one?"

Bob's furry gray eyebrows drew together suspiciously. "Why are you asking?"

"Just have a question for the person who gave her directions," she said mildly, giving him a smile.

After a glare that lasted long enough for Dahlia to start thinking Bob wasn't going to answer, he grudgingly did. "Could be Howling Falls Diner. Or the gas station on the corner. Think they both have maps."

"Thank you," Dahlia said graciously, even though she wanted to rail against the man. Thanks to him, she'd had *spiders* in her *hair*. Instead, she reminded herself that she and Winston—mostly Winston, to give credit where credit was due—had outsmarted Bob, so they had the upper hand—even though Bob may never know he'd been bested. She gave him another smile and a small pageant wave. "Have a nice day."

Winston held the door for her. When she paused right outside the motel office, he gestured to the left. She started walking that direction even as she shot him a curious look.

"Where are we headed?" she asked.

"Howling Falls Diner. Assumed you'd want to try there first."

"I do," she agreed, "except that I'm feeling like daylight's burning. Should we have started hiking to the falls at the crack of dawn instead of doing fruitless searches for you-know-whats and hanging out in crawl spaces with smallish bitey things and matching wits with Bob? Are we wasting valuable time?"

"What's the point of searching for your sister at the falls if she never made it there? Or never even left town?" he asked.

This struck her as extremely smart thinking, and she shot him an approving look. "Recruiting you to our team was the best thing I've done so far."

"Blackmailing," he countered. When she gave him a faux-innocent look, he clarified, enunciating each word. "You didn't *recruit* me. You *blackmailed* me."

Dahlia waved off his petty nitpicking. "Eh. You would've helped anyway. Anyone who cares whether I have spiders in my hair wouldn't have let me wander around the mountains alone and ignorant." She walked through the door he held open, assuming it was the diner. "Thank you."

"What you just said didn't make any sense at all," he grumbled, just loud enough for her to hear him.

She smiled, keeping her face turned away so he didn't see. There was no reason to poke the beast. *Okay, fine. Poking the beast is fun, so that's a reason. I just can't make him so mad he decides his rabid fans are the less-annoying option. So…limited beast-poking then.*

"Welcome to the Howling Falls Diner!" a cheerful server called out. The fiftysomething white woman had graying blond hair and the leathery tan skin that so many of the locals seemed to have. Dahlia figured it was from being high in the mountains, close to the sun. "Booth okay?"

"Actually, I wanted to ask—"

"Yes," Winston interrupted, drawing the server's attention to him. The woman's broad smile faltered as she took in his mountainous form.

"Oh… Mr. Dane. Nice to see you." Despite the server's best efforts, it was painfully obvious that she didn't find seeing Winston nice at all. Gathering up a couple of menus, she led them to a booth in the corner, away from the other occupied tables. Although Dahlia appreciated the privacy, she was amused at how the server made sure to give them—well, Winston really—a big bubble, like he was a mountain lion or something, and she wanted to ensure that the other patrons were all out of swatting reach. "My name's Susan—well, you know that, Mr. Dane." She made a small throat-clearing sound that was closer to a choke. "I'll be…um, back to take your order." She ran off as if a mountain lion was indeed after her.

Dahlia was momentarily distracted by the server's reaction to Winston, but she quickly refocused on their mission. "What are you doing?" she demanded in a whisper-yell as she slid into the booth. She was determined to stay on task, but she felt silly hovering outside the booth, especially because it appeared that all the other diner patrons' eyes were on them.

"Getting some breakfast," he said, not even looking at the menu.

"We need to keep searching for Rose."

"We also need to eat."

"I already ate. You made me oatmeal. It was delicious."

"You barely ate any of it."

She stared at him, frustrated by the delay but also by the fact that he was right. It wouldn't do Rose any good if they fell over in a faint. Besides, she wouldn't want to deal with a hangry Winston. He was growly enough when he was well fed. "Fine," she sighed, grabbing one of the menus. When he didn't move to do the same, she held up the second one in his direction.

"I already know what I want," he said, not taking the proffered menu. "I eat here *a lot*." He gave her a look.

It was her turn to raise her eyebrows. Unfortunately, she'd never mastered the art of lifting just one, but she did her best. "What's with the heavy emphasis?"

"Just more proof that I'm not a hermit. A hermit wouldn't come to the café to eat."

She gave a skeptical hum as she looked around. "I don't know. This place seems pretty hermit friendly. Did you sit by yourself or with friends?"

Leaning back, he crossed his arms over his chest and glowered at her.

Contrary as always, his pout made her want to pat him soothingly. "I'm just teasing. I'm sure you do lots and lots of non-hermit-y things."

His scowl just deepened, probably because her tone was more appropriate for a sulking six-year-old than a thirtyish one-ton truck of a man.

Feeling a little guilty for giving him a hard time, especially because he was helping her willingly after only the slightest threat of blackmail, she turned the conversation to easier topics. "So what's good here?"

Eyeing her suspiciously, as if he figured her innocent question was a lead-up to more teasing, he finally grunted, "Eggs."

Lifting her gaze from the egg-centric breakfast menu, she smirked. "Any eggs in particular?"

"The Lumberjack," he grumbled, although his arms uncrossed, making him look a little less defensive.

Dahlia found the menu item, and her heart almost gave up on life just from the description. "Wow. That's a lot of…meats."

His grunt sounded both affirmative and approving.

Susan reluctantly made her way back to their table. "Did you need more time?" she asked hopefully, darting a wary glance at Winston before refocusing on Dahlia.

"I'll take the breakfast burrito with a side of fruit," she said, handing the server both menus. "He'll have the Lumberjack, eggs over easy, extra meats."

Winston looked startled, and she reveled in being able to surprise him. "How'd you know?"

"The gleam in your eyes when I mentioned the plethora of meats," she said as Susan hurried away. "And you just seem like a guy who likes your eggs over easy."

His hum was thoughtful as he studied her. "What do you do?"

"As a job?" At his confirming nod, she settled back in her seat. She loved talking about what she did for a living. "I do makeovers."

He blinked once as he digested that. "Like...at a makeup counter?"

She laughed, weirdly loving the hit to her ego. "Nah. Makeup's just a small part of it. I help people find their style—clothes, hair, accessories, and yes, makeup too. By the time I'm done with a client, I want their outsides to mirror their insides." She paused, replaying what she'd just said. "That sounded more serial-killery than I meant it to. I just help people show who they really are and who they want to be."

"Isn't that kind of...shallow?"

She'd been asked that question so many times in so many ways that she didn't even get annoyed anymore. "Not at all. It's the most physical and basic form of self-actualization. People come to me because they feel trapped in a look that isn't truly *them*. They know they're stuck, but they don't know how to get unstuck. I help them find their way out."

Winston watched her intently, although the groove between his eyebrows deepened. "How can clothes do that? They're just...clothes."

"Have you ever had an office job?" she asked.

He gave a short nod, never taking his eyes off of her, and a very distracting mental picture of him in a well-fitted suit flashed into her mind. Shoving the image away so she could concentrate, she refocused on the conversation.

"Think about how it felt to wear a tie." He grimaced, and

she started to smile, knowing that she had him. "The feel of it wrapped around your neck, knotted and tightened so your top shirt button is pressed against your throat. What's the first word that comes to mind when you remember how it felt?"

"Trapped."

She grinned, triumphant and excited to share the thrill she got from her makeovers. "Exactly! Now tell me how you feel right now, in your flannel shirt and jeans."

He paused for a moment before answering, and Dahlia appreciated his thoughtfulness. "Fine. I mean, I don't really feel anything about them. They just…are."

"Exactly," she said again, this time with even more satisfaction. "They're just a part of you, like your pretty hazel eyes or your judgmental right eyebrow. They fit—not size-wise, although they do that too, but they fit who you are right now."

He didn't look fully convinced. "That's because they're comfortable."

"Physical comfort's a part of it. Clothes shouldn't be uncomfortable," she agreed. "But someone else might take comfort from wearing a necktie. They might gain confidence from the feel of fabric wrapped around their neck. Wearing a sloppy flannel shirt like yours, on the other hand, might make them uncomfortable."

"Sloppy?" That eyebrow was judging her again, but she just nodded firmly.

"Sloppy."

He hummed skeptically, but Dahlia saw the twitch at the corner of his lips as a smile tried to escape.

A movement in her periphery made her turn her head to see Susan watching their booth warily even as she delivered food to another table. "So…question," Dahlia said, returning her attention to Winston.

His stern poker face was back, but she remembered that tiny almost-smile and pressed on.

"Why is Susan acting like you're actually a vicious, people-eating alien stuffed in a human suit?"

He blinked, started to open his mouth, then snapped it shut and blinked again. After a few seconds, he regained his ability to glare ferociously. "I'm intimidating."

Dahlia tried to turn her laugh into a cough, but from the way his frown deepened, she hadn't succeeded very well. "Please. You're about as intimidating as a fluffy kitten."

He made a choking sound.

"How can you be intimidating when you're afraid of your own TikTok fans?"

"I don't have any TikTok fans."

"Denying your TikTok fans doesn't make them not exist." She decided the conversation wasn't going anywhere productive, so she changed the subject. She'd figure out the mystery of Winston's reputation in town later. "I've told you what I do. What do *you* do besides write and hermit it up?"

"Not a hermit."

"That was a dodge," she hummed.

"I don't do anything else right now."

The "right now" caught her attention. "What'd you do before? Besides being on *City Survival*, I mean. Just tell me one thing."

"I taught." His jaw tightened in a way she was starting to recognize when she made him talk about something he didn't want to discuss—which, to be fair, was most subjects. Therefore, she decided to ignore all the "do not enter" warning signs he was throwing up all over the place.

"A teacher?" Now she was picturing him all buttoned up and professorial, and it made her squirm a little as heat curled in her belly. "That was a good look for you, I'm sure."

"A what?" From his momentarily startled glance, she'd gone in a direction he hadn't expected.

"Did you have wire-rimmed glasses and a dapper waistcoat?"

"No."

That was a disappointment, but Dahlia decided she could still picture him that way for her own enjoyment. "What'd you teach?"

He paused long enough that she was pretty sure he wouldn't answer. "Urban warfare tactics and defense," he finally said.

It was her turn to blink. "Huh. So that's why they interviewed you on *City Survival*. How'd you get into the urban warfare thing?"

The split-second, supremely uncomfortable glance he shot her made her sit up straight. She'd been interested in his past before, but that quick look had shot her curiosity meter up to an eleven. To her extreme frustration, he just shrugged without answering.

"Nuh-uh. Now you have to tell me, or I'll die of not knowing."

He let out a groaning sigh. "You're aggravating."

"I know. Now tell."

"I played a combat RPG a lot as a kid." It sounded as if every word was dragged out of him. "I started researching different tactics to use in the game, and that got me interested. I enlisted when I was eighteen, got some combat experience, then got my degrees once I was out of the army."

There were so many questions she had about that short explanation, but the most important point had to be brought up first. Her voice hushed in absolute, complete awe, she asked, "Oh my god, were you a *nerd*?"

The back of his neck grew red as he glowered at her.

She stared back, unable to believe the absolute perfection that sat across from her. "How do you even exist? You're like a magical lumberjack nerd author hot-teacher hermit unicorn *dream*."

He closed his eyes for a long moment before resuming his glaring. "You're doing that thing again."

"What thing?"

"You put all of these words together in a way that makes zero sense."

"One Lumberjack." Susan was back with their food. "And one breakfast burrito and fruit. Anything else I can get you?"

"I think we're good," Dahlia said, the smell of the food making her realize how hungry she was. The ball of anxiety about Rose had stolen her appetite over the past couple of days. Winston had been right to insist that they stop to eat. She gave him an inquiring look, and he lifted his chin in one of his brusque nods. Turning back to Susan, she gave the server a smile. "Yep, we're good. Thank you."

As Susan hurried off, Dahlia admired the sheer quantity of food heaping Winston's plate. "That is indeed a lot of meats."

Picking up his fork, he paused and looked at her. She was confused for a second before she realized he was waiting for her to start eating. "Is that a manner I don't know about?" she asked, taking a bite of her burrito. When he gave her a confused look, she gestured between their plates with her fork. "A gentleman waiting until the lady takes a bite to start eating?"

He shrugged. "Just seemed rude to dig into my...meats." That right eyebrow bobbed, but it seemed more teasing than sarcastic.

Dahlia grinned and then took another bite. "Mmm... You were right. The eggs here are excellent. *Egg*cellent, in fact."

Although he rolled his eyes mockingly, both corners of his lips were twitching with an irrepressible smile, so she took it as a win.

———

After they'd eaten, Winston insisted on paying. A little annoyed that all her attempts to shove money at him had been refused—at the end, quite rudely—Dahlia trailed after him to the counter, where Susan and another server were wrapping silverware in napkins. When she looked up and saw them approaching, Susan dropped the knife, fork, spoon, and napkin, turning pale as they clattered against the countertop. "Was something wrong with your food?" she asked anxiously.

"Oh no," Dahlia hurried to reassure the server. "Everything was wonderful. Winnie here just told me that you might have maps of local trails?"

Looking relieved but still uneasy about Winston's scowling proximity, Susan nodded. "Sure, I can grab you one. Any trail in particular? There are lots of great ones around here."

"The one to Howling Falls—the actual falls, not the town, of course." Feeling a bit silly for making the distinction—since *of course* she meant the falls, as there wouldn't be trails from the town that led to the town—Dahlia ignored Winston's amused snort and kept her focus on Susan.

"Oh yes, we have a map of that trail. I'll get that for you," she said, before hurrying toward the empty hostess station by the door. She returned with a brochure matching the one at the motel—and definitely *not* matching Rose's map—and Dahlia deflated a little. Hiding her disappointment, she made sure the smile she directed at Susan was extra bright.

"Thank you so much."

She waited until they were outside the diner and heading toward the gas station to let out all her disappointment in a heavy sigh. "Well, I guess we have one more place to try." When Winston just grunted his agreement, she shot him a sly look. "Soooo… You never really answered earlier. What'd you do to Susan?"

He frowned down at her. "What? Nothing. I barely know her."

"Then why was she acting like you were going to bite her face off like a rabid mountain lion?"

"Rabid mountain lion?" His scowl deepened. "I thought I was a vicious alien in a people suit."

She studied him, keeping her expression serious with an effort. "Ah. Got it."

"What?" he demanded, just as she intended.

"Oh, nothing." She checked for traffic—not that the town of Howling Falls ever had any traffic—and then strolled across the road with Winston swelling like an impatient balloon next to her. "Just that I get it now."

"Get what?"

"Why Susan's scared of you."

"Why?"

"It's the whole...*face* thing." She sketched an oval in the air, as if outlining the face in question.

"What's wrong with my face?" he demanded.

"Absolutely nothing," she assured him. "It's what you *do* with it that can be terrifying."

"What?" Instead of waiting for her to continue, however, he just shook his head while mumbling angrily under his breath. "Never mind."

"The face thing isn't anything bad. You're just a bit...frowny."

"Frowny."

"Definitely frowny."

"You're so strange."

She smiled and linked her pinkie finger with his, half expecting him to pull away. She knew she was treating him like she'd known him forever, but that was how it seemed. Winston must've felt the same way since he'd finished her pancakes last night and the half of her breakfast burrito she couldn't manage to eat just now. That's not something a new acquaintance would do. An insta-friend, however, wouldn't care that her mouth had been on that burrito.

Now Winston went stiff, but he allowed the pinkie link.

They reached the door to the gas station too soon, in her opinion, and she reluctantly dropped her hold on his finger. She led the way to where the bored-looking clerk was sitting behind the counter. He was white, about her age, and mildly good-looking in a pasty ginger sort of way, but then his gaze ran over her with a mix of entitlement and slime, and he lost any sort of attractiveness and slid right down the appearance hill into total grossness.

Forcing a smile, Dahlia pulled out the map and a picture of Rose. "Hi…Fletcher," she read off his name tag before meeting his gaze again. "Mind if we ask you a few questions?"

Fletcher's greasy smirk disappeared. "You a cop?" He stood up as if preparing to run, and Dahlia barely kept herself from sending a meaningful glance Winston's way. This guy was giving a great impression of someone who was guilty of *something*.

Dahlia huffed. "A cop? Please." She swept a hand down her body, showing off her fitted cream cashmere sweater and Pip Corning leggings, which magically managed to be fleece-lined while still looking sleek. "Would a police officer be this fashionable? And look at my boots." She backed up so Fletcher could get a good look at how the soft-as-butter Newmarket leather hugged her calves. "They might be practical and warm, but they're still as far from ugly, orthopedic cop shoes as footwear could possibly be."

Although he looked confused, he relaxed a little and settled back on his stool. "What do you want then?"

"I was supposed to meet my sister here—in this town, not in

this gas station—but I was unavoidably delayed, and she started the hike to the falls without me. She left this map, but I'm a little confused by it. Were you the kind person who gave it to her?" Dahlia placed the map on the counter where Fletcher could see it, although she kept her fingertips resting on the paper, ready to yank it away from him if he tried to take it. Her gut was roiling, all her instincts sending up flares, shouting that this guy was one big red flag.

He didn't touch it, however. Instead, he glanced at it from his sprawled position on the stool. "Maybe." He shrugged. "I give out a lot of those maps."

Reluctantly, she showed him Rose's picture. Even though Rose was fully dressed in the photo—she even had on a beanie, for Pete's sake—Fletcher leered at the image like it showed her riding a mechanical bull in a bikini. "This is my sister. Do you remember giving her a map?"

"Nah." He rocked back on his stool, leaning his shoulders against the wall behind him. "Never seen her before."

Studying his face, Dahlia tried to determine if he was lying. "You sure?"

"Would've remembered someone that hot," he said. "Besides, I didn't work Monday."

Dahlia studied him for a few seconds before sighing and returning the map to her pocket. "Who else works here who might've given her this map?"

"Could've been Livvy," he offered, his eyes fixed on her chest. She had a feeling it wasn't because he appreciated quality fabrics and workmanship. "She's the manager. Or Carson works Mondays sometimes."

"Do you know their phone numbers?"

He looked uneasy. "We're not allowed to give out employees' numbers."

Although she gave a frustrated grimace, Dahlia couldn't help but agree with the wisdom of that policy. "Are either of them working later today?"

"Nah. I'm on until five today, then Greg has the evening shift—his first one after being out sick for a week."

Forcing a smile, Dahlia thanked him for his help, even if he hadn't actually helped them all that much. Grabbing Winston's hand, she left the store. It wasn't until they were halfway back to the Yodel Inn that she realized she was still holding on to him like he belonged to her. She gave their interlocked fingers a quick sideways glance, debating whether she should release her grip. His hand was warm, though, and felt rough and comforting against hers, so she decided to keep hanging on to him. If it bothered him, he'd pull away or say something. It wasn't like he was afraid of hurting her feelings or anything.

"Should we try to track down the other gas-station employees?" Winston asked.

Appreciating that he tossed the decision ball to her, she considered the idea before shaking her head. "I think it'll take too much time, especially since we might not learn anything new. Let's hit the trail."

He accepted this silently.

"I just need to pack a few things," she said, unable to resist giving their clasped hands a swing. "Then I'll be ready to go to your house and pick up our hiking stuff."

His side-eye definitely delivered a whole truckload of doubt at her statement, but he didn't comment except to say, "I loaded the pickup this morning after I dropped you at your car, so no need to go back to my place."

"Oh, efficient. I like that." It moved the whole timeline forward, which was good, since—thanks to the hotel room search and subsequent crawl-space escape, breakfast, and their map search—the day was edging toward midmorning. Dahlia was antsy, ready to hit the trail and find her sister.

He gave her that skeptical side-eye again. "What clothes do you have?"

Surprised and pleased, she grinned at him. "I'm so glad you're taking an interest in my mountain-chic collection. It was hard to put together at the last minute, so I'm pretty proud with the final result. My first ensemble is a Pip Corning—a new designer who I love, since they're very environmentally conscious without looking all smug and self-satisfied, and their winter line has a retro nineties ski-bunny feel that I just ado—" She broke off when he dropped his grip on her so he could hold up both hands like a panicked traffic cop.

"Stop. Talking."

Obediently, she stayed quiet and just looked at him curiously. He was the one who'd asked her about her clothes, so she wasn't sure what exactly the problem was.

"You have layers."

It was more of a statement than a question, but he seemed to be waiting for her to respond, so she nodded.

"Any cotton?"

This time she couldn't stay quiet. "Of course not. I might be from California, but I'm not an *idiot*. Cotton hangs on to moisture, which would make me cold and—even worse—*chafed*." She shuddered at the thought. "Fabrics are kind of my thing—well, one of my things."

"Good waterproof hiking boots?"

Although it almost killed her not to expound on her absolutely fabulous Takki Winter Explorer Hiking Shoes in roasted almond, she rolled her lips in and nodded.

"Warm socks?"

She almost managed to stay silent, although a tiny peep of distress escaped her as she nodded. After all, she'd managed to find the corgi design, the most popular and hardest to find WoolyBear Sock pattern, *and* she'd found it in the coffee and cream with red accents—her very favorite color scheme—*with* a matching hat.

"Gloves?"

Now he was asking for the impossible, because she was *very proud* of her gloves. "Tri-layer Guy Nuit Boarder Glittens in scarlet with tech-friendly fingertips" burst out of her. She would've had better luck holding back an avalanche with her bare hands than to keep from telling him about the very awesome glove-mittens.

By the way he was staring blankly at her, the amazingness was lost on him.

She sighed. "Yes."

"Hat?"

"Now you're just being cruel. Yes."

This time, his side-eye was confused. "How is it cruel to want your ears to not be frostbitten?"

"No, it's..." Within two words, she knew it was futile to try to explain her enthusiasm when it came to clothes. "Never mind. I even have a sleeping bag that is good for as low as negative thirty, which I think is just a made-up number because that would be ridiculously cold."

He smirked. "Just wait."

"It's a real thing?" They'd arrived at her motel door, so she dug out her key. "That can't be right." She gestured toward the bright morning sun. "At least it's not that bad yet. It's only November fifth. Rose was nice enough not to get herself lost in January." Shoving open the door, she went to step inside, but Winston was there first.

"Wait here," he ordered, leaving her in the doorway as he prowled around the motel room. After checking the bathroom and closet—even under the bed—he waved her inside.

As she closed the door, she tried to figure out why she'd enjoyed that little maneuver so much. Maybe because she'd never had anyone willing to check her room for monsters before. The emotions these thoughts brought up made her uncomfortable—and, oddly, too comfortable, at the same time—so she shoved them in a mental closet and focused on one of her favorite things: packing.

"What's that?" he asked, leaning over her shoulder.

"What?" She hadn't managed to put anything into her bag yet, so there was only one thing it really could be. "Um...a backpack?" It was a remote mountain town, but surely they'd heard of backpacks here. After all, the town had wireless internet and everything.

With a cranky grumble, he left the room, closing the door behind him with a heavy thump.

Dahlia watched him go. "That was weird." With a mental shrug, since what else should be expected from a weird hermit besides weird behavior, she started transferring her hiking clothes from her suitcase to her pack.

Winston quickly returned with a bigger backpack, which he held out to her.

"Ohh," she said as realization sank in. "You were mocking my little backpack. I thought you hadn't seen one before."

"Of course I've seen a backpack," he scoffed, sounding offended. "What do you think I use when I hike?"

She shrugged, concentrating on a pair of waterproof ski pants so he wouldn't see her smile. "I don't know—a bandana on a stick?"

To her surprise, he laughed at that. To her even greater surprise, it was irresistibly contagious, and she couldn't hold back her own laugh upon hearing his. She looked at his still-smiling face, and her stomach erupted in an explosion of giraffe-sized butterflies, which killed off any trace of amusement in her.

"Oh no," she said, staring at his not-scowling face as horror overcame her. "I'm in trouble."

"What's wrong?" All the amusement disappeared from Winston's expression, replaced by a concerned frown.

Dahlia wanted to groan, but she held back, since Winston already thought she was dying, and there was no way she was going to tell him the truth about *why* she was in trouble. "Oh, sorry. I'm being dramatic. I'd just forgotten about Rose for a second, and then it all came rushing back—the fact that she might be in trouble and that we have to hike and camp, which I've never done, but it never looks all that comfortable on TV."

He gave her a sharp look, but he didn't challenge her excuse, so she gave a silent sigh of relief. There was no way she was about to admit that she'd just fallen a teeny-tiny little bit in love with the weird hermit she was currently blackmailing.

They were both quiet as she packed up her borrowed backpack, which was less fashionable but possibly a bit more practical than the one she'd brought. She was almost done when he spoke.

"What's that?" he asked again.

This time, she knew exactly what he was talking about, and she held it up excitedly. "It's a compact makeup case, built for airport-approved-sized containers. I love how organized it is. See?" She unzipped the case so it opened flat, revealing all the bottles and tubes and tools and compacts, each one tucked into its appropriate spot. It was a thing of well-ordered beauty.

"You don't need that."

She laughed even as she tucked the case into the backpack he'd provided. "Of course I do. I know exactly what I need. Besides, I'm the one who'll be carrying it, so why do you care?"

He opened his mouth, looked at her face, and then apparently changed his mind and shut it again.

"Good idea," she said, knowing her smile had a hint of sharpness. Gathering up the last of her hiking clothes, she took them into the bathroom to change. Remembering how they'd escaped from her sister's room, she checked to find that, sure enough, there was a plumbing-access panel in the floor of her bathroom too. Not liking the idea that someone lurking in the crawl space could pop up at any time, she stood on the access panel while she put on her silk long underwear, a pair of her adorable corgi socks, her fleece middle layer, and her waterproof outerwear. A glance in the mirror revealed that, although not the most flattering, the outfit was definitely cute. She braided her hair into two thick ropes, since straightening it would be impossible out in the wilderness, and then she pulled on her WoolyBear cap with the tongue-in-cheek earflaps and an adorable pom-pom on the top.

As she left the bathroom, she fanned her face with her hand. "I'm sweating already."

"Get your boots on, and we'll go," Winston said, and she did so, having just a little trouble bending over to tie her fantastic hiking shoes, thanks to all of her layers. Doing a final check, she zipped up her backpack and attached her sleeping bag to the bottom with the intended straps.

"Only two-thirds full," she said proudly, hefting the bag and very carefully not grimacing at the weight.

Winston grabbed the bag, lifting it with enviable ease. "Not after we put in food and water."

"Oh." She suspected he'd try to crowd out her compact makeup case, but it wasn't getting left behind, even if she had to engineer a special strap to hang it off her pack. He had his idea of what he considered essentials, and she had hers. She wasn't about to go the good part of a week without floss or tampons or her skin care products. It wasn't the apocalypse, after all, and even if there *had* been zombies, she liked to think she'd still take some time for self-care. Otherwise, what was the point of surviving?

"You need to check out?" he asked.

"Nope. I've extended my stay for a week."

"We could be gone for five days," he warned as she tucked her room key into one of her jacket's nifty pockets. "Sure you want to keep paying for the room?"

She nodded. "I want to make sure I have a place to go when we get back, no matter when that is. This is the only motel in the area, and I have a feeling I'll be wanting a real bed and indoor plumbing immediately."

Instead of mocking her for her city ways, he just held the door for her silently. She appreciated his restraint enough that she wasn't able to resist giving his arm a pat of thanks as she passed him.

"What was that for?" he grumbled.

"You're an excellent sport," she said, amused. "If I had to pick anyone to go with me on this rescue mission, you'd be a strong contender."

"A strong *contender*?" Now he was the one sounding amused as he closed the door and stepped aside so she could lock it. "You have another preferred option?"

"I did say *anyone*," she teased, zipping her key securely in her pocket and heading for his pickup. "Think of all the possibilities." Her dreamy sigh was just a show, since strangely enough she couldn't think of anyone else she'd pick over the weird hermit currently tucking her backpack behind his seat.

By the time Winston started the truck, Dahlia was sweating under all her layers of clothes. Pulling off her hat, she wiggled out of her coat and unzipped her fleece, exposing the thin silk top that covered her sports bra.

"How much are you taking off?" he asked as he drove out of the parking lot. There was the tiniest hint of panic in his usual cranky rumble.

Curious, she turned her head to eye his profile. "Enough so that I'm not about to bake like a soufflé. Why?"

"No reason." Again with the teeniest bit of panic.

Forgetting about her discomfort, she turned fully to face him. "Why are you being weird?"

"I'm always weird," he grumped, his fingers tightening on the steering wheel. "Isn't that why you call me the weird hermit?"

"But now you're being weird in a weird way."

He laughed, and she was distracted from her initial distraction. The guy was positively beautiful when his face wasn't twisted up in a scowl. "Weird in a weird way?" he repeated, and she had to smile, since his laugh was contagious *and* because he was right to mock her nonsensical words.

"How long before we get to the trail?" she asked, giving up on what had started this whole convoluted conversation.

"Ten minutes." He seemed relieved by the subject change, igniting her curiosity again. "Trailhead's just out of town."

A thrill went through her. Although they'd been looking for Rose in Howling Falls the town, it felt like their search was just beginning now. It was a beautiful day, the sun warm enough to dissolve the trace of snow that'd been blowing about the previous night and bright enough to bring out the vivid colors of the sky and mountain peaks and evergreens. It looked like a movie backdrop, too perfect to be real. The pickup cab was toasty from the sunlight, reminding her that she was very, very warm. She wiggled out of her fleece layer, not missing Winston's quick glance.

"That's it, I promise," she said, anticipation for their search and the gorgeous day pushing away any desire to tease him.

He shot her another sideways glance before focusing through the windshield, letting out what she thought was an acknowledging grunt, although it was a bit higher-pitched than his normal bass tones. She cocked her head, but when he didn't say anything else—or even look at her again—she shrugged and went back to admiring the scenery.

The drive went quickly, and soon he was pulling into the trailhead parking area. A handful of other vehicles were scattered around the gravel lot, and Dahlia's heart rate quickened at the thought of one of those being Rose's rental car. As soon as Winston backed into a parking stall and the pickup came to a stop, she hopped out and hurried to examine the other vehicles.

She pulled a small notebook and a pen out of one of her many jacket pockets and jotted down the license numbers. Three—two cars and an SUV—had rental stickers, and Dahlia focused on those, peering in the windows and even trying the doors. All were locked, to her disappointment. The only one with anything visible inside had a hard-sided cooler and a blanket, but there was nothing to indicate which car—if any—was Rose's.

"Careful," Winston said from his spot by the open doors of his pickup. "This lot is visible from the road. Someone's going to think you're about to break into those cars."

Reluctantly, she joined him, although not for the reason he gave. It was because he had her backpack and another larger one open, and he was in the process of rearranging the contents of both. "You better just be adding to mine, and not *subtracting* anything," she warned as she made it to his side.

His side-eye glance was so mischievous that it took her breath away. "If you want to carry useless deadweight, that's on you."

Maybe that look wasn't quite so adorable. "Not useless."

"Don't want to hear any whining on the trail about it being too heavy," he warned sternly.

Swallowing a "Yes, Dad," since her brain was already in some pretty risky unchartered territory and she didn't need to catapult herself even farther into the tangled weeds of unfathomable attraction, she just widened her eyes innocently and sketched an invisible X over her heart.

Something about her expression or gesture made him flush, a dark-red slash along each cheekbone. "Go put your jacket back on."

His words reminded her that she only had a thin silk top on over her sports bra, and she gave a shiver as the sharp wind cut through the fabric to slice at her skin. "Good plan."

She hurried around to the other side of the pickup. Leaving

her fleece middle layer off, she pulled on her jacket and immediately felt the difference. Knowing she'd be walking soon and getting even warmer, she unlaced her boots and peeled off her top two bottom layers.

"Are you undressing *again*?" he asked with a long-suffering tone and odd emphasis on the *again*, as if she made it a habit of whipping off her clothes every five minutes.

She gave him a glare that wasn't as sharp as it should've been, since she was trying to balance on top of her unlaced boots so she didn't have to stand on the cold ground in her socks. "You sound like I'm constantly getting naked. I'm just losing my middle layer since it's warmish right now." It felt strange to consider the temperature—which she would've pronounced as frigidly freezing and unbearable back home— "warmish," but she had a feeling this would be as good as it got on their hike. "Make sure to leave a little room in my pack for these." She held up the fleece pants and made them do a little pants dance.

His flush reappeared when she said *naked*, but she somehow resisted the urge to say the word a bunch more times for the fun of seeing Mr. Grumpy Hermit get all flustered. He grumbled something that she was pretty sure she misunderstood.

"Did you just say that's a good idea?" she asked. "Because I'm going to write this in my diary as soon as we get back—and I actually get a diary. *Winston Dane admitted that I had a good idea! Oh, wondrous day!*"

"You're very odd."

"Yes," she said, distracted as she balanced on a single hiking boot while putting one leg of her waterproof pants back on. "Maybe as weird as you."

His unexpected laugh brought her head up, and she wobbled, forced to grab the inside handle on the open door to regain her balance. The resigned—and maybe fond?—look on his face didn't help her equilibrium any. "Yeah," he admitted. "We're quite a pair, aren't we?"

Thrown completely off-balance by his reaction, she could only grin back at him, her outer pants halfway on as she clung to the pickup door. "That we are."

FIVE

Despite Winston's warning not to whine about the weight, Dahlia's backpack didn't feel heavy at all. She was grateful for the loan of the pack, since hers—although much more stylish—didn't distribute the weight over her shoulders and back nearly as well. "Hiking isn't bad at all," she said cheerfully, lengthening her stride to keep up with Winston. "In fact, I might like it."

He snorted. "We'll see how you feel once we've made it out of the parking lot."

"Fair enough." She saw a large trail marker with a map, so she hurried over to it. It looked comfortably familiar, since she'd studied Rose's map so much. "I don't see the trail from the falls."

He leaned close behind her so he could peer at the map, and she fought the urge to rest back against him. "It's not shown on here, but it runs about like this." He traced a line with his finger for several inches before tapping where she assumed the X would be.

"Nothing's there on this map either." She frowned at the unlabeled green expanse surrounding Winston's fingertip as disappointment filled her.

"Did you expect a marker showing where your sister is?"

"No." She paused to dig a reproving elbow into his side and consider the honesty of her answer. "Sort of. This map is very large and official-looking. I was hoping there'd at least be an arrow or something, pointing us in Rose's direction. Otherwise, what's the point of putting this map here? It's just not logical."

"You're the one not being logical."

"Yeah. But then hope's kind of the enemy of logic."

He stared at her, and then gave a half shake of his head at the same time he raised one shoulder in a semi-shrug, which she interpreted as him deciding to just leave it and move on. "Let's go."

She gave a little skip to catch up with him. "Since we're out of the parking lot, can I say that I like hiking now?"

"No. Give it ten more minutes."

"Got it." She didn't speak for a few minutes, but everything was just a little too quiet. The wind rustled a few dead leaves still clinging to a tree, and her footfalls made what seemed like an inordinate amount of noise every time her new hiking shoes connected with the dirt path. Winston, on the other hand, managed to move completely silently, which was surprising, considering that he was about two of her, size-wise. "How is it that you move like a ninja?" she asked, curious but also wanting to fill the too-quiet space around them.

"Practice." The rumble of his voice was soothing, and she

was tempted to request that he keep talking. Maybe he could tell a story, or recite an epic poem he wrote in high school, or sing.

Ohh, yeah. I bet he can sing like a burly bass angel.

Rather than request that he break out his favorite sea chantey, however, she instead blurted out, "Doesn't the quiet creep you out?"

He shot her an incredulous sideways look. "No."

"But it's so ominous."

"No, it's not. It's peaceful."

"Nope." This was nice. Talking was much preferable to that eerie stillness. They needed to continue the conversation, and Dahlia felt very much up for the task. Scary silence? Not on her watch. "It means the killer is about to strike again, or the asteroid is about to hit, or everyone else has been beamed up into the spaceship of a hostile alien army and we're going to be next. Silence is always, *always* a sign that something terrible is about to happen. Don't you watch movies?"

"Not as many as you do, apparently," he muttered.

"Do you have a TV?" she asked. Maybe he only liked the quiet because he didn't know any better. Maybe his life was constantly quiet. She shuddered at the thought. "Or a phone?" She hadn't seen him use one, but the very idea of not having a cell made her panic a little. She patted her own phone in her pocket—currently turned off to save charge—reassured by the familiar feel of the hard rectangle.

"No TV," he said, tossing her a glance that was almost amused, in a surly sort of way. "But of course I have a phone. *And* a smartwatch even."

"Good." She gave a relieved sigh, even as she realized she'd already known about his tech. "That's right. You need it to know when a poor marmot has fallen into your death pit."

"Not a death pit."

"Mmm," she hummed skeptically, although she let it go as another question occurred to her. "Have you always lived out there in your fortress of doom? Were your parents nature-loving mountain people? Did your mom give birth to you in a home-made metal bathtub in the very kitchen where we were standing with only your dad as a midwife?"

"No." The answer wasn't much more than a grunt, but he still managed to make it sound both exasperated and bewildered. Before she could ask him to elaborate, he said, "Your imagination is…vivid."

"Thank you." She grinned at his profile, happy about the compliment even though he hadn't really answered any of her questions. "So… Where are you from? Unless your 'no' was in reference to the whole bathtub-birth thing and you really have lived on your own personal prepper compound your entire life?"

He huffed an impatient sigh and was quiet long enough that she was pretty sure he wasn't going to answer. Just as that freaky silence started creeping her out again, he startled her by actually speaking. "Maryland."

"When did you move here?" She wasn't sure how long he'd participate in her question-and-answer game, but she was willing to press her luck.

"Three years ago."

She waited for him to elaborate, but that was apparently too much to ask for. "Why Howling Falls the town? I mean, don't get me wrong, it's pretty in a rustic way, and every place has a pervy gas-station employee or two I would assume, so I can't hold that against it, but it's not exactly going to make the Top Ten Best Places to Relocate To list or anything."

"Acreage was a reasonable price and met my qualifications."

That told her…absolutely nothing. "What were your qualifications?"

His shoulder closest to her twitched in an annoyed shrug. He acted like conversing was painful, rather than an entertaining way to stave off the death-portending silence. "Reasonably accessible but remote. Over forty acres. Close enough to town to get supplies, but not too close. Open home site not directly in the trees. Standoffish neighbors."

"Wow. I have so many questions about several of those. Why didn't you want to be in the trees? I would've thought it'd soothe your hermit-like soul."

"Security risk," he answered, pulling out one of his water bottles and taking a drink. "Besides, falling branches can do damage to the roof. Make sure you're drinking a lot."

The non sequitur made her blink.

"Don't wait until you're thirsty." He scowled at her as if she were refusing to drink, rather than just a bit startled by his demand. He started reaching for the water bottle on the near side of her pack, but she grabbed it before he could.

"I'm drinking! I'm drinking!" She sucked down some water while glancing over at him.

Apparently, he really had strong feelings about getting

enough water. Not that dehydration wasn't a good choice of nemeses, just a bit…unusual for that degree of passion. Once she'd finished half the bottle, and his scowl had lightened to his usual level of snarliness, she tucked her water bottle back in its holder.

As soon as her mouth was available again, she asked, "Why'd you leave Maryland?"

His shoulders dropped in a silent sigh. She figured he'd hoped she would've forgotten what they'd been talking about. As they followed the trail around a curve, he pointed out in front of them. "Look."

"Wow," she said, honestly awed by the view. A break in the evergreen trees allowed them to see the sprawling vista, the jagged cliffs striped with white and rusty red and even violet, offset by the green of the pine trees. The sky was infinitely blue, and everything looked bigger and deeper and richer than anything she'd ever seen. "Where'd we start?"

He scanned the scene before them before pointing to a spot far below and to the left of them.

"We've come a long way." It hadn't felt that long—although she had noticed they'd been walking uphill the whole way. Her legs were feeling a little fatigued, and her shoulders, unaccustomed to carrying a pack, ached slightly, but overall, the hike so far had flown by. She was very happy with her hiking shoes, since she hadn't had a chance to break them in before her rushed trip to Colorado, but so far, she couldn't feel any tender spots that might mean blisters were forming. She made a mental note to leave a positive online review when she got back.

"Better keep moving," Winston said, and she realized that she'd come to a halt at the breathtaking view. He waited for her to start walking again before he fell in next to her.

"So far, I'm torn about hiking," she said conversationally. "Not a fan of the creepy silence."

"Not creepy."

Ignoring the interruption, she continued. "If we get to see views like that, though"—she gestured back the way they'd come—"the eerie lack of noise is almost worth it."

"You *like* city noise?" he asked, sounding as if he couldn't believe how it was possible. "You're from LA?"

"Close enough, and I love the sound of a city," she said honestly. "It's a constant reminder that other people are around. I can be alone without being, you know, *alone*. I mean, when someone's playing the bagpipes under my bedroom window, maybe I don't especially love city noise in that specific moment, but even bagpipes are preferable to *this*." She waved her arms broadly at the too-quiet wilderness surrounding them. "This is just…wrong."

He barked a laugh that, as usual, made her laugh along with him.

"Sooo…" She drew out the suspenseful pause until he shot her some curious side-eye. "Why'd you leave Maryland?"

"You're like a pit bull."

"Adorable and playful, with the jaw strength of a thousand men?"

He laughed again. "Sure. That's what I meant."

"Well?"

"It's going to be a long hike."

"Exactly!" Now he was getting it. "A long, *quiet* hike unless we do a little chitchatting."

This time, his sigh wasn't silent. "Fine. My job was…stressful, so I left."

"But to move two-thirds of the way across the country? Maybe even three-quarters?" She hopped over a small pile of rocks that had tumbled across the trail, feeling like a true hiker. She'd even mastered *obstacles*. "I get quitting your job, but why did you have to leave your home?"

A muscle in his jaw flickered, making her assume he was grinding his teeth. "I wanted a change," he finally said, which really told her nothing.

"Hmm." She hurried her stride to keep up with him, since apparently Winston was a speed walker when he was annoyed. "So you built your house?"

"Had it built, but yeah." His speed eased a little, telling her that he was on more comfortable conversational footing.

"I really like it." She remembered the whimsical furniture that managed to both stand out and fit with the rest of the house and smiled. "You did a wonderful job furnishing it."

"Thanks." His voice was gruff, but she got the impression he was pleased with the compliment.

A couple of people came into view, walking toward them. Although the path was wide enough for her and Winston to walk side by side, he moved in front of her and nudged her into place directly behind him. It felt protective and kind, since Dahlia assumed he did it just in case the approaching white man and woman were serial killers instead of the sweet—albeit some-what grubby—college-age kids they appeared to be. She peered around his thick arm and waved at the other hikers, pretending like she'd moved behind Winston to make room on the trail for them to pass.

"Hey," she greeted when they got close enough she didn't have to yell like a weirdo. "Did you go all the way to the falls?"

"Nah," the woman said with a stoner-like laugh that matched the smell of pot wafting off of the pair. "Just went out for a couple hours. Too nice of a day to pass up, you know?"

"Definitely." Feeling pretty confident that the hikers weren't any sort of danger to anyone who wasn't a family-sized bag of chips, Dahlia started to shift out from behind Winston. He subtly reached his right hand behind him and caught a fistful of her coat before yanking her back into position. "*Uff,*" she grunted at the unexpected move. Rolling her eyes at Winston's overprotectiveness, she kept her body behind him but peeked her head around his arm again. It was just too weird to talk to someone while hiding behind her hiking companion.

"Storm's coming," the guy warned, the beads in his braids tapping lightly against each other as he turned his head toward the bank of dark clouds edging the bright blue of the clear sky. "Might want to set up camp early if you're staying out here overnight."

"Thanks," Dahlia said when Winston stayed silent, still watching the two hikers as if they were going to pull some poison darts out of what looked like a fanny pack around the guy's skinny waist. The two seemed oblivious to Winston's suspicious glare, smiling at Dahlia with slightly dopey smiles as she continued. "Did you see anyone else on the trail?"

"A few coming back as we were starting out," the guy said.

"A blond woman?" Dahlia pressed hopefully. "About my age?"

Both the man and woman squinted at her for a long moment as if thinking hard before the woman finally said, "I don't think so?"

The guy looked at his companion. "There was that mom with the kids. Wasn't she blond?"

"Yeahhh?" The woman drew out the word doubtfully. "But she was, like, forty."

Dahlia also didn't know where Rose would've come by random children, and the little spark of hope that'd flared died down again. "Well, thanks anyway."

With a final wave, the two passed them, and Winston tugged on her coat until she was side by side with him again.

"Probably overkill," she said once the two hikers were out of sight. "They seemed harmless."

"The harmless-looking ones are the most dangerous," Winston muttered.

She couldn't help snorting at that. "Sorry," she apologized when he leveled a glare at her. "You just sounded like the weathered old sea captain warning about impending catastrophe. I'm surprised there wasn't a clap of thunder right after your ominous pronouncement."

His offended expression only deepened. "Old? I'm thirty-two."

"If you don't want people to call you a leathery old sea captain then maybe—hear me out now—try to sound *less* like a leathery old sea captain?" she teased.

He grumbled something, but a gust of wind snatched up the words before they could reach her. Her unzipped jacket billowed out, and cold air needled her skin through her base layer.

"*Brr!*" She shivered, hurrying to zip up the coat she'd been considering taking off just ten minutes earlier because she was too warm. "I think the weather just switched to winter mode."

"The guy was right, even high as a kite." Winston frowned at the sky, once again resembling that sea captain. "It's going to snow soon."

"But it was really nice just thirty seconds ago," she said, baffled as she huddled in her newly zipped coat. She even debated whether to put on her fleece middle layer again, but since that would involve partially stripping down, which *brrr*, she decided against it. "And snow? It's barely November!"

"Welcome to the mountains," he said dryly.

Winston's pace increased, and she scrambled to keep up with him since the incline of the trail had ramped sharply upward. Suddenly, hiking didn't seem so easy and fun as she'd thought at the beginning. Since she needed all her breath just for walking, she couldn't keep the conversation going. Instead of the eerie silence, however, the wind howled through the trees, and the tallest evergreens creaked and moaned, sounding like they were one soft breeze away from crashing down on their heads.

"Should I be worried?" she asked, having to almost shout to

be heard over the wind. It was almost—but not quite—enough for her to miss the creepy quiet from earlier.

"Yes," he said.

"I haven't even said what I should be worried about." The trail narrowed, and she fell in behind him. She had to focus on the ground in front of her to make sure she didn't trip on a protruding rock or root, or step on the loose shale and slip, so she missed it when Winston stopped. "Oof," she grunted as she ran into his backpack. "What do you have in there? Bricks?" She rubbed her sore nose.

Ignoring her question, he pointed to a narrow trail leading off to their left. "You think Rose would've taken the main trail to the falls or the more adventurous route?"

Her stomach dove as she stared at the path. Had her sister gone that way? Is that where she ran into trouble? "Knowing Rose, the adventurous route. So this way?" Although she meant for the words to come out firmly, like a solid statement, her voice betrayed her, turning up at the end in uncertain question.

His right eyebrow wasn't happy about that plan, she saw. "I don't know that path well. Not sure if there'll be a good place to set up camp."

That made her insides twist even more. "But what if she went this way? We can't just stay on the main trail because it's more comfortable. We're not hiking for fun. The whole point is to find Rose." The last bit was more of a reminder to herself than to Winston, since she felt guilty that despite the weird silences and cutting wind, she was kind of enjoying the trip so far. Rescue missions weren't supposed to be fun.

"She told me she wanted to go to the falls," Winston said hopefully. "That was the whole point in her coming here. Maybe she went the fastest, most direct route."

That was true. Dahlia felt hope bubble up inside her, but then reality poked that floaty sphere with a sharp pin. "We still need to check. If we wait until we're headed back from the falls, that'll be three more days. It's already been two since her text asking for help. Rose is smart, but sometimes she's a little too adventurous for her own good."

Still looking grumpy in a worried sort of way, he dropped his shoulders in a resigned sigh before turning onto the narrow trail. "I'm going to regret this," he grumbled.

Dahlia swatted his hip. "Knock off the portentous predictions. Everyone knows that the leathered old sea captain's warnings always come true."

Although he snarled, she was pretty sure he was holding back a smile.

SIX

THE NEW TRAIL MADE THE previous one seem like a paved sidewalk. The narrow path was rutted and rocky, and she found herself watching where Winston stepped so she could follow his route exactly. Even copying him, it was rough. She caught her toes on uneven rocks, and loose stones rolled under her soles, making her slip. More than once, grabbing on to Winston's backpack saved her from face-planting, so she stayed close behind him. Trees pressed in on either side of her, and scratchy bare branches caught at her coat and pants, making her grateful for the slick material.

The wind picked up, following the trail like a pipe, giving Dahlia yet another reason to stay close to Winston. For not the first time, she was grateful that she'd blackmailed him into coming with her. The thought of wandering around this mountain on her own… She shuddered. She'd already be eaten by a bear or—at best—curled up in a bush, sobbing her eyes out.

"Ow!" Something bit at her cheek, sharp and painful. It

was quickly followed by a sting on her chin and then—worst of all—on the sensitive skin right under her eye. She squinted to keep whatever was hurting her out of her eyes, confused when she saw the tiny white pellets. "Is that…snow? Ouch! Why didn't anyone tell me that snow was evil?"

Winston turned, pulling off his pack in the same movement. He stood close to her, and Dahlia didn't hesitate to bury her face against his chest, protecting it from the wicked snowflakes.

"Hallmark movies make it seem like snow is gentle and fluffy and angelic, but it's obviously demonic. People send their kids out to *play* in this? What kind of parent *does* that?"

His chest shook a little, rumbling quietly in a way that was either a laugh or a growl. Knowing Winston, it was probably the latter. He moved her back just enough that he could pull off her hat.

"Wait!" she protested, grabbing for it too late. Her vulnerable head was immediately bombarded by the demon snow. "Hang on. I need that!"

Instead of returning her corgi hat, he tugged something else over her head. At least it was covered, so she stopped her demands, especially when he pulled the thin knitted fabric down over her face. There was a single oval opening for both her eyes, but her nose and mouth were covered.

"Excellent," she said, her voice slightly muffled by the tightly knit fabric. Her face did feel warmer, although she still had to squint against the angry flakes trying to smack her in the eyeballs. "We can stay warm and rob a bank. Well, we could if there was a Bank of the Boonies around here."

With an amused huff, he fit ski goggles over her eyes.

Now that her vulnerable skin was completely covered, she let out a relieved breath. "Thank you."

With a short lift of his chin to acknowledge her thanks, he yanked his own face mask and goggles on much more roughly than he'd put on hers. In fact, he'd been positively gentle with her, which made her insides squirmy in a warm and unfamiliar way. She would've thought that having him dress her in her face mask and goggles would've seemed infantilizing, but instead it just felt…nice.

She shook off her introspection when she realized he'd shouldered his pack and was walking again, soundless and oddly graceful for his size. Hurrying to catch up, she stifled a frustrated sound as a branch caught in her coat and jerked her arm back before she could get loose. Yanking herself free, she heard a small tearing sound that sent a flash of rage through her. As illogical as it was, she had an almost overwhelming desire to fight the tree that dared to rip her new coat that she already loved.

"Dahlia." Winston's voice brought her head around. He was quite a bit ahead of her on the trail, watching her with confused impatience. "What are you doing? Let's go."

"Sorry," she called out, before giving the offending tree a final glare. "Don't think you've gotten away with anything." Her voice was a low mutter that only the tree could hear. "Karma will get you. Maybe it'll be a lightning strike, maybe a deer will chew on your tender bits, but mark my wor—"

"Dahlia!"

"Coming!" She hurried to catch up.

"Are you drinking water?" He'd waited for her, but started walking as soon as she'd caught up with him.

"Um…" She grabbed her water bottle and pulled up her face mask before taking a long drink. "Yes."

His grunt wasn't the amused one she expected, which made her worry.

"Everything okay?"

"No."

She blinked. "You can't just say 'no' and then leave it at that," she instructed him. "You need to elaborate, or I'm going to come up with an imagined scenario that is ten times more terrible than whatever the real problem is."

He shot a look over his shoulder that was a mix of bemusement, amusement, and exasperation. He gave it to her so often that she was starting to think of it as her signature look, one he only gave to her. During their limited acquaintance, she'd only seen him give other people his flat, blank stare, occasionally tinted with impatience, but nowhere near as expressive as the one he focused on her at regular intervals. "Told you earlier. I don't know this trail."

"You're worried about where we're going to put the tent?" she extrapolated.

This grunt was affirmative, and his pace sped up, as if discussing his concerns was making them even more distinct. "It's going to get dark fast," he grumbled, making her glance up through the bare branches arching over them at the sky. Rather than the bright-blue expanse that'd been there just a short time earlier, steel-gray clouds hung heavy and ominous, appearing so low that they looked like they were almost sitting on the tops of the tallest trees. "Don't want to walk us right off a cliff."

"Yeah, that wouldn't be good." *Maybe I shouldn't follow Winston* quite *so closely*, she thought, dropping back a couple of steps. Then she promptly tripped on a rock and almost fell on her face, so she closed the distance between them again so she could grab his pack the next time she stumbled. Besides, if he did walk off a cliff, she wasn't sure she'd want to be left to wander the dark wilderness alone—especially since he was carrying the tent.

Tucking in close behind him, Dahlia concentrated on her feet. Each step became a challenge as the snow fell more heavily. Although it mostly melted when it touched the ground, the moisture made the surface slick, and any hard BBs of snow that remained rolled like ball bearings beneath her hiking shoes.

She found herself continuously clutching a strap on Winston's pack, even more for the comfort of knowing he was right in front of her rather than to help her keep her balance on the slippery ground. The thicker the snowfall became, the darker it got, creating shadows between the trees that could hold any number of watching predators—human or animal. She pressed closer in behind Winston so that his pack was all she could see.

When he stopped, a hundred of the very worst scenarios filled her mind. She forced herself to peek around his bulk, figuring that his abrupt halt meant that they were facing at least eleven full-sized grizzly bears—if not an even dozen. Instead, the small clearing in front of them looked to be empty except for a few stray branches and some long-dead and dried-out weeds.

"Are the bears hiding in the trees?" she whispered, tightening her grip on his backpack as she squinted through her ski goggles at the shadowed evergreens.

Winston turned his head so he could look at her. Despite his goggles, she saw that his right eyebrow was being judgmental again.

"Why'd we stop then?" she asked, assuming by his expression that there weren't, after all, a full dozen bears wanting to throw hands...paws.

"This'll work," he said, sliding off his pack.

She followed suit, hope flaring. "We're camping here?"

At his short nod, she gave a relieved groan, reaching toward the snow-laden clouds before bending at the waist to let her spine stretch. "You okay?" he asked.

The position felt too good, so she stayed in forward fold, only turning her head so she could see Winston's concerned face. "Yeah, just need to stretch. That backpack is well designed, but I'm a city girl. I'm used to carrying about a third the weight with about twice the oxygen." She took a deep inhale, feeling the cold, thin air fill her lungs as she rose to standing. "Okay, camp master. Just tell me what to do and how to do it, because I'm going to be honest. This is my first time camping."

"Really?" His sarcasm was as thick as peanut butter. "I wouldn't have guessed."

She gave a Cheshire-cat grin. "That's because I'm dressed like a pro." She paused. "If there is such a thing as a professional camper."

His grunt wasn't impressed. "We'll set up the tent, then eat and hang our food."

"Umm…" She almost didn't want to ask and sound like an idiot, but then she realized she'd just told him she knew nothing about camping. Pride would only keep her ignorant. "Hang our food?"

"Between two trees," he explained. "Protect it from bears."

"Ohh." She mimed wiping sweat off her forehead in a move that she instantly knew was extremely dorky. "I thought for a second it was some weird method of hunting, and I'd rather just eat what you brought. No fresh meat needed." She paused, eyeing his pack. "Ah… What food *did* you bring?"

"None. We're going to hunt and forage." She froze, but he didn't even last ten seconds before he lost his poker face and laughed. When she propped her fists on her hips and gave him a glare, he smirked at her. "Tent first," he ordered. "Then you can look at the food."

"Yes, Camp Master," she agreed.

He gave her a look she could only describe as smoldering, but she didn't understand what caused it. It was over in a second, and Winston focused on pulling the tent from his pack, but Dahlia felt a warm tingle in various parts lingering long after he'd broken their gaze.

"Put these together," he ordered, piling black pieces of what she assumed were the tent poles into her arms.

Crouching, she connected the pieces, creating three arching poles while watching Winston as he unfolded and flattened the tent on the ground. The wind fought him, making the material—as heavy as it was—flap and billow with each gust. He drove silver stakes that looked like huge nails into the ground, distracting her from her task. Even with multiple layers hiding his body, she'd never seen anything sexier than Winston hammering tent stakes.

Once she was done, he attached the poles with a rhythm and ease that spoke of frequent tent pitching. Once he'd attached the last strap and stood back, she eyed the finished product with some doubt.

He must've seen it in her expression, because he asked, "What?"

"It's just...not how I expected." She cocked her head the other way to get a new perspective. "It looks like a stubby burrito."

With one of his snort laughs, he turned away and picked up both of their packs. He tucked hers into the little triangular porch next to the tent door before shouldering his. "C'mon. Let's eat."

She hurried after him, since her stomach had been shrieking at her for what felt like hours. Also, it was even darker now, so she didn't want her wilderness guide to disappear into the night—especially since he had all the food.

"Can you tell if anyone else has camped here recently?" she asked once she fell in behind him. "Also, why can't we eat in the tent?"

"Doesn't look like it." He wove his way through the trees as she struggled to keep up. She thought she'd been doing pretty well before they'd arrived at the clearing, but now that they'd stopped moving for a few minutes, her body had decided that she was done for the day...and maybe the next week. It took everything she had to put one foot in front of the other instead of sinking into an exhausted heap. "And bears."

"Where?" She stopped abruptly, her head whipping from side to side as she tried to spot the angry bear—or hungry bear. She wasn't sure which would be worse.

Winston's chuckle made her frown at him. Amusement didn't seem like the correct response when discussing angry, hungry, or—even worse—hangry bears. "That's why we're cooking and putting the food away from the campsite. So there aren't any smells there to attract bears."

"Oh." She abruptly started walking again, using the residual surge of adrenaline to propel her exhausted body. "How far exactly do we need to go?"

He didn't answer for a minute, but then he finally stopped in a spot that looked like every other spot since they'd left the campground—since they'd left the trailhead parking lot, in fact: evergreens and rocks, coated with snow, making dark shadows and creepy, lurking shapes in the dim light. "This'll work."

What Dahlia really wanted to do was sink down on the inviting-looking log—as inviting as a log could look, at least—but she didn't want to act like a princess. There was only so much hassle Winston would take before deciding that his rabid fans were the lesser of two evils. They were already standing in a blizzard—well, maybe a blizzard-lite—about to eat camping food, whatever that may be. This likely wasn't his ideal evening, not when he could be at home doing...whatever weird-hermit things he normally did.

So she remained standing. "What can I help with?" she

asked, trying to sound a little peppy rather than exhausted to her bones.

She wasn't sure how well she succeeded when he looked up from where he was rummaging in his pack to give her an assessing look. "Sit," he commanded, which meant that she'd completely failed in hiding how done she was with the entire day.

She was happy to obey, plopping down on the log. It wasn't comfortable, cold with bumps and ridges that seemed to dig into her most tender spots no matter how much she squirmed. Giving up, she tried to convince herself it was therapeutic, like the world's worst massage chair. Subsequently giving up on *that*, she tried to distract herself from her discomfort by watching Winston set up a small camp stove. He poured water into a tiny saucepan and placed it on the single burner.

"Watch this," he commanded. Although she knew she should give him a hard time about his bossiness, she couldn't seem to work up the energy. Besides, her tired brain actually appreciated the simple, clear orders. "Tell me when it boils."

She stared at it, hypnotized by the tiny bubbles forming around the edges. Normally, she would've found waiting for water to boil impossibly boring, but now it was soothing, almost meditative. For the past two days, her life had been a frenetic race, filled with stress and worry and fear. It was a relief to not think about anything. All she had to do was watch the bubbles roil in the water.

Hang on. When did it start boiling? You had one job here, Dahl. "Winston," she called to where he was doing something involving white cord and a couple of trees. "It's boiling."

He finished knotting the cord and returned to her log. She watched, now mesmerized by his efficient movements, as he turned off the stove and divided most of the water between two pouches, leaving just a half inch in the pot. He sealed the two foil pouches, set them on the log next to Dahlia, and checked his watch.

"Is this dinner?" she asked, waving toward the two pouches.

Lifting his chin in one of his man nods, he said, "Twelve minutes."

"Good. I'm starving. My stomach feels like it's eating itself." A yawn took her by surprise. "Sorry. You're working, and I'm zoning out watching water boil. Sure I can't help?"

To her surprise, he patted her on the knee. "You did well today. Take a break." As she stared at him, shocked by that simple friendly gesture and a *compliment*, of all things to come out of his grumpy mouth, he returned to his cord and trees.

Twelve minutes passed in what felt like a blink, and he nodded at the two pouches. "Pad thai or spaghetti?"

Pad thai? Too tired to glance at the labels on the packets sitting next to her for the past twelve minutes, she'd been expecting something more along the lines of baked beans or stew or something rustic and...mountainy. She realized Winston was still waiting for an answer and shook off her surprise. "Pad thai, unless you loathe spaghetti?" She reached for the pouch but then paused for his answer, which was, unsurprisingly, a snort.

"Why would I buy spaghetti if I don't like it?" he asked.

"Fair enough." She grabbed the pad thai pouch and took the fork he held out. "Thank you." She opened the pouch and gave it a stir. The smell made her mouth water as her stomach twisted with frustrated hunger, so she didn't hesitate to pull her face mask out of the way and take a bite. "Not bad," she said after swallowing.

He grunted in acknowledgment, his own mouth full of spaghetti.

She shoved in another bite, both because she was hungry, and also because she wanted to hurry up and get into the burrito tent. It wasn't her own bed back home, but at least it would be a little warmer…she hoped. Despite her raging hunger, her stomach protested after just a few more mouthfuls, and she was only able to finish a quarter of the pouch. Glancing at Winston, she saw he'd finished his whole meal. It made sense, she figured, since there was a lot of man to fuel.

"Want the rest of mine?" she asked, holding the pouch out. Without refrigeration, she figured there was no saving leftovers.

He accepted it, checking to see how much was left before raising his right eyebrow at her. "That's all you're eating?"

"That's all that fits." When he continued to frown at her, as if unsatisfied with that non-explanation, she admitted, "It's like all my worry about Rose is balled up in my stomach. It doesn't leave much room for food."

Although he gave an unhappy grunt, he didn't argue anymore. Instead, he finished her pouch with impressive speed. He washed their forks in the remaining hot—well, probably lukewarm by now—water and returned the stove, pot, and forks to his backpack. Tucking the two empty meal pouches into a plastic bag, he headed back to his tree-and-cord project.

Although she felt even more exhausted with some food in her belly, she forced herself to stand and join Winston as he tucked the plastic bag into a large nylon one that was already packed pretty full. "What's this?" she asked.

"All our food." He pulled one of the cords, and the nylon bag rose above their heads, suspended between two trees.

"Ohh," she breathed as the cleverness of the method struck her. "Because bears can climb trees, but they can't walk a tight-rope." She paused. "Most bears, at least. I'm assuming there's at least a couple in Vegas who've mastered the skill."

Winston huffed a laugh. "C'mon, Punchy. Time to sleep."

SEVEN

Camping, Dahlia was realizing, was extraordinarily inconvenient. Not only the obvious things, like a lack of plumbed toilets, but a dozen of other actions she usually did multiple times every day without thinking, like washing her hands or tossing her used floss in the garbage can or brushing her teeth at a sink or flicking on an overhead light or being able to stand up to undress.

"Ung," she grunted, wiggling out of her snow pants while sitting on top of her sleeping bag. She'd already stripped off her face mask and coat and had removed her hiking shoes, so she was left in her silk long underwear and socks. The struggle with her clothes at least left her warm—sweating a little, even—as she finally managed to work the elasticized cuffs over her feet. "How far should I take this?"

Winston, who for some reason was busy putting her shoes in a nylon drawstring bag he'd called a "stuff sack" earlier, looked at her. The harsh illumination of the flashlight emphasized the grooves of his scars and furrows of his questioning frown.

"Should I get naked?" Dahlia grabbed the hem of her top as if to give him a visual aid of what she meant.

He choked. It was obvious even in the poor light that his face had turned red.

"In the sleeping bag," she clarified, feeling a bit guilty for embarrassing him. "I read somewhere that you stay warmer in a sleeping bag if you're…ah, naked." She hesitated to say the word again, and sure enough, he choked a second time. She immediately had the contrary urge to repeat *naked, naked, naked* to see what would happen, just like she always felt the compulsion to push buttons that were clearly marked *do not touch*.

He cleared his throat, concentrating intently on pulling the drawstring of the bag holding her shoes. "No. The more layers, the warmer you'll be."

"Should I keep my fleece on then?" She frowned, dreading the thought of wrestling with clothes in the small tent again, this time to get them *on*.

"No. Don't want you sweating. What you're wearing now is fine." He gestured at her without really looking, which she thought was adorable. A shy Winston was unexpected and a little unfair. She hadn't thought he could be any more attractive.

"Okay." She started to wiggle into her sleeping bag, but stopped when he handed her the sack he'd been fiddling with. She accepted it, confused. "Um… What do you want me to do with my shoes?"

"Put them at the bottom of your sleeping bag." Once she obeyed, he handed her the fleece top and pants he must've pulled out of her backpack at some point. "These too."

"Oookay." She shoved them down to join the shoe sack. "Anything else?"

He shook his head seriously, although she'd been mostly kidding.

"Why am I sharing my bed with my clothes?" she asked, wiggling into the sleeping bag. It was a tight fit, making her glad she wasn't claustrophobic.

"Keeps 'em warm. You'll be glad tomorrow."

"Makes sense." Once again, she was very glad Winston was her hiking buddy, especially because he'd brought *two* pads for underneath their sleeping bags. She'd already figured out that the ground was cold and shockingly lumpy, so she was very happy he'd thought of it. She zipped her sleeping bag most of the way, and then tucked her arm back in. "Zip me up?" Dahlia wanted to laugh. She'd requested that numerous times in her life, but always in reference to getting dressed. Asking such a familiar question in this foreign environment was both funny and strangely comforting.

Reaching over her, Winston did as she asked before arranging the portion of the bag that went over her head. He pulled the drawstring, narrowing the round opening over her face until just her eyes, nose, and mouth were exposed.

"Thank you," she said, wiggling around, trying to reach her usual sleeping position—on her left side with her knees bent and her fisted hands tucked under her chin—but it wasn't working in the mummy bag. She growled and grumbled under her breath as she rolled from side to side. "I'm an upside-down roly-poly bug."

Winston, who'd been watching her with a sort of amused

and yet horrified fascination, reached over again, this time to move her onto her side. She made a sort of startled squeak at the ease with which he lifted her, as if she didn't weigh any more than that metaphorical potato bug.

"Thanks," she said again, this time a bit more uncertainly. Then her brain blanked because Winston was undressing. She could only stare as he stripped out of his layers until he was down to his long underwear, which looked much different on him than it did on her. Strangely enough, he seemed to get bigger rather than smaller with each item he took off, as if his clothes were containing him somehow, like he'd been shrink-wrapped and was only now inflating to his actual size.

He shoved his own shoe sack and middle layers down to the bottom of his sleeping bag, plus he added a stuff sack with their water bottles in it before zipping himself in. He seemed to maneuver more easily inside its confines than she'd managed to. Dahlia could only assume that he'd found an extra-extra-*extra* large size, since those shoulders were much too wide to be accommodated by a normal-sized bag.

Before tucking his arms in, he flicked off the flashlight. The darkness was so complete that Dahlia blinked, illogically checking whether her eyes were open or closed. Winston rustled around for a few more moments before settling into stillness.

"Good night," Dahlia said softly, not exactly sure why she was whispering. It seemed like the thing to do in the darkness.

His grunt was weirdly comforting, the familiar casualness of it cutting through the darkness to make this decidedly not-normal situation feel less strange. She smiled as she snuggled down, closing her eyes. If someone had told her she'd be stuck in a tent in the mountains in *winter* with a weird hermit who was one step up from a stranger, she would've called that person a dirty, dirty liar. And yet not only was all that true, but she was oddly content.

My life is strange.

———

The cold woke her. More specifically, her cold nose woke her. It was a weird feeling, one she definitely didn't care for. Gray light was just beginning to fill the tent, turning everything monochromatic. Dahlia tucked her face into her sleeping bag.

"Don't."

At the growl, she jumped and tried to sit up, but she only managed to roll to her back like the potato bug she was. Subsiding onto her back, she let her galloping heart ease back into a normal rhythm as she recalled all the details—Rose, Colorado, hermit, tent. *Got it.* "Dude. Next time give me some warning."

"Wouldn't the warning just startle you too?"

Since it was too early for reason and logic, she just groaned a response, engaged her abs, and managed to lever herself up to sitting. It was only then that his earlier command filtered through her brain. "Don't what?"

"Don't breathe in your sleeping bag. You don't want the condensation to make it damp in there. If your face is cold, I'll get you a scarf."

She yawned wide enough that her jaw cracked. "Thanks, but I'm going to get up. Lots to do before we hit the trail." Working her hands up by her chin, she untied the drawstring and then grabbed the tab of the zipper. Instantly, she was sorry. "Oh, it's cold."

Although Dahlia was tempted to zip right back up, she really had to pee, and her sleeping bag didn't have a back flap. She forced herself to grab her fleeces from by her feet and yank them on, followed by her coat and snow pants. Her boots were next, and then she tugged on her wool hat and all three layers of her glittens. It didn't sound like the wind was still blowing, so she didn't think the face mask and goggles were necessary.

Once she was fully outfitted, she glanced at Winston, who was sitting up. He'd freed his upper body from the sleeping bag but didn't seem to mind the frigid temperature. Instead of rushing to dress, he was watching her with hooded eyes. The tent, which was truly very small, suddenly felt unbearably tiny— mouse-tent sized, even—and the man in here with her seemed overwhelmingly large.

"Sooo," she said, since she never could stay quiet when she was feeling uncomfortable. "I'm going to go find a nearby bush, while you…" Her voice trailed off when every morning ablution she could think of suddenly had suggestive undertones. "While you do whatever you need to do." *Why does that sound even worse?* Giving up on attempting to ease the awkwardness, she gave him a goofy abbreviated wave and unzipped the door.

"Don't forget toilet paper."

She took a page out of his book and grunted. His reminder made the atmosphere in the tent both stiflingly intimate and, at the same time, reminded her that they'd just met two days ago. It was also necessary, since she would've indeed neglected to bring toilet paper with her, and then she would've been sorry indeed when she was forced to use a frozen dead leaf instead.

Shuddering at the thought, she grabbed the toilet paper and bolted for the nearest trees. To her surprise, there was only a dusting of snow on the ground. After all that spitting snow during the last part of their walk, she'd expected it to turn into a true blizzard. It definitely felt cold enough, especially when parts of her were bare that never should be bare outside, especially during winter.

When she returned, Winston was dressed and out of the tent. He watched her walk toward him, his eyes scanning over her in that assessing way he had.

"Why does this all feel so unnatural?" she asked, waving an arm at their campsite.

His eyebrow asked for further elucidation.

"Up until just a couple hundred years ago, people ate and peed outside all the time, but now it seems weird and wrong. That seems really fast, evolutionarily speaking."

Instead of answering, he just squinted at her for a few moments before taking the toilet paper from her and tucking it into her pack.

"Thanks," she said absently, still thinking about how modern plumbing felt more natural than nature. "That toilet paper is worse than the stuff they offer at the grungiest truck stop, by the way."

"Yeah."

"Should just use cotton candy instead. Bet that wouldn't dissolve as fast as this stuff."

His mouth twitched.

"It'd be stickier, though. And we'd probably attract more bears."

Shaking his head in put-on exasperation, he chuckled. She joined in, his laughter as contagious as always, watching his face with something that felt weirdly like awe. She was tempted to keep talking to him, see if she could make it happen twice, but they had trails to hike and a sister to find, so she dove into the tent instead.

"Hungry?" he asked as she leaned out the door—which really couldn't be called a *door*, since it was just a zippable flap of fabric—to grab her makeup and toiletry bags.

"As one of those aforementioned bears," she said. "Give me ten minutes, and then I'll help cook. I promise I won't be a lump on the log like I was last night."

"You were fine." He paused, eyeing the bag she was unzipping as if it was an offended porcupine ready to stab him full of quills. "You're still fine. No one around except me and those aforementioned bears. No need for all…that." He waved toward the makeup bag.

Despite her tight nine-and-a-half-minute time frame, she used ten seconds to give him a flat look. It was important to really impress upon Winston exactly how much of a yo-yo he was being right now. "You forgot me."

"What?"

"There's no one around except you, the bears, and *me*. So there is a need for all…this." Rather than the dismissive wave he'd made, she gestured toward her bags as if presenting the finest treasure. "I like to look good for *me*. I want to decide what I present to the world, even if my current world is just you and the bears and the squirrels."

Aware that time was a-wasting, she pulled out her pocket mirror and hairbrush and set to work. After rebraiding her hair, she applied her makeup with a quick, assured hand. Despite his earlier grumbling, Winston did not find anything better to do with his time than watch her through the open tent door.

Since he seemed grudgingly fascinated, she started talking him through it. "I'm shooting for an easy, natural look that works for a day of hiking, and I'm going with more earthy tones to fit the theme."

"What's the lighter for?" he asked, seeming honestly curious.

A teacher at heart, she forgave him for his condescending mini-lecture and grinned as she flicked on the lighter. "Since it's as cold as the abominable snowman's pink bum, I'm warming this eyeliner, turning it from a pencil to more of a gel. That way, it goes on more smoothly and the lines are crisper. It also feels toasty and nice." She turned her face up to show him the result. "See?"

His grunt wasn't really a definitive yes or no, but she continued her tutorial for her reluctantly fascinated audience of one.

"I like this Candy Floss gloss." She paused to smooth it over her lips. "It's not sticky or obnoxiously shiny, but it helps keep my lips from chapping, *and* it has a fun pink tint to it." She laughed as the name registered. "Guess the theme of the day is cotton candy."

Winston cleared his throat as he gave her an odd look. She

wasn't sure if he was annoyed or interested or what. "Ready for breakfast?"

At the question, she gave up trying to guess his internal monologue and hurried to zip up her makeup case. "So ready. What're we having?"

"Oatmeal with pecans and dried blueberries."

"Yum." She tucked her bags back into her pack as Winston shouldered his. "Any chance there's a coffee shop on the trail? Maybe just a kiosk? Or a cart?"

"No." Before she could explain that she really hadn't expected a coffee shop to be plopped down on a cliff out here in the middle of nowhere, since she wasn't *that* much of an idiot, he added, "But I can make some."

She actually gave a little hop of excitement at that. Since coffeemakers seemed to be one of those very useful appliances that needed to be plugged in, she'd figured that she'd be cranky and caffeine-deprived until she could make it back to her room at the Yodel Inn and the little two-cupper there.

"It won't be fancy," he said, but she waved a casual hand, dismissing his warning.

"I usually get it straight and black anyway."

As they walked toward their woodsy dining room, she caught his side-eye glance—his third in as many minutes. It didn't seem judgmental, but she still felt her skin prickle from his attention, so she asked, "What?"

One of his shoulders rose in a half shrug, and that was his only answer for so long that Dahlia thought she'd have to tackle the man into the pathetically small amount of snow in order to

get an answer. To her surprise, he spoke again without being wrestled into submission, which was good, since the ground looked
much too rocky to be comfortable to roll around on. "If I hadn't
watched you apply it, I wouldn't think you had any makeup on."

It was one of the best compliments she could remember getting from an assumedly straight guy, and she clutched her hands
over her heart. "Thank you!"

"No, I mean…you're welcome, but why wear it if you can't
see it?"

"Ah, but just because you don't notice it doesn't mean it's
not doing its job." She smiled at him, still completely tickled by
the compliment. "The whole idea is to apply makeup in a way
that makes it seem like I just roll out of bed all fresh-faced and
pretty. That's the beauty—heh—of the natural look."

His grunt clearly said that he still didn't get the point, but
that was okay. It actually made her feel better to know more
about something than Winston Dane did. He was so intensely,
ridiculously competent that she knew she came off as the fluffi-
est ball of fluff to ever float past, but in this, she was the expert.
She might not know how to bend a stick to find water—or
whatever wilderness skills the man had—but she could nail a
perfect natural look, and in a freaking *tent* at that.

That wasn't to say she didn't want to learn how to take care
of herself in the wilderness, because if there was one thing Dahlia
hated, it was to be bad at something—especially at something
so important. To that end, she resolved there'd be no more log-
sitting while he worked like she'd done the night before. From
now on, she was going to be his useful hiking minion.

"Want me to make the oatmeal?" she asked. When he shot her a look, she rolled her eyes. "Despite appearances to the contrary last night, I'm not total deadweight." The need to be honest niggled at her, so she qualified that statement. "Just about eighty-seven percent deadweight."

Although he wore his usual scowl, there was a hint of… Was that disappointment? She got the impression he *wanted* to cook for her.

"I don't have to make the oatmeal," she hurried to backtrack. Something inside her really wanted Winston to be happy. She didn't know why, and nothing like this had ever happened before with someone who wasn't her sister, but the compulsion was strong enough that it was impossible to ignore. "I can do whatever. Just give me a job."

"I'll cook," he said, heading for the suspended bag holding all their food. "All the other jobs are at the campsite, and you shouldn't go off on your own. Just sit there."

With a sigh, Dahlia settled on her log—which was even more uncomfortable than she'd remembered it being the night before—resigned to upping her deadweight percentage to eighty-eight. At least the rising sun was starting to warm the air, and her snow pants protected her from the dampness of the melting snow.

As Winston set up the tiny stove and pan, she watched him, noting his satisfied expression.

"Ah," she said as the mental light bulb turned on.

"What?" he asked.

"I just realized why you insisted on cooking," she explained, glad there was a reason that was more about him than it was about Winston thinking she was useless. "Men have a thing about cooking outside."

"A thing?"

Ignoring his sarcastic tone, she nodded amicably. "If I were to light a grill in the middle of nowhere—somewhere like here, in fact—twenty guys would immediately appear to give me advice and then just take over. Even though that's more of a camping hot plate, the same idea applies. Outdoor cooking turns guys into cavemen."

He made a show of slowly looking around the area. "Nineteen other guys didn't magically appear when I lit the stove."

"Exactly," she said, gesturing in a eureka-type way, since he'd just proven her point. "*You* lit the stove. To draw the male masses, the grill—or camping stove—lighter must be a woman. Those are the rules, as messed up as they are."

He blinked at her for a long moment before shaking his head and turning back to his oatmeal making, muttering under his breath.

She watched for a few moments before the silence started to make her itch. "Tell me more about your job before."

"What?"

"The teaching one. In Maryland." She picked up a small twig by her feet and absently played with it while keeping her gaze on Winston. He seemed to be focused on making their breakfast, but she couldn't seem to look away from his expressive right eyebrow. It was strangely fascinating.

He made her wait for his answer, and when it came it was grudging. "I was more of a consultant."

With an amused snort, she tossed the tiny twig at him. She was aiming for his chest, figuring she'd have no problem hitting her target, since it was wide as a barn, but the small stick bounced off his forehead instead. He glared at her as Dahlia covered her mouth with both hands, attempting to physically block her laugh from escaping. "Sorry," she said, doing her best to sound contrite. "It's just...a consultant? That's your answer?"

"What's wrong with it?" he grumbled, leaving off glaring at her so he could stir the oatmeal.

"It's so vague." She picked up another twig, widening her eyes at him innocently when he gave her—and the little stick in her throwing hand—a warning look. "I mean, I'm a consultant too. Did you do makeovers? Best looks for...what did you call it? City fighting?" She got the name wrong on purpose, willing to accept a condescending lecture if it included interesting bits about him.

He made a grumbly sound, and she figured that was all she was going to get, but then he actually elaborated. "I taught urban warfare tactics and defense."

"That's right," she said, rolling the twig between her thumb and fingers as she mentally organized the thousand and one questions that had been rolling around in her head since basically the moment she'd met him. "To the military?"

He gave a short nod, his hands busy with preparing their food. "Not just ours. Plus law enforcement and civilian groups too." Every word seemed to take an effort on his part to force it out. Apparently, the guy had been hermiting too long. Hanging out on that booby-trapped property all alone, he'd forgotten how to make casual conversation.

That made her curious about something else. "Have you ever been married? Kids?"

Tipping his head back, he seemed to be muttering something to the brightening sky, probably a prayer for patience… or deliverance.

She hoped he'd realized that if he'd let her make breakfast like she'd offered, she'd be too occupied by that to be giving him the third degree. *He'll learn*, she thought, amused.

"Here," he grunted, shoving a bowl filled with oatmeal at her.

"Thanks." She accepted it, as well as the spoon he held out, but her expectant gaze never left his face. He was going to satisfy her curiosity. There was nowhere to run to escape from his fate. She glanced around at the trees surrounding them. Okay, so there were a *few* places to run, but she had a feeling his conscience wouldn't let him abandon her in the wilderness, even if she was a bit nosy. At least, she hoped it wouldn't. "Well? Do you have a wife tucked away in that house of yours?"

He shoved a bite into his mouth instead of answering.

Her stomach growled, reminding her to do the same. "Oh, wow," she said through a mouthful of oatmeal, nuts, and dried fruit. "This tastes so good. You're a god among camp cooks."

A tiny smile twisted up one side of his mouth before he shoveled in another spoonful.

"Not sure how many women would agree to move to the middle of nowhere and become co-hermits," she said casually once her stomach resisted the idea of any more food. "Want the rest?" She held out her half-full bowl.

He frowned, although she wasn't sure which topic had

caused his annoyance—likely both. "You need to eat more," he said, taking her bowl reluctantly. It was the latter that had bothered him then.

"I'll work on it," she promised, taking a drink from one of her water bottles to appease him. "So…wife?"

"No."

"No, you won't discuss it? Or no, you don't have a wife?"

With an aggravated huff, he finished her oatmeal. "Both."

"Any mini-Winnies running around?" When his right eyebrow jerked up, she rephrased. "Kids?"

"No."

"Me neither." She resisted the urge to tell him why she didn't have any offspring, and her reasoning, but then she reminded herself that she'd met him two—*two*—days ago, even though it was starting to feel like she'd known him forever, and the poor man didn't want to hear all of that.

His grunt was flat, ending the conversation, but that right eyebrow of his very obviously wanted to know more. To be contrary, since he'd made her drag every single detail out of him, she smiled obliviously.

"Can I at least help clean up?" she asked, but he'd already given everything a quick wash and wipe, and he was currently stashing the stove and dishes in his pack. She grabbed the food bag from him before he could tuck it in as well. "Nope. There's plenty of room in my pack. Not total deadweight, remember?"

"Only eighty-seven percent."

Shocked that he'd remembered—and repeated—her joke, she paused for a moment before correcting him. "Eighty-eight.

I had to add another percentage point when you wouldn't let me cook *or* clean up after."

"Didn't want nineteen random guys hanging around," he muttered, deadpan, as he shouldered his pack and gestured impatiently for her to stand and head back to their campsite—at least the sleeping part of their campsite.

Instead, she stared at him a moment longer before laughing and getting to her feet. "You're a funny guy, Mr. Weird Hermit."

"No." Now why did he sound panicky? It'd been a compliment.

"Yes, you are." She headed toward the tent, feeling more confident about her sense of direction now that it wasn't dark outside.

Except for his grumbles, they were quiet. Dahlia didn't mind his muttering since it covered the eerie wilderness silence she hated so much. Looking around at the towering evergreens, she had to admit that the scenery was stunning. The mountain peaks circled around them, providing a backdrop for the pines that covered the slope with all shades of green, reminding her of a packed theater audience, with their camp as the stage. The hush from the wilderness around them seemed to echo, it was so quiet.

"Too bad there's not a soundtrack," she mused as they reached the campsite. "This place would be perfect with just a little background music."

His scoff sounded awfully close to a laugh, but she didn't call him out on it.

EIGHT

THEY PACKED UP AND WERE back on the trail in short order. Dahlia immediately felt the evidence of their previous day's hike in her sore muscles and feet. They walked for a few minutes in silence as the trail narrowed to almost nothing.

"Ugh," she complained when an evergreen branch snagged in her hair. She tried to free herself without losing a handful of strands. "Trust Rose to attempt the worst path on the mountain…maybe. If she did go this way."

Winston's mouth quirked up as he moved to help. "This isn't the worst trail." His fingers were gentle and sure as he worked to separate her from the clingy branch.

"Close enough," she grumbled, then laughed.

"What?"

"Just that we switched roles for a conversation." When he looked confused, she explained, "I'm being crabby, and you're being reasonable and helpful. It's like we swapped bodies."

"I'm always reasonable," he said…crabbily. "And helpful."

To illustrate the last point, he gestured toward her newly freed hair.

Trying to smooth down the damage the branch had done to her neat braids was useless, so she gave up. "Helpful, sure. Reasonable…eh." She held out her hand, turning it side to side in a maybe, maybe not gesture, but then grinned when his scowl returned. "I'm just teasing you, Grumpy Smurf."

The sound he made was skeptical as he continued glaring down at her, and she suddenly realized how very closely they were standing. Normally, she hated when tall people loomed over her, but with Winston, she didn't feel like he was trying to intimidate her. It was hard to assign less-than-great motives to a guy who'd just freed her from a tree so gently that he hadn't even yanked one hair from her head in the process.

This close to him, she noticed things she hadn't before, like his ridiculously long eyelashes and his full bottom lip. She normally wasn't a fan of beards, but his looked like it might be soft, and she had to grab one hand with the other to keep herself from yanking off all three layers of her glittens to feel for herself if her guess was accurate. She distracted herself from her sudden beard obsession by meeting his gaze but quickly realized that was a tactical mistake when she was unable to look away.

When he was scowling at her, his eyes looked very dark, but with the morning sun hitting them, they were more hazel, with a green rim that blended into the brown around the pupils. Despite the lush eyelashes that she would've given both ring fingers to have, they were just normal eyes, but somehow they sucked her in.

Dahlia, who wasn't a blusher, found that heat was working its way up her neck and into her cheeks. Her heart was beating a thousand miles an hour for absolutely no reason at all, and she couldn't seem to slow down her breathing. It didn't help *at all* when he flicked his gaze to her lips and then back to her eyes, because despite their surroundings, she knew exactly what that meant.

Winston Dane was thinking about kissing her.

Mistake! The sensible part of her brain was screaming. *This is a mistake!* Dahlia knew that the inner voice was correct, as usual. It would be incredibly stupid for her to kiss her conscripted wilderness guide. Even as she warned herself of all the reasons why it was incredibly stupid, she couldn't stop herself from leaning toward him.

Those riveting eyes were getting closer, which could only mean that he was bending down, bringing that tempting full bottom lip closer to her own.

I'll feel whether his beard is soft, the very *not*-sensible part of her brain whispered, and the sensible part gave a shriek of frustration, threw up its hands, and stomped off to sulk in a dark brain closet, though hopefully not the one where she'd stuck her insecurities or childhood fears. The not-sensible part of her smiled wickedly at the feel of his breath against her lips. Heat radiated from him, so much that she was surprised he didn't walk around steaming all the time—literally, not meta-phorically, since he was almost always metaphorically steaming. *Seriously, eyelashes that luxurious should be illeg—*

A branch cracked, and Winston straightened abruptly

and whirled, backing her into the tree as he scanned the area. Although she was dying to know what was happening—since all she could see was the broad expanse of Winston's back, and, as nice as that was, it wasn't very informative—she stayed quiet, questions itching at her throat.

His shoulders dropped as he audibly let out a breath, so Dahlia figured it was safe to whisper. "What is it?"

"Deer," he grunted, stepping to the side and pointing at a spot between the trees. She peered in the direction his index finger indicated, frowning when she didn't see anything but trees and rocks. Then the deer moved, and Dahlia flinched, since the animal was much closer than she'd expected. She watched, entranced, as the deer bounded away from them, navigating through the trees like a slalom skier.

"Oh, he's beautiful," she breathed, trying to catch a glimpse even as the deer moved out of sight.

"She," Winston corrected, starting to walk again. "It's a doe."

Dahlia started to follow him, but her head jerked back, stopping her in her tracks. "Hang on," she called. "I'm stuck again."

He immediately turned and gave her an exasperated look.

"It wasn't my fault," she protested. "You're the one who shoved me back into their twiggy little grasping fingers. Although I can't blame them, because my hair is quite irresistible. Even trees want to touch it. My hair is both a gift and a curse sometimes."

Grumbling, he returned to her and once again freed her from the branches. This rescue, however, wasn't nearly as much fun as the last, since he carefully didn't meet her eyes, and his hands—although still gentle—moved impersonally and quickly. Once he'd released her, he turned and stomped away, and she grinned at his thumping footsteps.

"Wow," she said, unable to resist poking at him just a bit. She knew it would've been a mistake to kiss Winston, but there was still a disappointed pang in her chest, and teasing him eased the ache. "So loud. Where's your usual ninja stealth?"

He shot her what was supposed to be a quelling look over his shoulder, but it just encouraged her.

"Normally, I feel like an uncoordinated elephant compared to you, but I think I'm actually making *less* noise than you right now. Could you hold it down a little? I'd like to see another deer, and you're scaring them all away."

He actually growled this time, but he returned to his usual noiseless movement, and she was disappointed again. Not only had he taken away her fun, but his crashing and stomping had drowned out that creepy silence. Now, it returned with a vengeance. With a sigh, she debated whether reciting a dramatic monologue or singing every show tune she knew at least some of the words to would be more likely to convince Winston to hold a conversation with her.

As if he could hear her thoughts, he spoke. "Keep your eyes open for spoor."

"Spoor?" she repeated, wrinkling her nose. "Isn't that poop?"

He gave an amused-sounding huff. "It can be, but you're thinking of scat. Spoor is trace evidence people—or animals—leave behind. Tracks, hair, litter, damaged vegetation, and yeah, poop."

"I'm pretty sure Rose wouldn't poop on the trail," Dahlia said, frowning at the thought even as she started looking more closely at the ground and surrounding brush and trees. "She'd more likely bury it or even carry it out in a bag. She's lectured me about leave-no-trace hiking more than once, even though she knows it'd take zombie hordes overtaking every city in the world before I'd venture into the wilderness." She paused. "Guess Rose disappearing is equivalent to a zombie apocalypse." It was true. Rose was Dahlia's person, her *only* person, and she'd do pretty much anything to keep Rose safe. Shaking off her thoughts, since she hated how her chest threatened to collapse in on itself when she contemplated the idea of living in a world without Rose in it, Dahlia cleared her throat. "She definitely wouldn't litter."

"Could be unintentional," he said.

She fixed a skeptical gaze on the back of his head. "Unintentional poop?"

A laugh escaped him before he reined it in. "Unintentional *litter*. She might've taken something out of her pocket, and a protein bar wrapper falls onto the ground, for example."

Dahlia just hummed, since she had a hard time believing that her sister could be that careless, not when Rose was positively rabid about the environment.

"Your sister's blond, right?"

"So blond. Almost white blond."

"Keep an eye out for strands caught on branches," he suggested.

She immediately took her eyes off the ground and started

looking at the trees on either side of the trail. "Yeah, that's a good idea. Rose's hair is almost as tempting as mine. These jealous grabby twigs wouldn't be able to resist."

He shot her a flat look over his shoulder. "And you call *me* weird."

————

Time flew now that she had a task. It could've been boring, since she didn't find any sign that her sister had been through, but once she started looking, there was a ton of interesting things to see. She asked Winston a whole slew of questions, and he knew the answers to every one. It made her a little suspicious that he was making things up, and she wished she had cell reception so she could check his facts.

"Wait," she said, bending to peer more closely at a plant that looked suspiciously like a deflated cactus. "Is this a cactus?"

He gave it a quick glance before refocusing on the path in front of him. "Yeah."

Despite the urgency of her goal, she couldn't resist stopping to get a closer look, then she had to jog to catch up with him. "But it's cold here."

He didn't answer, probably because it was such an obvious statement he didn't feel it deserved a response.

"How does a succulent survive?" she asked, figuring she had to specifically spell out her question. "They're all water. Don't they turn into cacti pops when they freeze?"

The glance he gave her was considering, which annoyed her as much as it amused her.

"Don't look at me like you're surprised I'm capable of having a logical thought," she scolded. "I'm very obviously brilliant, so your shock is more a reflection of your intelligence than mine."

He cleared his throat, his gaze focused on the path in front of him. "I know you're smart."

Ignoring the flush of pleasure that coursed through her at this compliment—despite having to drag it out of him—she said, "Like I said, it's obvious."

With a snort, he gave her a bit of side-eye over his shoulder, which was a *very good* look for him, she decided. "Cacti shrink into the ground, or at least drain out most of the water and go limp."

The mental image struck her as comical. "Flaccid cactus. Flactus."

He barked out a laugh, shaking his head. "Focus on finding spoor."

Even though he couldn't see her, she saluted his back. "Yes, sir."

This time, the side-eye was filled with a flashing heat that sent a lightning bolt of shocked awareness through her. Although the glance was brief, it knocked the words out of her for a full eight minutes, when she finally collected the scattered pieces of her brain enough to ask her next question.

"What's that weird twisty tree?"

"Bristlecone pine."

"Very beautiful in an ugly way."

His grunt was skeptical, but Dahlia didn't know if he was protesting the beautiful or ugly designation. Either way, he moved on. "Really long-lived. Oldest tree in the world is a bristlecone."

Although her feet kept moving, her gaze stayed on the twisted, knobby tree. "That makes sense. This one looks ancient." When she tripped over a rock, she refocused on the narrow trail in front of her. "Are you seeing any sign that Rose came this way?"

"No." He paused, and she was certain that was the entire answer she was getting, but then he continued. "Don't think anyone has come this way in a while."

"That's because most people are smart enough to take the other trail to the falls," she said, ducking under a branch before it could snag her. Her hair had been yanked out enough for one day—one *year* even. "Ha! I've managed to evade your evil clutches, you dastardly tree-villain!"

This time, his look was hard to read.

"What?" she was forced to ask, since her Winston-interpreting skills had failed her.

One of his shoulders lifted and fell in a half shrug. "Sometimes you sound like you came out of a comic book."

She beamed at him, pleased. "You give the *best* compliments."

————

Just as the trail started a broad curve, Dahlia heard a sound that was both immediately familiar and, at the same time, ridiculously out of place. "Is that a car?" she asked, stopping and tilting her head as if that would help her hear better. "A car missing a muffler?"

Winston stopped too, listening for a moment before saying, "ATVs."

"Plural?"

"Two or three." He looked around before leaving the path and weaving through a stand of aspen trees.

Dahlia hurried after him, not wanting to be left behind now that there wasn't a trail to follow. She caught up with him as he was scaling a rocky ledge. When she paused to eye the mini-cliff, he turned, holding out a hand to help her climb up next to him.

She scrabbled up the incline, happy to find that there was enough of a slant to make the climb manageable, especially with Winston's help. His strength was impressive, hauling her up alongside him with little apparent effort. Once they reached the top, the ground leveled off, but he still kept hold of her hand. Dahlia was pretty sure he'd forgotten that he was holding it, but she didn't draw his attention to it. She liked it, liked the connection, especially out here in the wilderness with nothing but a narrow tree-choked path and wild animals for miles.

Well, and the three people on ATVs heading toward them.

"Is this an actual road?" Dahlia asked, eyeing the wide gravel path in front of them, the sight of it sending her a little off-center. Just a second ago, she would've sworn they were in the middle of actual nowhere, alone except for the bears, when they'd been a short cliff climb away from civilization…or at least semi-civilization.

"Logging road," Winston said, his eyes following the ATVs as they slowed, rolling to a stop next to them.

Yanking off his helmet, the fiftyish Latino man in the lead smiled affably at them. "Hey. How's the hiking?"

When Winston just studied the strangers, not answering as per his usual with everyone they encountered, Dahlia figured it was up to her to carry on the conversation. "Good," she said, even though she had no idea if the hiking could be considered "good," since she had no previous experience to compare it to. "How's the...ATVing?" She wasn't sure exactly what the verb was for what they were doing, so she improvised.

The other two took off their helmets as well, revealing another man and a Latina woman approximately the same age. The two men looked too much alike not to be brothers.

"Great!" the first man answered.

"Cold," the woman said at the same time, and all three—and Dahlia—laughed. When Winston didn't join in, they threw him cautious looks. She wanted to assure the strangers that he wasn't dangerous, he just had a bad case of resting grump face, but it was more urgent she ask about her sister.

"Have you run into anyone else?" Dahlia asked. The chance of them crossing paths with Rose was low, she knew, but it didn't hurt to check.

"Nah," the first guy said. "This time of year, it's just diehards like us."

"And a diehard's wife who lost a bet," the woman said, deadpan, although she shot an amused look at the man next to her.

Even though she'd not really expected any information, Dahlia still had to hide a ping of disappointment. "Well, enjoy the rest of your ride," she said. "We'd better get hiking if we want to make it to the falls tonight."

"Howling Falls?" the guy who'd been quiet until this point

asked. "This road won't get you there. It turns west instead of north and dead-ends at the ranger station, miles from the falls."

"We're following the trail over there," Dahlia said, gesturing vaguely behind them. "We just heard the ATVs, so we figured we'd say hello."

"Good timing," the first man said. When Dahlia looked at him curiously, he explained. "This is the only point where this road and the trail get close. Otherwise, they're nowhere near each other."

"Where does this road start?" Dahlia pointed in the opposite direction of the ranger station.

"Duff Road, right outside of Howling Falls—the town," the first guy hurried to clarify. "We're from Glass Lake, just ten miles south, and this is one of our favorite local routes."

For some reason, this information brought home the fact that Rose could be anywhere, and Dahlia had to work to keep her smile in place. "Nice chatting with you," she said, giving the trio a wave as they put their helmets back on and rolled away, all three returning her wave before they rounded a bend in the road and disappeared.

Dahlia watched the spot where they'd disappeared, her mind running over all of the possible catastrophes that could've befallen Rose.

Winston gave her arm a gentle tug, pulling her out of her panicked thoughts.

As they turned to make their way back to the trail, she glanced at him. "You were awfully quiet just now. Did you get a bad feeling from them?"

"No."

"Yeah, me neither." They'd seemed just as they appeared—locals out for a leisurely ATV ride. That didn't explain Winston's reticence, though. "Why don't you ever talk to people we meet?"

"I'm not a big talker." He grabbed a narrow tree trunk to hold his balance as he started down the short but steep incline. "You know that."

"You're not Chatty Cathy, sure, but you talk." She wished he'd offer her a hand down, but he seemed to be focused on his own footing. With a mental shrug and sign of the cross, she started to make her way down after him. "Why is downhill worse than uphill?" she asked, already breathless as her feet skidded down the smooth rock before she could grab the same small tree as Winston had.

"Stay right behind me," he grumbled. To her surprise, he picked up their conversation again without her having to prod him. "I don't like talking to strangers."

"But even when we were strangers, you talked to *me*." Her feet skidded again, and she almost face-planted against his back before she caught herself. Having his huge form as a wall reassured Dahlia. She might mash her nose against his iron-hard lat muscles, but she at least wouldn't plummet to her death. "In fact, I was an uninvited stranger who'd just climbed your obnoxious fence."

One shoulder twitched in what might've been a shrug. "You're different."

If she hadn't needed both hands to clutch anything in reach, she would've propped her hands on her hips. "What does that mean? Everyone we've encountered wa—" She broke off with a tiny shriek as the clump of dead weeds she was using for a handhold came loose. Quickly grabbing a sapling, she paused until she knew it was going to support her before finishing her sentence. "Everyone was very nice. I'm a lot of very impressive things, but I'm not all that nice."

She started puffing a little from exertion as she hurried down the last few feet of the incline. Finally able to put her hands on her hips, she concentrated on catching her breath for a few moments. Once she was breathing a little bit closer to normal, she focused on Winston again. He was waiting for her, but he wasn't even breathing hard. It was annoying. "Why did I get words when no one else does?"

"If you want me quiet, I can be quiet," he grumbled, turning abruptly and walking toward the trail they'd abandoned earlier.

She snorted, chasing after him. It felt much better to walk on semi-flat ground. "Don't threaten me with a good time."

He shot her a baleful look over his shoulder, which again made her want to laugh.

"You don't have to explain," she allowed—benevolently, she felt. "I'm just curious why you thought me worthy of words."

He twitched his shoulders in one of those shrugs that made him look like he was trying to rid himself of pesky flying insects. "I don't know."

"You must have an *inkling*."

"You're a pest."

"Yes." She fully accept this truth.

His sigh was loud and long, making her snort. Who knew

Winston Dane the weird hermit could be so *dramatic*? "You're just…easy."

She cleared her throat.

The look he threw her was a bit hunted, so she hid her smile and arched her eyebrows instead, hopefully giving off the stern-nun vibes she was shooting for. When he flinched, she was satisfied that she'd achieved her goal. "Not *easy*. Just simple."

It was too hard to hold back, and a bark of amusement escaped before she reined it in. "So now I'm *simple*?"

"Not…uh… You're…" His hands grasped at nothing, as if he could literally pull more tactful words from the air, and she basked in the smug satisfaction of making Mr. Stoic trip over his own tongue. His next sigh sounded even more exasperated than the first. "You're not being very easy now."

Her laughter broke free, filling the too-quiet forest with the ringing sound of her amusement. "Sorry," she apologized once she'd gotten herself under control. Winston didn't look too offended. In fact, there was a suspiciously upward tilt to the right corner of his mouth, and his shoulders were relaxed rather than stiff and bunched. "I shouldn't tease you. I know you didn't mean anything by it," she assured him, not wanting to drag out his torture any longer. "I usually hear 'difficult' and 'high-maintenance' and 'disrespectful' and 'stubborn' and—"

"You're not, though," he interrupted.

Now it was her mouth that was twitching with amusement. "I'm not difficult? Really?"

He cleared his throat. "You're not high-maintenance. You jump in to help and are eager to learn things. You're not whiny or demanding, and I–I actually like having you around. I'm *comfortable* with you."

"Thank you." Now *she* had to clear her throat, unexpectedly touched. "Seriously, Winston, that's a skill."

Tossing her a confused glance over his shoulder, he asked, "What is?"

"You're the *best* complimenter."

The back of his neck flared red again as he grumbled something under his breath.

"You don't take compliments well," she said, even though she enjoyed his flustered growliness. "But you're the king of giving them."

He abruptly stopped and dug in his pack.

"Everything okay?" she asked, startled by his sudden halt.

Instead of answering, he thrust a bag of trail mix and a strip of jerky at her. "Eat. And you need to drink more water."

"Oh!" She slid off her own pack as realization dawned. "Lunchtime!" It seemed more like midmorning to her, but she was no expert at reading the position of the sun, and her phone was off, so she wasn't positive. "Or is this more like second breakfast? Morning tea? Elevenses?"

His lips twitched right before he shoved a handful of trail mix in his mouth. She had a strong suspicion that he was using the food to hide a smile.

With a mental shrug, she follow suit, ripping off a bite of jerky. After chewing the dried meat for what felt like fifteen minutes, she finally swallowed and asked, "How close are we to the main path?"

"Twenty minutes," he answered once his mouth was empty, and then immediately ate another fistful of trail mix.

"Hmm," she hummed, eyeing him narrowly. "I'm beginning to think this food break is just to get out of talking to me for five minutes."

Although he didn't say anything, the sly twist to his right eyebrow confirmed her suspicions. However, Dahlia wasn't willing to say no to food after hiking for-freaking-ever, so she bit off another chunk of jerky. As she chewed, she made a mental list of conversational topics for the walk ahead. He could silence her for a minute or two, but there wasn't enough food in the world to keep her quiet for long.

The snack and water brightened her mood, however, so she wasn't feeling particularly revenge-focused once they headed down the trail again. Instead, she hummed quietly to herself and started her search for Rose-related spoor. Even though they were fairly certain Dahlia's sister hadn't come this way, it felt neglectful not to continue looking for evidence.

As she eyed the path in front of her, she frowned. "What if Rose was on the other path to the falls when something happened to her, and we miss seeing any clues?" Before he could answer, she winced. "Sorry. Nasal. Glut." She gagged a little on her two least-favorite words. "We're even again."

"You're not making any sense."

"Since we went on this trail, we're missing any evidence on the other path," Dahlia tried to explain, but he waved impatiently.

"I get that part," he said. "It's all the nonsense words after— never mind. If we don't find your sister at the falls or on that highlighted trail, we'll follow the other path back to the trail-head, check it then."

"Okay." She wasn't entirely happy with the plan, but that wasn't Winston's fault. Dahlia felt her strictly repressed worries slip free just a bit, and her brain flashed to all the terrible things that could've happened to Rose. She firmly corralled those thoughts before they could spiral into panic. "I'm sure she's fine. She always is. Once we find her in that hippie bear commune, we'll all have a good laugh about me thinking she might've been eaten by a mountain lion."

"We'll find her," Winston promised. The confident way he spoke, as if there was no question what he'd said was true, reassured her.

"I know." After a moment, she had to ask, "No comment about the hippie bear commune?"

He just grunted, which made her smile.

Her mood lifted even more as the trail widened. "This feels positively luxurious," Dahlia said, stretching her arms out at her sides just because she could. "It's almost as good as a paved road." She spun in a circle, enjoying the freedom of movement. When she came to a dizzy halt, she saw Winston had tromped on without her, and she chased after him. "Think we'll make it to the falls tonight?" she asked once she'd caught up.

He shook his head. "Tomorrow before noon if we don't waste time spinning in circles for no reason."

"There was an *excellent* reason." When he gave her an inquiring look that was more pointed than she would've preferred, she explained, "The path is wide."

Since they were walking side by side, she could see his expressions and not have to guess what he was thinking by the way he held his shoulders. His profile told her he was bemused, which was better than annoyed, she supposed, since they had to share a tiny tent again tonight. "Doesn't take much to make you happy, does it?" he asked.

"Nope." It was her turn to give him just the tiniest bit of side-eye. "Like you said, I'm pretty simple."

"I didn't m—" He broke off with a huff when she couldn't hold back her grin. "Save your breath for walking." As if to encourage her silence, his steps sped up.

That made her chuckle and give a little skip as she caught up with him. "Oh, please. Don't you know me well enough by now to realize I have enough breath for both hiking *and* talking?"

Although he sighed heavily, he couldn't hide that betraying twitch of his mouth. As much as he wanted to pretend other-wise, the man was entertained by her chatter, and that was good, since there was absolutely no way Dahlia was going to listen to the creepy forest noises for *hours*. Besides, she liked talking to him. As unexpected as it was, this gruff mountain man was quickly turning into one of her favorite people.

NINE

SHE MANAGED TO KEEP UP ninety-five percent of the conversation for quite a while, but after lunch, the clouds crowded in and the wind picked up. That wouldn't have been so bad, except that the temperature jumped off a cliff as well. Even with all Dahlia's layers on, including the borrowed face mask and goggles, the wind found gaps in her clothes and bit at her skin.

"It's so cold." Her teeth chattered on the words, emphasizing her statement.

"You've already said that," he said, although mildly for him. "Seven times."

"That's because it is *that* cold—seven times cold. Exponentially cold, cold to the power of seven." She tried to put some bounce in her step to warm up from the inside, but that just emphasized how the frigid temperatures tightened her joints and made her bones brittle, like they'd shatter if she stomped her foot too hard. "Besides, all other thoughts have been frozen out of my brain."

"Fine," he grumped in that way she was beginning to suspect wasn't a real grumble, but was more of a faux-growl. She was pretty sure he didn't really mind, but he thought he had to keep up his reputation as a sourpuss.

"Fine what?" she asked when he didn't elaborate.

"Fine, we'll make camp early."

"Oh, good." Although she worried that she'd get even colder—it that was possible—if she stopped walking, the lure of her sleeping bag and the shelter of the tent was tempting.

True to his word, after only ten more minutes of walking, he turned off the main path onto a small tributary trail marked with a pictogram of a tent. The trees pressed in on either side, helping to block the wind, but there was no escape from the surrounding cold. Her fingers and toes were numb, and despite the face mask, she couldn't feel her cheeks. Why anyone would live somewhere they couldn't feel their extremities on a regular basis, she couldn't even fathom.

After just a couple of minutes, they reached the tiny campground with a cold, blackened firepit and even several stumps set around it to use as chairs. There was just enough room for two or three tents in the little clearing, but no one else was there. She was grateful they wouldn't have neighbors since it was much too cold for friendly chitchat with strangers. In fact, it was too cold for any sort of chitchat, so she was silent as she followed Winston's orders for setting up camp.

Her fingers fumbled with the tent poles, but they didn't require any fine motor skills, so she eventually got them assembled. Once their tent was up and her pack was stored in the vestibule, she followed him the short distance to the food area. Her head spun—from hunger or tiredness or the elevation—and she paused until the dizziness eased. There were more stumps there, and Dahlia lowered herself onto one as Winston set up the stove and started the water—slushy ice at this point—heating. She reached over to warm her hands with the heat radiating from the sides of the pan.

When he didn't move away, she looked up to see that he was eyeing her with what looked like concern. "What's wrong?" he asked.

"Wrong?"

"You're too quiet."

She smiled, even though it made her numb cheeks feel weird. "I would've thought a break from listening to me talk would make you happy."

"No." His right eyebrow scrunched toward the left. "It's creepy."

She threw her hands in the air, ignoring the cold for a moment as she wallowed in the joy of being right. "Yes! That's what I've been *saying*!" Her fingers missed the warmth of the stove, so she quickly moved them close to the pan again.

He snorted but kept his eyes focused on her. When she returned his gaze, not quite sure what he was waiting for but enjoying the chance to look straight at him and admire him for a while, he growled out an impatient, "Well?"

"Well…what?"

"Why aren't you talking?"

Although it was tempting to remind him that they were,

in fact, in the process of talking right this minute, she resisted. "It's so cold. I need to conserve my energy for heat. Besides, my frozen lips might fall off if I move them."

"Hmm." Instead of looking reassured by her answer, he seemed even more concerned. "It's not really that cold for this time of year. You're just not used to it."

She stared at him in consternation. "Do you mean it's going to get even *colder*?" She wasn't sure how she'd survive that, since she already felt like her body had been lowered into a vat of liquid nitrogen. It was enough to make her cry, except that she was afraid her tears would freeze on her face.

His grunt, she was horrified to hear, was definitely an affirmative. "Water's boiling."

He'd already set out and opened two dehydrated food pouches, so she carefully added water before sealing them back up. Starving and already sick of jerky and trail mix, she didn't even care what meals he'd picked for them. As long it was warm and filled her belly, she'd take it. She huffed an impatient sigh as she eyed the pouches, willing them to be ready quickly.

"You staring at them isn't going to speed things up," Winston said. His ability to read her mind was a little unnerving.

He wasn't wrong, however, so she forced her gaze away from the rehydrating food. "Do you have any sisters?" she asked. "Or brothers?"

"No." He paused, then modified his answer. "Not really."

That was interesting. "It's usually a yes or no question. How can you sort of have a sibling?"

One of his shoulders twitched in the shrug he brought out

when he was uncomfortable. She was struck that she knew that fact. Even if he *was* starting to read her mind, she was also starting to know him. Maybe it was the hiking and camping and spending every minute together, or the urgency of their errand, but she felt like she'd known him a very long time, rather than just a few days. "I was an only child, as far as I know, but my foster families had other kids."

"Ah." She gave a nod. "That's definitely a way you can sort of have a sibling. Did you like any of them?"

"My foster families?" he asked. "Or the kids?"

"Either. Both." She suddenly wanted to know everything about him. He'd always been interesting to her, even when he was just an unknown weird hermit who'd talked to her sister, but now he was fascinating. This realization made her uneasy for some reason, but she tucked away that reaction to pull out and examine more closely later. Right now, she was learning things about Winston, even if those things were only that he grew stiff when discussing his past and that his right eyebrow flattened out when he was uncomfortable.

"They were fine. Nice enough." He grimaced as if the words tasted bad, as if he hated the feel of the term *nice* in his mouth as much as he did the word *clue*. "Just wasn't that close to any of them. None would've chased after me like you did for your sister."

His shoulders twisted awkwardly again. Knowing how much it sucked to talk about subjects she'd rather internalize until they warped her psyche, she took pity on him and brought the focus back to her and Rose. "We're half sisters, but we're close—probably because everyone else in our family either died or is objectively terrible."

Although he looked interested at that, enough to possibly ask a personal question even, his watch beeped, interrupting whatever he was going to say. "Food's ready."

"Did you set an alarm?" Why she found that adorable, Dahlia wasn't sure, but she did.

He shot her a sideways glance as he handed her one of the pouches and a fork. "Yeah?"

"That's adorable."

Even in the moody gray light of the cloudy afternoon, she saw color creep under his beard to land on his sharp cheekbones. "Why is that…? Never mind." He concentrated a little too hard on opening his meal pouch.

Smiling, feeling a little lighter and even a bit warmer, Dahlia followed suit, checking the label to see what she was about to eat—beef stroganoff—before digging in. "You know, these aren't bad," she said as she rooted around for her next bite. "My expectations for rehydrated pouch food were pretty low, but this is definitely not gag-worthy."

He didn't respond, but she took his inhaling his food as agreement.

"A nice change from jerky and trail mix."

He grunted as he shoveled in another bite. To her surprise, he swallowed and asked, "You mentioned your stepmom isn't great, but *everyone* in your family is terrible?"

The continuation of the pre-food topic surprised her, and she blinked silently for a moment before answering.

Dropping his head to refocus on his meal, Winston muttered, "Sorry."

"Oh no, I don't mind." She waved her fork hand as if dismissing his concerns. "I can't remember my mom, but my stepmom and father, the aunts and uncles, and even the cousins are all fairly horrible people. And I mean it when I said they are *objectively* awful, since this isn't coming from an emotional place. Both Rose and I accepted that we're the only decent people to come out of our family, and now we keep our distance from them so we're able to find them ridiculous rather than monstrous."

He studied her silently, already done with his food.

"For example," she said, poking at her stroganoff, not wanting to hand it off to Winston yet since it would make him worry she wasn't eating enough. "Rose and I are only three weeks apart in age."

His right eyebrow twitched, and Dahlia took it as a sign of sympathy.

"Not sure what you'd call us. We're not twins or even Irish twins. Twins from a dickwad, maybe?"

The corner of his mouth twitched.

Lowering the remains of her meal to her lap, she shrugged. "Rose and I both have our issues, but overall, we consider ourselves lucky. We had each other and strong enough personalities to come into adulthood fairly intact. We managed to avoid the billionaire curse."

"Billionaire curse?" When his gaze flickered down to the pouch on her lap, she held it out.

"Want my leftovers?"

With a concerned frown, he finished them off as she explained.

"Too much money often makes people into huge assholes—see my family for Exhibits A through M or so. Rose and I managed to avoid that. We're only *moderate* assholes."

His fork paused halfway to his mouth. "Weathersby. As in Weathersby Tech? *Those* Weathersbys?"

She grimaced. "The very same. Weathersby Tech and Weathersby News and Weathersby Financial Services and a whole lot of nasty Weathersby scandals. I never wanted anything to do with that whole mess. I think that's why I got into makeovers. I wanted—still want—to present myself how I want others to see me, rather than people hearing the name and thinking that's me in my entirety."

Although Dahlia was expecting more questions about her famous—and sometimes infamous—family members, Winston just looked at her with a penetrating gaze before silently going about his business. He used the rest of the hot water to fill their water bottles and clean their dishes, while she, happy to stop talking about her unpleasant family, returned everything that wasn't food or smelled like food to his pack, as he put their food and bag of garbage—and even their toothpaste—into a stuff sack. It felt strangely domestic, and a prickling warmth spread through Dahlia's insides. Deciding that was just the beginning of hypothermia, rather than some unfamiliar emotion that would be very inconvenient for her to start feeling, she jumped up and hopped around.

When he arched that right eyebrow at her, she shrugged. "Trying to warm up somehow."

For some reason, that made him look a bit grim. Grabbing his pack and the food stuff sack, he strode across the small clearing in the opposite direction of the campsite.

She trotted after him. "I can carry something," she offered, but he didn't respond, not even with a growl.

They quickly reached another clearing, this one with a tall metal pole. At the top, metal rods protruded, making the whole thing look like a messed-up postmodern tree sculpture.

"What's that for?" she asked, but her question was answered quickly enough when he hooked the food sack onto the end of another pole, lifting it up to hang on one of the protruding "branches."

"Bear pole," he said, leading the way out of the clearing.

"Much better than having to make your own food clothesline," she said approvingly, glancing back at where their solitary bag hung. "Or food line, I suppose."

Once they reached their campsite, Winston shooed her into the trees to pee. Twigs and frozen weeds crunched beneath her hiking shoes, loud in the hush of near-dusk. When Dahlia realized she was tiptoeing, trying to preserve the silence as if she were in church or a library, she intentionally stomped, making as much noise as possible. The last thing she wanted to do was surprise some wildlife, especially one with big teeth and claws.

She picked a good-sized tree and tried not to think too much about the stillness around her. As much as she teased Winston about the creepiness of the quiet wilderness, it wasn't really *bad*.

It was just…different from the bustling city she was used to. She could even understand how some people could find the silence peaceful. It was just when she started thinking too much about what might be hiding in the gloom beyond her chosen tree that her heart started to beat too quickly, and she hurried to finish so she could get back to the safety of Winston.

Dahlia finished performing one of her least-favorite camping tasks—she was seriously going to worship her toilet once she returned to civilization—and moved around the tree she'd been hiding behind. Immediately, she ran right into someone.

Clenching her teeth, she held back her startled shriek as she recognized the brick wall she'd just mashed her nose against. "Winston!" That instant of fear transformed to annoyance, which she released by pinching his arm. Unfortunately, thanks to his multiple thick layers of clothes and her glittens, the move wasn't very effective. "Why are you lurking? You scared the crap out of me." Her heartbeat settled, although the adrenaline-fueled jitters still remained.

"It's getting dark." He seemed extra-grumpy, which didn't make sense, as *he* wasn't the one who'd just had the bejesus scared out of him.

"It was nice of you to be concerned," she said, moving around him to get to the tent. Now that the shock was waning, the encroaching cold was all she could think about. "But I don't need a pee guard—not one that close, at least. I'll yell for you if any peeping-Tom animals try to intrude on my private time."

"Not just wild animals to worry about," he grumbled, following her back to the tent and waiting while she grabbed her water bottles, makeup, and toiletry bag. "Doubt Rose got abducted by a bear."

She jolted and then froze for a moment. Even though Rose and what might've happened to her was always on Dahlia's mind, she hadn't considered that whatever danger her sister had encountered could be lying in wait for her too. "You think Rose was abducted?"

"Probably not, but it's a possibility. Sorry," Winston growled.

"For what?" Dahlia said, trying for insouciance but hearing her words come out a bit thin instead. "You're not telling me anything that I shouldn't already be considering. I appreciate the reminder." She scooted into the tent, wanting to burrow into her sleeping bag, even though she was aware this new coldness seeping through her wasn't a physical reaction.

It was fear.

Winston sighed but didn't say anything else as he joined her in the tent. They completed their pre-bed routine in silence, except for him reminding her to add her water bottles to the collection of items at the foot of her sleeping bag to keep them from freezing. She also created a skin care and cosmetics stuff sack that went in with her too, since freezing couldn't be good for them. The water bottles were still warm from the hot water he'd added, and she pressed her socked feet against them.

Before zipping herself in, she pulled out a small mirror and the package of makeup-removing wipes.

"Are those scented?" Winston asked, watching closely as she cleaned her face. "If so, we should hang them up with the food."

"Nope." Dahlia was extremely glad they weren't, since she

would've cried if she'd had to get dressed and trek to the bear pole. "None of my products are scented."

"Huh."

His grunt sounded a bit skeptical, and she paused, giving him a challenging look as she held up the package of wipes. "See? Scent-free."

He waved away the pack she was shoving at his face. "I believe you. Just confused."

"About what?" she asked absently, occupied with returning the pack to her toiletry bag and zipping it closed.

"If nothing you use is scented, how do you smell so good?"

She froze, her hand still on the zipper of her bag, feeling pleased and weirdly flustered at the same time. "You think I smell good?"

His grunt was displeased. "Forget I said anything."

His grouchy growl just made her smile widen. "What do I smell like?"

"I don't know," he huffed, focusing on arranging the stuff sack that held his boots, even though she was pretty sure it didn't need reorganizing.

"I'm going to die of curiosity if you don't tell me," she said, adding her toiletry bag to the collection at her feet before scooting down in her sleeping bag and zipping herself in. Despite the cold and their very rudimentary accommodations, she couldn't stop smiling. Winston Dane thought she smelled nice. "Worse than that, I'm going to keep nagging you about this until you tell me."

"Or you die."

"Right," she said without blinking. "Although I'm pretty sure that if I die before you tell me, I'll stay on the mortal plane so my ghostly self can continue to nag you about this."

The sound he made was both a groan and a huge, gusting sigh, and the exaggerated drama of it made her smile. "I don't even know what you smell like. It's just…nice."

"Hmm," she hummed. "I suppose I can live with that."

"Finally," he grumbled.

"I think you smell nice too. Like vanilla cake."

"What?" He sat up, and his sleeping bag fell to his waist, showing off his broad chest covered in just a thin layer that didn't hide much. Even as she voraciously took in the view, she cuddled deeper into her sleeping bag with a shiver. The air was much too cold for dramatic gestures. "I do not."

For some reason, his refusal made her snicker. "You do. Why are you complaining? It's a good smell—delicious, even."

He flushed. "Guys are supposed to smell like… I don't know. Pine needles and woodsmoke, not baked goods."

Her eyebrows flew up. "There are gender rules on smells?"

"Of course."

"Oh." The ridiculousness of their conversation struck her, and she giggled. "Too bad. You're a weird hermit who smells like vanilla cake fresh out of the oven, and that's just how it is. You can't argue with reality and cold, hard facts."

He huffed and flopped back down, making her roll her lips in to hold back yet another laugh. "You're wrong." There was a pause, and then she heard the sound of a sniff.

Completely losing control of herself, she burst into gales

of laughter. "Did you just...*sniff* yourself?" she asked once she could speak coherently again.

His growl sounded self-conscious, sending her off again. "Go to sleep."

TEN

ALTHOUGH DAHLIA DOZED OFF EASILY, the creeping cold woke her soon after. No matter how small she curled up inside her sleeping bag or how tightly she drew the drawstring closure over her face, she couldn't seem to get warm. The icy air soaked right through her sleeping bag. Judging by the sound of Winston's steady, deep breathing, he wasn't having any issues staying warm.

"Rated for temperatures as low as thirty below, my foot," she grumbled under her breath. Although her words weren't much louder than a breath, she went still for a second, listening to make sure she hadn't woken her tent buddy. Listening to him breathe brought back the memory of how his thinly covered chest appeared in the dim light earlier, and her heartbeat sped up, making her blood whoosh in her ears. That should've warmed her, but Dahlia was pretty sure she was beyond hope. She was destined to be a fashionista-shaped icicle for the rest of her life. *A fashionista pop.*

Once she was reassured by the audible sound of Winston's breathing—not quite snoring but loud enough to convince her he was still asleep—she wiggled a little closer to him. All that muscle mass had to work like a furnace, she figured. If she could get close enough, it'd be like having a huge, warm rock next to her. If it worked for a cold-blooded lizard, then why not for her?

The problem, she decided in frustration, was all the layers of extremely insulating materials separating them. Two sleeping bags blocked Dahlia's warm-rock access, and having a heat source so close that she couldn't access was making her wild with frustration. She considered herself a reasonably considerate person who respected other's boundaries, but this was the very definition of an extreme situation. Forget personal space—her feet were frozen.

"Winston," she whispered, and his breath immediately caught and went silent. Not a deep sleeper then. She opened her mouth to make her request but then shut it again. As cold as she was, she was suddenly embarrassed and had no idea how to phrase such an intrusive question.

"What?" he asked at a normal volume. His voice was a little huskier than his usual growl, but overall he sounded shockingly awake for someone who'd been asleep a literal second ago. "Dahlia? You okay?"

The concern in his tone, as rough as it was, eased her awkwardness until all she felt was cold again. "I'm freezing. Let me in."

His pause was louder than his words had been. "Let you in…where?"

"Where do you think?" Bracing herself for a rush of cold air, she whipped her sleeping bag zipper down and kicked her feet free. It was terrible, but she reassured her goose-bumped skin that she'd soon be in a much warmer place. "Your sleeping bag. Open up."

"My…what?" It was the most bewildered she'd ever heard him, which was quite impressive, since they'd spent several days glued together at the hip. She needed to start upping her day-time game.

"Sleeping bag. Please?" She was rapidly approaching a fully frozen state, so she wasn't going to shy away from a little begging. "C'mon, Winston. You have tons of extra room in there, and I'm not-so-slowly freezing to death by myself. Lend me a little of your sun-warmed rockiness."

"My…?" There was a click as the flashlight turned on, and he made a sound awfully close to a disapproving cluck when he saw her. "What are you doing out of your sleeping bag? You'll freeze."

"I was freezing *in* my sleeping bag," she informed him through chattering teeth. Her whole body was shivering uncontrollably. "That's why I want to get in yours."

He let out a groaning growl and jerked down the zip on his sleeping bag. "Hurry up then."

He didn't need to invite her in twice. She shoved the stuff sack holding her cosmetics and toiletries at him, impatiently waiting as he tucked it with his by his feet, and then scrambled into his heavenly warm bag. Barely hearing the *burr* of the zipper as he closed them both in, she burrowed into his chest, tucking her icicle hands between them, her icicle feet under his calf, and icicle nose into the crook of his neck. With each cold contact, he grunted and flinched—although if that was because of the shock of her icy touch or for some other reason, she wasn't sure.

She wasn't really thinking logically at all. The only thing that mattered at the moment was warmth, and she was finally, luxuriously, surrounded by it. Her skin prickled as she slowly thawed, but she appreciated even those tiny pains, since that meant she was no longer frozen. She gave a moan filled with contentment and raw pleasure, and his entire body stiffened into a plank—well, a thickly muscled and gloriously warm plank.

"Dahl," he growled her name in thick protest, but she just wiggled closer.

"If you were just a little softer and squishier," she said as her nose flattened against his collarbone, forcing her to turn her face into the space under his chin instead, "this would be *perfect.*"

"You wish I were...*squishier.*"

"Mmm," she hummed in agreement. When her lips accidentally brushed against his throat during her burrowing process, she discovered that she wasn't the only one with goose bumps. "Sorry. This must be miserable for you, like sharing a bed with a woman-sized Popsicle. Your poor balls are probably sucked so far inside your body that you'll never see them again."

His entire body jerked. "Dahlia!"

Her chuckle was sleepy. "Sorry again. My brain-to-mouth filter is already asleep. I'm sure your balls will reemerge someday. Maybe not this winter though, since it's awfully cold here."

"Please stop talking about my balls."

"Right." Her words were a mumble as sleep sucked her in

now that she was deliciously warm. "Inappropriate. Sorry. No more ball talk."

When she tucked in even closer to him, she felt him shiver, which made her feel bad for torturing him this way. Winston, trouper that he was, gave a heavy sigh that sent a gust of warm air down the back of her neck as he wrapped his arms around her, surrounding her with his heat.

She'd never been all that cuddly, but this…this was *luscious*. Humming with contentment, she let herself drop into sleep, but not before she felt a light pressure on the crown of her head that felt suspiciously like a gentle goodnight kiss from none other than Winston Dane.

———

A howling woke her, although she fought to hold on to sleep. Her body was warm and heavy, and she was snugged tight against Winston's hot rock of a body. It was a good place to be, and she didn't want to leave that cozy, comforting place, but it was too noisy not to wake.

"Who's screaming?" she mumbled, keeping her face buried in the crook of his neck. "Can you ask them to be quiet please?"

"Don't think the wind will listen to me," he said, sounding like he'd been awake for a while. His voice rumbled in his chest, and Dahlia enjoyed hearing him in stereo—inside and out.

Focusing on his words, she frowned. "The wind?" With a soundless sigh, she opened her eyes and raised her head. The morning light was muted by the tent walls, but she could tell it wasn't all that bright outside to start with. "Is it snowing?"

"Blizzarding," he corrected.

"Oh." She wiggled a hand free so she could rub at her still-sleepy eyes. "That's going to be fun to hike through."

"No." When she looked at him in surprise, he elaborated, "We're not hiking in this." As if to emphasize the wisdom of his words, the wind screeched again, and the tent fabric snapped and rippled. Dahlia eyed the walls around them in concern.

"Will the tent hold up in this?" she asked.

"Yeah. It's made for it."

She snorted. "And my sleeping bag was made for keeping me warm, and we see how well that worked out."

"It should've," he said, and she frowned at him for taking the sleeping bag's side over hers. In response, the corner of his mouth twitched in that way it did when he was holding back a smile. "You're just used to a warmer climate."

That tiny quirk of his lips made her realize that they were still plastered together from the chest down and that his arms were wrapped around her and that his hands were stroking over her back, with only the thin silk layer of her long underwear top as a barrier. All he'd have to do was slip one of those broad hands under her shirt, and then they'd be skin to skin, his callused fingers gliding over her sensitive back… "Enough of that!"

The words came out loud enough that Winston froze, and she felt bad. She'd just meant to startle herself out of that very distracting and dangerous train of thought, not scare the spit out of him. "Sorry," he said. "I didn't realize…" His hands lifted off of her back as he cleared his throat.

"No, sorry, I didn't mean… I meant enough of…uh, lazing

around. I need to get up." The problem was that she didn't actually want to get up, and there wasn't a good reason—except to maintain what was left of her self-respect. Her bladder gave a twinge, and she seized on the excuse. "I need to pee!" It came out a bit more excitedly than the task really deserved, but she pretended like she didn't see the way his right eyebrow shot toward his hairline. Instead, she gestured for him to unzip the bag.

After a final wary look, he obeyed. Despite knowing that some distance was called for, it still felt tragically wrong for him to unzip their shared sleeping bag, letting in the frigid air and destroying their warm nest. With a sigh, she scooted out and over to her abandoned sleeping bag. As she fished out her clothes, she groaned.

"What's wrong?"

"I didn't move my clothes over to your sleeping bag, so now they're all cold." She yanked on her fuzzy fleece top and shivered, hoping that her body heat would kick in sooner than later. It was too bad she couldn't stay wrapped up in Winston for the rest of her stay in this mountain-filled icebox. The thought made her blood rush more quickly through her veins and her face grew warm, so at least one part of her wasn't freezing. She'd never thought she'd be grateful for blushing, but this trip had introduced a lot of firsts. Dressed, she pulled a water bottle out of the stuff sack and sighed. The water inside was frozen solid.

"Here." Winston held out one of his bottles.

"Thanks, Wins." When he didn't react to the nickname, it was her turn to cock an eyebrow. "No objection? That's a win. Heh. Wins is a win."

"Better than Winnie, anyway."

Although he grumbled, it sounded halfhearted. Either he'd given up on arguing or was actually starting to like being teased by her. Although she had a strong feeling it was the former, Dahlia decided to be optimistic and believe the latter. She drank the unfrozen-but-still-too-cold water while eyeing him thoughtfully as he dressed, and then shivered when the icy liquid hit her empty stomach.

"Hurry up," he demanded, gesturing toward the door. "Sooner you're done, the sooner you'll be back in your sleeping bag. Hypothermia's a real risk."

Handing him back his water bottle, she unzipped the door and stuck her head out…and then immediately retreated like a scared turtle back into her shell. Turning to stare at Winston, she said, "That's, like, a full-out blizzard."

"It's not 'like a 'blizzard.' It *is* a blizzard."

"I know, but I didn't expect *that*." She pointed at the door, eyeing it like Sasquatch was squatting right outside, waiting to pounce. "It's all so…*white*."

The corner of his mouth raised even as his right eyebrow twitched with impatience. "That's why it's called a whiteout."

Ignoring his condescending statement, she dared another peek outside. "Should I tie a rope around my waist? I read a book once about an Old West pioneer who got lost on the way back from the barn and froze to death. I'd rather not die in such an anachronistic sort of way, if possible."

By the way his mouth twisted down ferociously, he was losing control over his smile. "No rope needed. Just stay close to the tent."

She offered him a bit of side-eye. "Seems gross to pee right in our front yard."

He huffed a little. "It's just going to freeze anyway."

That reminded her of another danger. "My butt's going to be bare. I could get frostbite."

"You won't get frostbite if you hurry." He flapped both his hands, shooing her out like she was an entire flock of chickens. "Go."

Since her bladder was also encouraging her to just get on with it, she forced herself out the door. The wind immediately smacked into her, forcing her to close her eyes. The snowflakes were larger than they'd been the first day of hiking, but they still managed quite a sting.

"Hurry up!"

Winston's bellow spurred her into motion, reminding her that the quicker she took care of business, the quicker she could be back in her sleeping bag—or, even better, back inside *his* sleeping bag. She probably should've been embarrassed by the way she'd wheedled her way into his bed, but when it came to seeking heat, she was as shameless as a pampered cat.

Keeping her glittened fingertips brushing against the fabric of the tent, she scooted around to the side. Despite Winston's assurances, she wasn't going to pee in their front yard. The wind shoved at her from multiple directions, as if it was a gang of bullies trying to intimidate her, and she had to admit that she wanted to run back into the tent to get away from it. Clenching her teeth, she bared what she needed to bare and endured the slicing wind on parts that she never thought would be exposed on a winter mountainside.

"Rose, when we find you," she said in a conversational tone that was snatched away by the howling wind as soon as the words left her lips, "I'm going to kick your ass twice—once for scaring me, and a second time for my frostbitten fanny." The thought of Rose being alive and well enough for an ass-kicking cheered her, and she yanked up all her layers as she plotted her future revenge.

A dark form appeared out of the snow in front of her, and she shrieked.

"It's just me," Winston shouted over the wind, and she slapped him on the arm. Even though she knew he'd barely be able to feel the smack through all of his layers, it still made her feel better.

"You jerk!" she yelled, which also released some of the unnecessary adrenaline coursing through her from the scare. "I thought you were a bear!"

To her shock, he grinned, his white teeth matching the snowflakes caught in his beard. "I do fit the description."

Now she was laughing, and she smacked him again for deflating her anger. "Why are you over here in my bathroom?"

"I heard you talking," he said, ushering her back toward the tent entrance. Happy to oblige, she rushed to get out of the wind. "Thought you might need help."

"Just talking to future Rose," she explained, crawling into the tent and exhaling in relief at the instant cessation of the wind. "Threatening her, actually. She's going to pay for many things, including having to bare my ass in a blizzard."

"As she should."

Winston's unexpectedly prim and proper tone made her laugh again, and she hurried to shuck her outer layers and boots before crawling back into her sleeping bag. "Actually…" she started, eyeing Winston's bag, which was perfectly roomy enough for two.

"No," he said flatly, unzipping his coat.

"But you're so *warm*," she protested.

"Too warm," he muttered, softly enough that she was pretty sure she wasn't supposed to hear him.

"Fine," she huffed. "Can you grab my makeup bag from your bag, please?" She scooted deeper to her sleeping bag and then zipped herself in. She kept her arms and shoulders free of the bag, tugging it so it covered most of her chest.

Winston, bless him, didn't argue, instead fishing out the stuff sack with her toiletry and makeup bags. "We're going to have to wait on food," he said, handing her the sack, which she took with a nod of thanks. "I don't want to risk making it to the bear pole and back."

She pulled out a box of wipes and pointed it at him. "That's good. Learn from that pioneer guy's mistakes. He probably left a wife and seven kids behind, all because he thought he knew where he was going."

"Dahl?" He sounded a bit tense, as if he was gritting his teeth together.

"Yes, Wins?"

"You going to be okay without food?"

"Oh yes," she assured him without looking up from her hand mirror. "I might borrow some more of your water though, just until mine thaws." She winced as her feet pressed against the chilly stuff sack.

The water bottle was suddenly right in front of her face, and she looked up in surprise. "I didn't need it right this minute," she teased, although she did take it and drank. Handing it back to him, she refocused on her reflection. "Since we probably have a couple of hours of tent time, I'm thinking I'm going to do a more complex look today."

Winston drank and then got into his own sleeping bag. She didn't miss how he leaned closer to see what she was doing, so she started explaining each step, giving him a tutorial.

"Even though I want to be a bit more dramatic," she explained, smoothing on foundation with the ease of long practice, "this is still a day look, so I don't want to go too OTT."

"OTT?"

"Over-the-top." She held up a dark-brown shadow so he could see. "I'm going to do the tiniest wing, but to make it subtle, I'll use this matte shadow instead of an eye pencil."

"No melting makeup today then?" he asked.

"Nope." She smiled.

Despite his small tease, he was watching her with an interest bordering on fascination, and she absorbed his attentiveness as hungrily as she had his warmth the night before. After him looking at her like that for just two makeup application sessions, she already wanted to bring him home with her in her suitcase so he could go with her on every job. His fascinated regard was just that addictive.

Dahlia drew out the makeup application process as long as

she could, but she eventually had to call it done. "What do you think?"

He'd inched closer and closer during the process, so it was easy for him to catch her chin in a light grip and tip her face first up, then right and left slightly. His smile was slow and absolutely devastating. "It's perfect. You look completely different, but I can't tell how."

"It's the touch of shininess on my lids and cheekbones," she told him seriously before allowing herself to beam at his reaction. She couldn't seem to look away, and his eyes grew hotter and heavy-lidded. He leaned in closer until she felt his warm breath on her lips, making her realize how chilled her face had gotten.

A loud gust of wind screamed as it rattled the tent, and Winston jumped, leaning back. His expression looked startled, as if he'd just been woken up from a dream.

Dahlia didn't move for a moment, hoping he'd come in for a second try, but his attention seemed to be fixed on the weather outside the tent. She pouted a little, more annoyed with the blizzard than ever. "The wind is a total cockblock."

His head jerked around and he stared at her before erupting into laughter. Of course, his laugh led to hers, and soon she was giggling uncontrollably even though nothing was all that funny, especially when she never got the kiss that Winston's hungry gaze had promised.

"Well, since the weather's not cooperating," she said once she got herself back under control, "we need to find our own entertainment."

Winston froze.

Rolling her eyes, Dahlia came to his rescue, even though she thought his shy panic was kind of cute. "Do you have any games? Pack of cards?"

"No." The word came out rusty, and he cleared his throat. "I normally camp alone."

"Haven't you heard of solitaire?" she asked, but then waved off the question. "How about I make you up?" Although she asked the question casually, she'd been dying to take a brush to his face since she'd gotten her first glimpse of the weird hermit she'd searched out.

"Make me up?" He sounded bewildered, as if the thought had never occurred to him. "With makeup, you mean?"

That made her snort. "Yes, make you up with…makeup. What do you say?"

"But…why?"

"No reason." She waved toward the tent walls that were still rippling from the fierce winds. "Something to do since we're stuck in a tent in a blizzard on a mountain." When he continued to stare at her blankly, she wheedled, "What will it hurt? I have plenty of makeup-removal wipes. No one except for us will see or know, unless you want to leave it on. Even then, I doubt we're going to see anyone else on the trail, except hopefully Rose, and she'd never judge. She has a weakness for guyliner, in fact, so she'd probably appreciate the effort."

"I don't care about that," he said.

"Then you'll let me?" She gave her best wide-eyed, pleading gaze, and he finally twitched his shoulders in a shrug.

"Fine."

A tiny squeak of excitement escaped her before she bit her lips to hold the torrent of words in. She didn't want to scare him off now that she'd gotten him to agree. Rolling to her knees, she got tangled in her sleeping bag and paused for a moment to consider the best way to arrange them both without freezing. Coming to a decision, she unzipped her bag and tossed a leg over Winston's lap so she straddled him on her knees.

It was his turn to make a squeak, and his eyes widened as he stared at her. "What are you doing?"

"We *just* discussed this," she said in an exaggeratedly patient tone. She arranged her opened sleeping bag around her like a throw blanket, tucking the edges under her socked feet and knees to keep drafts from sneaking in. Satisfied that she was as covered as she was going to get, Dahlia pulled her makeup bag close and then rubbed her hands together to warm them—since she couldn't wear her glittens unless she wanted Winston's face to look like an expressionist painting.

"You're *sitting* on me," he said tightly.

"Sorry." She lifted off his thighs a little so that she was kneeling. "Am I too heavy?"

He gave her his are-you-an-idiot look, which wasn't her favorite of his expressions, to be honest. "No. You weigh nothing."

She offered his look right back as she settled onto his thighs again. "Sure I do. Ready?"

"No, I…" With a grimace and a short shake of his head, he seemed to give up. "Yeah."

She tipped his chin up and studied his features close-up, as excited to have an opportunity to stare at him as she was to have his face as a canvas.

"Still not sure what the point of this is."

"The point"—she rubbed her thumbs over his brows, smoothing them down, feeling the ridge of the scar on the left side—"is to enhance your outside to better represent your insides, remember? So when someone looks at you, what do you want them to see?"

Although he shrugged, he carefully didn't move his head, staying perfectly still under her exploring fingers. "Don't really care what they see. Doesn't matter."

"What if that someone is a person you care about?" She swept her thumbs over his temples and across his cheekbones. With the beard, her canvas space was limited, but she could use it as contrast for the non-hairy parts. "What trait is most important to you? Strength? Intelligence? Fun-lovingness?"

His mouth quirked for a moment, but he went serious as he thought. "Honesty," he finally answered.

"Ohh," she breathed as ideas flooded her, making her so excited that she couldn't stay still. "We definitely can do that."

With a bitten-back grunt, Winston grabbed her hips, stilling her wiggling. "How?" His voice was gruff, and his expression almost pained. "Isn't the whole point of makeup to be *dis*honest? To change how I look and cover things up?"

"Nah, that's just incel whininess," she said, grabbing her moisturizer. "Although it can be a bit of the chicken and the egg. For example, a woman might pick a confident, powerful look for a job interview, and that makes her feel more confident and powerful, since she knows that's the image she projecting. Different looks aren't lies; they're representations of different parts of ourselves, the parts we want to bring to the forefront at the time. We humans are complex beings."

That hungry, intense look of his was back, and she gave him a smile before chickening out and dropping her gaze to her makeup bag, pretending like she had to search for the concealer, even though it was tucked in its proper place.

"Makeup is an excellent survival tool," she said, picking up the thread so she didn't lose herself in the feel of his skin beneath her bare fingers and his powerful thighs flexing under her. "We use it to become who we need to be in the moment. It's sometimes camouflage, sometimes battle armor, sometimes a costume, sometimes a tool, sometimes just a fun toy, sometimes a little of all those things."

She fell into the familiar rhythm of contouring. Whether it was from sharing Winston's body heat or the distraction, she wasn't feeling as cold as she had been earlier.

"Do you always have a beard?" she asked absently as she blended shades below his cheekbone with her thumb.

"No." He spoke without moving his lips, even though she wasn't working on his mouth at the moment, and for some reason she found that absurdly cute. "Just in winter. It's warm."

"Makes sense." She was overcome with curiosity about what he'd look like beardless. Hot, of course—there was no way Winston could ever *not* be hot—but the beard was such a big part of his mountain-man, lumberjack-meets-hermit style that it was hard to imagine him without it. He'd always have his flannel, of course, but he wouldn't be the same. She'd felt his face enough to know that he had a strong chin and jawline under the hair, so she decided that proved her initial hypothesis—a beardless Winston would be hot. "I wouldn't be able to take the beard sweat. Doesn't that get itchy?"

"No, like I said, I shave it in summer." Even without moving his face, he managed to scowl at her dumb question as he slowly finished, "Because it's hot."

Digging out her tweezers, she held them up. "Okay to pluck a bit?"

He grunted with a wary nod. "Just don't take too much."

"Don't worry," she soothed, even as the tweezers flew. "I'm just opening up the area above your eyes. I'd never do anything to harm your right eyebrow. It's perfect as it is."

The eyebrow in question scrunched up. "What's wrong with my left one?"

"Nothing at all." She moved to work on the eyebrow in question, careful not to pluck too much on this side, since the scar already had carved a smooth path through it. "Your right brow is just especially expressive."

His grunt sounded uncertain, as if he couldn't decide whether she was complimenting or insulting him.

"Most people's eyebrows are more like sisters than twins, but yours are cousins—maybe even cousins twice removed." She smoothed aloe with her fingers over the skin around both brows to sooth any irritation as she studied them. His eyes closed and his mouth softened, and she was reminded of the way her client's anxious golden retriever relaxed under gentle repetitive stroking.

Plucking out a few more hairs, she asked, her voice a little softer, as if not to startle him, "Does that hurt?"

His words were slow to come. "Not really."

"Probably because it's so cold out. It's like we iced your face before plucking."

He huffed out a laugh but then immediately stilled his face, as if she'd stop if he moved, and he really, really didn't want her to stop. It was both flattering and alluring, and she had to force herself to continue applying the cosmetics, since she just wanted to rub his face all day and watch his tight cheek muscles go slack with pleasure.

"Once we're back in civilization," she said, returning the tweezers to their spot in her makeup bag and finding the eyeliner she needed, "I'm going to give you a facial. I think you'd really like it."

He grunted again, but any suspicion was gone. She had him completely under her spell. It was an addictive feeling, like she was the goddess of cosmetic application and he was worshipping her. Biting her lip, she held in a pleased smile at her ridiculous thoughts, not wanting to break the spell they'd somehow created.

Feeling like she was falling a little too deeply, a little too quickly, she picked up her tutorial monologue, grasping for safety in the familiar patter. "One thing that signals honesty is higher brows and more open eyes—also more defined cheekbones for some reason, so contouring and a bit of shine help with that—which is why I cleaned up this area." She very lightly brushed the ridge above his closed lids. "I'm going to build on that with a nude liner and a light, shimmery shadow that goes all the way up to your brows."

"Shimmery?" he repeated, cracking open one eye. His glare fell short of its usual ferocity though, so he appeared more resigned than anything.

She smiled widely. "Shimmery. Just wait. You're going to be goooor-geous."

With a sigh, he closed his eye again.

She used her lighter to heat the tip of the eye pencil before lining his lids. "Since this is nude, the sharp definition doesn't really matter, but I thought the warmth might feel nice."

"Mmm-hmm." The drawn-out sound was more of a moan than a grunt, sending a shiver of arousal down Dahlia's spine. The sudden awareness shocked her, and she barely resisted the urge to squeeze her thighs together, knowing that he'd feel the pressure on his legs and realize exactly what his pleasured groan had done to her. Instead, she swallowed hard and steadied her eyeliner hand with sheer force of will.

"There," she purred as she finished lining the second lid, and now *she* was the one sounding like a fully baked sex cake. Clearing her throat, she focused way too hard on gathering the shadow palette she wanted. It helped to concentrate on what she was doing, turning him from a desirable man—a way-too-desirable man—to a collection of canvases: eyes, cheeks, lips. Breaking him up into manageable bites—*great, now I want to bite him*—she managed to finish the eye shadow and moved on to his lush eyelashes. Closing the curler over the thick fringe, she cupped the opposite side of his jaw with her free hand to hold him still. "Don't move, okay? I don't want to rip all of these glorious lashes out."

He froze in place. "What are you doing?" He seemed to be making an even greater effort not to move his lips when he spoke, which was equally hilarious and adorable.

"Curling these lashes. Another way to open up your eyes and make you look more trustworthy."

His face twitched under her hand in what she was pretty sure was a stifled frown. "Do I usually look untrustworthy?"

"Of course not. Maybe a little bit scary, but a trustworthy type of scary," she reassured him. "All this will just make you look *more* trustworthy."

"There is no trustworthy type of scary," he grumbled as she curled the lashes on his other eye.

"Somehow you managed it." She stroked the first coat of mascara on his curled lashes and then sat back on his abs to admire the affect. "Okay, look at me. Holy guacamole. People would give their left kidney for these eyes." Even though she knew the enhancing effects of makeup, she was still shocked by the effect. The chocolate-brown iris around his pupils transitioned to a bright-green outer rim, the vivid color made even more dramatic by the frame of his heavy lashes. Not made up, Winston was objectively gorgeous, sure, but with a little cosmetic assistance, he could stop traffic with his eyes alone. It was almost impossible to look away, but she finally managed to squeak out, "Close, please." It was only after he complied that she could breathe again, and it took two more coats of mascara before her heartbeat slowed to something close to normal.

I've created a monster. A breathtakingly beautiful monster.

She focused on his mouth, trying to break him into manageable sections again so she could catch her breath. Unfortunately for her racing heart, his full lips were much too luscious to make her comfortable. With a silent sigh, she gave up her attempt at casual immunity to his beauty and just tried to fake it. Applying lip balm to his soft mouth immediately tested her resolve.

"Lip pencils got a bad rap for a while," she said, trying to ignore how husky her voice sounded as she swapped balm for liner and traced his bottom lip. "People were using disparate shades and not blending, but just because someone misuses a tool doesn't mean we should toss the kitten out with the bathwater." She switched to a slightly darker pencil for the inner corners of his lips.

"You just combined about six different metaphors," the grump grumped without moving his lips. His crankiness would've been more effective if he hadn't been leaning into the hand cupped under his chin to hold him steady.

"Three, max," she corrected mildly, swapping the pencil out for lipstick. "Used correctly, liner is actually an excellent tool to make lips look fuller—not that you need much help in that department." She swept the lipstick on, the creamy color gliding smoothly over his relaxed lower lip, and this powerful, guarded man's trusting passivity under her hand flooded her body with a giddy rush of heat. The simple process of applying lipstick to Winston felt more erotic than anything she'd ever done, clothed or unclothed. Slightly panicked by her strong reaction, she shifted her weight—and then immediately remembered that she was sitting on him, and everything became that much more intense. "Need to blend!"

Her slightly too loud exclamation made him jump and give her a chiding look.

"Sorry," she mumbled, trying to straighten out her tangled, lusty thoughts. Using her thumb, she blended the liner and lipstick. "Your beard is surprisingly soft," she blurted out, which didn't help her composure any. "I've never dated a beardy before." Immediately, she flushed, since she'd made it sound like they were dating, which they definitely were not. They were strictly camping buddies—blackmail camping buddies, at that.

He didn't respond, not even a grunt, but just studied her with that steady smoldering stare.

Rattled, she cupped both sides of his jaw to gently nudge his face left and right so she could study her finished work. "Not bad for a tent in a blizzard," she finally said proudly. "Want to see?" She reached over to grab her hand mirror and hold it up in front of Winston's face. His eyes, which already looked big thanks to her styling, widened even more.

"Whoa." He took the mirror from her without looking away from his reflection, turning his face this way and that, studying himself with a fascinated interest that previously she'd only seen directed at her.

She flicked him in the chest. "I really have created a gorgeous monster, haven't I? I have a feeling I'm never getting that mirror back."

Despite his new look, his right eyebrow had opinions, just as it always had. "I'm impressed."

"I can tell."

"Not with myself." Despite his denial, his gaze was still fixed on his reflection. "With *you*."

The way he said *you* made her lungs catch, and when he finally dragged his gaze from the mirror to meet her eyes, her ability to breathe left her altogether.

"You did exactly what you said you'd do," he continued, which was good, since talking was beyond her at the moment. "I look like me, but *more*." To her relief, his gaze dropped back to the mirror. "It doesn't look like I'm wearing lipstick, but my mouth looks really good."

Yeah, it does, Dahlia's brain agreed enthusiastically, but she firmly brought it back in line as his gaze returned to meet hers again. "That's my favorite neutral color—radiant plum. I call the neutrals 'interview lipstick,' since they're just the tiniest bit more flattering than nudes." Even though she knew she was babbling and he probably didn't have a clue what she was talking about, he was still staring at her like she was brilliant. And a genius. A brilliant genius. And even though she'd called herself exactly that before, she'd meant it more as a self-effacing humble-brag, but there was no filtering the compliment with him. Every line of his face screamed open honesty, and part of that was her fault. They were going after the honest look, after all.

"I actually look...good. And more trustworthy." He sounded awed. She, Dahlia May Weathersby, had *awed* him. She was prouder in that moment than she'd ever been during her entire—extremely successful—career, which was kind of messed up, she knew, but what could she do? She felt what she felt.

"You do," she said, ignoring the breathiness caused by all these emotional revelations and his drop-dead gorgeousness. "It's just science. Certain aspects of people's faces lead others to make assumptions. We opened up those beautiful eyes of yours, exaggerated your cheekbones, and added some kick to your already attractive face—since people are shallow and trust good-looking people more, which is messed up but that's reality—and *voilà*! People would be happy to give you their money." *Especially if you were dancing on a stage in a G-string.* The mental image of Winston stripping almost shorted out the thinking part of her brain, so she quickly shoved that to the back of her mind to use later when she was alone and in an actual bed in a heated room.

"That's incredible." His gaze was back on his reflection. "*You're* incredible."

Dahlia knew that she couldn't take any more compliments mixed with intense eye contact from him without melting into a lava puddle or possibly plastering herself against that fantastically broad chest, so she pretended to search for the packet of makeup wipes even though she knew exactly where it was. When she couldn't delay any longer without looking even more like a complete ding-dong, she grabbed the wipes and forced a smile. "Ready to get naked?" Immediately, the temperature of his gaze shot up a thousand degrees. "Your face, I mean. Get your *face* naked. Not any of this." She waved her hands up and down his body, which somehow made a mortifying situation even worse. "Not that there's anything wrong with getting all of *this* naked, but it might be…cold! Yes, that's it. Better to keep the clothes on."

Although his gaze still had a gleam she could only call a *smolder*, there was a lip twitch too. At least her babble was amusing one of them, because it just frustrated Dahlia. Pulling out a makeup wipe, she warmed it in her hands as she studied his made-up face. Struck by a desire to keep a memento—it really was some of her best work—she reached for her jacket and dug out her cell phone.

"Mind if I take a picture?" she asked.

Immediately, he looked wary. "Why? Is this going to be part of your plan to reveal my location to my online stalkers?"

"Nope." She made an X on her chest with the hand holding her phone. "Just for personal use—and by use, I just mean to look at occasionally in a professional and not-creepy way." *Seriously, Dahl?* her brain demanded, exasperated. *Again with the babble?* There was just something about Winston that brought out the blathering fool in her.

"Fine," he grumbled, glaring the entire time she turned on her phone and took a picture. She smiled at his scowl, glad she'd have the visual reminder of her grumpy hiking partner once they'd returned to their respective homes. The thought made her sad, so she turned off her phone and went to work removing Winston's makeup.

She took her time, wanting to draw it out, since once his face was bare, she wouldn't have any excuse to touch him. "Close your eyes." Once he did, she kept her touch gentle as she removed the mascara, liner, and shadow. "Okay, you can open them," she said reluctantly. She'd enjoyed being able to look her fill without having to monitor her expression in case she gave too much away. With a few fingers on his jaw, she tilted his face so she could see if she'd missed any foundation.

His eyes closed again as he leaned into her touch. "I liked that."

"Watch out," she teased. "It's addictive. You're going to be trying new looks every day."

"It's not that." He kept his eyes closed as a small smile tilted his lips. "I like when you touch me."

ELEVEN

She froze as his words smacked her right in the middle, where a herd of butterflies had just lost their entire minds and were stampeding through her nervous system.

When she didn't respond, he opened his eyes and straightened his head away from her fingers. "Sorry. Didn't mean to make you uncomfortable. I don't have much experience with…this."

He was the one who sounded uncomfortable, and Dahlia shook off her shock. Cradling his face with one hand, she dabbed at a spot along his cheekbone that she pretended still had foundation on it. "You didn't, and I know what you mean." Focusing a little too hard on that imaginary smudge, she admitted, "I grew up without much touching, except for the occasional hug or noogie from Rose. Sometimes I think that's another part of why I ended up doing makeovers—all the nurturing contact I want without looking like a weirdo. It was either this or becoming a nurse, and that involves a lot of stray body fluids I don't want to be responsible for."

He was watching her with that laser-focused look again—the one that made her feel like she was the most fascinating, gorgeous person on earth. "I get it."

Even though it was a generic thing that people said a lot, especially when they were trying to pretend like they understood when they really didn't, the little she knew about his past convinced her that he did, if fact, truly get what she meant. "I know you do."

Dropping the wipe, she quit pretending that she was still clearing makeup off his face and touched him the way she wanted to. She ran her fingertips over his cheeks and along his temples, circling back to smooth his brows—the animated right one and the scarred left. *It's strange*, she thought, *how attached I am to a pair of eyebrows.* It wasn't just any pair of eyebrows, however—they were Winston's, and she was having all sorts of feelings for all of his body parts.

His eyelids had gotten heavy, but he still managed to keep his gaze on her. "You can touch me, if you want."

She laughed, low and husky. "I thought I already was."

When his mouth quirked in response, she slid her fingers beneath his hat and into his short hair. The cap, which she'd already shoved high on his head to get it out of the way for her makeover, lost its battle to stay on and dropped to the tent floor. Reveling in her increased access now that she had been granted permission, she ascertained that his hair was indeed as soft—softer, in fact—than his beard. She also discovered that touching the rim of his ear ever so lightly gave him goose bumps. There was a powerful headiness in giving this big, strong guy the good kind of shivers with just the brush of her fingertip.

"Can I touch you?" His normally low voice was now deep in the gravel pits, and it was her turn to get the good shivers *and* goose bumps.

"Yes, please." She meant the words to come out teasing, but instead they sounded even to her own ears like a desperate plea.

To her surprise, since she was expecting him to start at her face, mirroring what she was doing, he reached under her draped sleeping bag and grasped her hips. Her fingers tightened in his hair, tugging strands just barely long enough for her to get a grip on. He grunted, his hands kneading just hard enough to make her ache in the best way.

Since her hands were conveniently on his head, she tugged him down. The entire makeup session—their entire *hike*, in fact—felt like drawn-out foreplay. If she didn't get to kiss him within the next five-eighths of a second, she would most definitely shatter into a thousand unfixable pieces.

Thankfully, he seemed to feel the same way, because he bent down willingly. She wasn't sure which one of them closed the final inch of space, but it didn't matter. Nothing did, except the feel of his lips against hers.

For an abrupt, take-charge guy, his kiss was strangely tentative—gentle even. He explored, rather than plundered. Despite the sense of urgency driving her, she settled back on his thighs and enjoyed the process, the slow brush of his lips against hers, the nibble on her jaw, the softest bite to her throat. She wound tighter and tighter as he teased. Finally, gripping her two bare handfuls of hair, she yanked his mouth back to hers and kissed him hard.

His chuckle buzzed against her lips, but the sound of warm amusement soon shifted into a groan. With his grip on her hips, he pulled her in tightly against him, and the muffling layer of his sleeping bag soon became an unacceptable blockade.

Pulling back with some effort, she asked, "Let me in?"

He had to blink a few times before his eyes cleared and comprehension shone through. "Uh...right. Yeah." His cheekbones darkened to the color of a brick, and she frowned at him, unsure why her grumpy and opinionated Winston had gotten all tentative on her.

"You okay?" Despite his agreement, she didn't move to get into his sleeping bag with him. Sometimes, she got excited about things and dragged along unwilling participants, and she didn't want that to be the case this time, not with something this big and important. "If you'd rather not, I could get in my sleeping bag, and we could play...I don't know, twenty questions or something. Up to you." The excited part of her howled in protest at the suggestion, but she firmly ignored that as she waited for him to respond.

"No, I want to." The urgency in his answer made her smile. "I just..." He tipped his head back with a groan, but it didn't sound like the happy groan from just a few minutes earlier. "I haven't exactly done this before."

Since he'd delivered the last sentence in a rushed and grumbly mutter, she wasn't sure if she'd heard him right. "You haven't done this before? Sex, you mean?" She didn't mean to sound skeptical, but how in the universe could that have happened? Winston was a walking, talking wet dream of a man.

"Yeah." He released her hips and ran a hand over his face, his fingers rasping against his beard.

She was *extremely* patient and waited almost an entire three seconds before demanding more information. "Are you not interested in sex?"

His laugh was rough, but she still loved the sound of it. "Oh, I'm interested." The heat in his gaze flared back to life, searing her skin and underlining the truth to his words.

"Then why? How?" She tried to put together a more coherent question, but she was truly flummoxed that the gorgeous, fascinating Winston Dane could be a virgin.

"You said it—I'm a hermit," he said a bit defensively. "I'm alone most of the time."

She snorted. "Hermit-shermit. You have a whole town of people who are almost certainly panting to get into your pants. *Especially* since they're in a limited dating pool like Howling Falls the town. You can't tell me they weren't trampling each other to get to your door when you—a hot out-of-towner with muscles—moved in."

His grumbly answer was unintelligible, but she knew it didn't contain a good explanation. It couldn't.

"And you've just been here a couple of years, right? What about when you lived in actual civilization?"

He heaved an exaggerated sigh that Dahlia was pretty sure was meant to tell her how incredibly aggravating she was being, but she didn't care. He was a mystery, and she was curious, so she was going to Nancy Drew his ass until he spilled the true story. It didn't help that she wanted to know every single detail about him, and this was a *fascinating* one, enough so that she didn't mind delaying her personal gratification in the form of an orgasm for a few minutes. When she continued to watch him expectantly, his shoulders dropped in defeat. "I was a late developer," he said as if that explained anything. "I already told you I spent a lot of time by myself playing video games growing up."

"Okay," she said slowly when he left it at that. "But even if you were gawky or spotty or a loner or whatever, you were still *Winston Dane*."

He blinked at her, looking blank. "What does that even mean?"

"Fishing for compliments?" She waited for him to grumble denials in a flustered way before she grinned. "Don't worry about it. I'm happy to talk about your magnificence. I don't care what you looked like as a teen or in your early twenties. *This*"— she held her spread hands out toward him—"didn't come from nothing. And *this* is pretty incredible."

Although she could tell he fought to hang on to his scowl, she caught a brief pleased expression before he quickly masked it.

"And what about after you developed?" Somehow, she made *developed* sound the tiniest bit kinky, and he flushed again.

One shoulder twitched up in a stiff shrug. "There were a few who offered, but I didn't feel comfortable enough with them."

She studied him, extrapolating from the bits of information she was yanking out of him. "I'm guessing there were hordes interested, but only a few brave enough to ask."

"Brave?"

He gave the slightest offended huff as he repeated the word, and Dahlia looked back at him, amused. "Please. As if you don't try to drive people away with your frowns and Oscar the Grouch impression."

"Not an impression," he grumbled.

Grinning at him openly now, she squeezed his cheeks gently, taking advantage of the blanket permission he'd offered earlier. He didn't seem to mind, going still in that way he always did when she touched him, as if he thought she'd stop if he moved even a millimeter. "Why'd you say no to those brave souls who asked?"

"Like I said." This time his shrug was very intentional, and his gaze shifted to a point over her head. "I didn't feel...comfortable with them."

"I get it," she said, letting her fingers roam because the mystery was solved—and she couldn't seem to stop them. She followed his hairline down to his ears and then proceeded to give him goose bumps. "It's hard for people like us to be vulnerable, especially with a stranger."

He shivered as she petted the rim of his ear. "People like us?" he repeated in a rough voice.

"Yeah. Us tough-shelled badasses with squishy-soft middles."

His shoulders twitched in shrug, but he didn't deny the description was accurate. "You're different from anyone else before. I feel safe with you. I can talk—or not talk—and I know you won't judge me."

She gave a gentle snort at that.

"Okay, so maybe you judge me when I say thoughtless things, but it's *kind* judgment. I feel like the more you know about me, the more you want to learn."

His description took her breath away, so she could barely get the words out. "I really do. I want to know all about you." All the passion she'd banked in order to satisfy her curiosity came roaring back, and she scrambled off his lap and into his sleeping bag.

"Wait," he protested, and she froze halfway in, afraid that he was about to kick her back to her sleeping bag and tell her never to touch him again, which would be horrible. Despite what he said, however, his hands were urging her to finish crawling in with him. When she did, he wrapped an arm around her tightly, pulling her against his chest even though the roomy sleeping bag would've allowed more space between them. With his other hand, he zipped them in together. "I know the mechanics, but there's a difference between knowledge and firsthand experience."

"You'll do fine," she assured him, wrapping her arm around him in return and slipping a hand up under his hem so she could flatten her palm on his lower back, skin to skin.

"But my lack of muscle memory wi—"

She interrupted him with a snort that probably was more honest than sexy. "Please. I'm more turned on by a glimpse of your snarling face than I've ever been with anyone else. You'll be just fine. We both will. Tell me when something feels good, and when it doesn't, okay?"

He studied her, as if checking her sincerity, before giving her a slow, single nod. "I will. And I want you to tell me if I do something wrong. I take valid criticism well, so don—"

"I will," she promised, interrupting him again. If she let him talk, spring would roll around before they'd get to do anything fun. "I'll also tell you when you do something…right."

His eyes flared with heat, and she couldn't resist. She had to kiss him immediately.

The tent and snow and howling wind outside all disappeared as she sank into the kiss. Without taking his lips from hers, he lowered them both to the mat beneath his sleeping bag. For some reason, knowing that she would be his first made Dahlia slow things down. She didn't want to rush it. Every moment should be perfect, and she couldn't wait for his first actual-sex orgasm to blow the top of his head off. She'd never thought of herself as especially egotistic or possessive, but she wanted to burn herself into Winston's memory so that all he saw and smelled and felt with any future partners was Dahlia.

They explored each other's lips before he demanded entry with his tongue. He invaded her mouth like a pirate, and she loved every moment of being plundered. His lips were shockingly soft, and it seemed strange that they were the origin of such grumpy words and frowns. Then his teeth nipped her lip, and she smiled against his mouth. *There* was his sharp edge.

"Why are you smiling?" he asked, pulling away just enough to speak, but still close enough that his lips brushed hers with each syllable.

"Because I like you," she answered honestly. Then, because it was unbearable not to be kissing him, she dove in again.

Soon, he took over the kiss like he had before, rolling them both over and taking the sleeping bag with them. The tentativeness from earlier was gone, and now he was just as bossy with this as he'd been with pretty much everything else.

When he abandoned her mouth in favor of her neck, she said breathlessly, "I bet you learned to swim by just jumping in the deep end."

Pulling back enough that he could meet her eyes, he lowered his eyebrow. "Why do you say that?" His words were a gravelly growl that zinged right through her, almost taking away her ability to speak.

Almost. "Just a guess. Am I right?"

The corners of his mouth drew up slowly, curling into a mischievous grin that made her want to kiss him even more—and she hadn't realized that it was possible to want him more than she already did. "Yeah."

"What are you waiting for then?" She smiled back at him. "Dive right in."

With a gritty chuckle, he did just that, returning to her mouth with a wild intensity that had her clutching his head to hold him against her. Soon, that wasn't enough. She allowed her hands to roam and immediately became irritated at the clothes blocking her access to his bare skin. Grabbing the hem of his shirt, she tugged upward but wasn't able to get very far with their bodies pressed so tightly together.

"Off," she demanded.

He tried, but the sleeping bag bound them together. With an impatient sound, he unzipped the bag and sat up, straddling her hips. Grabbing the back of his shirt, he hauled it off in a swift movement that was way hotter than it ought to be.

A sound escaped Dahlia that was embarrassingly close to a whimper.

"What's wrong?" he immediately asked.

"Absolutely nothing." She reached to pull him back down, cold without him. "I just really liked watching you take off your shirt."

"Yeah?" Only one side of his mouth curled up that time, and that tiny smirk instantly became Dahlia's new favorite of Winston's expressions.

"Oh yeah."

"You think that's good, just wait until I take off my pants."

Laughter burst from her even as her temperature soared. "Hmm." She tried her best to sound skeptical, but she knew her expression was ravenous. "We'll see."

With a challenging expression that blended surprisingly well with the latent heat in his eyes, he stripped down the long underwear, not being careful at all as he yanked them over each knee and then off over his feet. The sight of his thick, hard, absolutely *luscious* erection made her surge toward him without any sort of chill. "No," he said, catching her hands in his and pressing her back down to the mat. "You need to lose some clothes too."

"I'm perfectly happy with that plan," she said honestly, although having her hands trapped above her head with a gorgeous bare Winston hovering just over her wasn't half-bad either.

He released her, to her disappointment, straightening to give her room. Even as she started inching her silky long underwear up, however, he went still. "Wait."

She froze, her belly exposed to the cold air, worried. His expression was nothing less than tragic. "What's wrong?"

"No condoms." He said the words like she would imagine he'd say they were out of water in the middle of an endless desert.

Her stomach dropped, and she immediately agreed with his tone of gloom, but then she started thinking about it. "I'm on birth control, but I haven't been with anyone since Cody, the absolute worst boyfriend in the universe, cheated on me with my much-hotter neighbor six months ago. I was tested for everything after since Cody was being sluttish, and I'm clear. You're a virgin, so we're good to go." She started inching up her top again, but stopped when Winston shook his head. "Why?" The word came out much too whiny for comfort, but she couldn't help herself. He was so close and so hot and she was so horny for him, plus she really, *really* liked him.

"I wasn't saying no to sex," he explained. "There's just no way your neighbor was hotter than you."

To reward him for that very sweet—albeit completely false—statement, Dahlia pulled off her top in one motion. Winston looked flatteringly thunderstruck by the sight of her— even though she was still wearing a sports bra. She stripped it off as well, and his eyes bugged out of his head. It was extremely satisfying to see his dramatic reaction. "I thought that just happened in cartoons."

"Uhng?" The sound he made was a strangled nonsense word, but she took a guess at what he was asking.

"The eye-bugging-out thing." She expected him to stiffen up at that teasing, but he seemed to be too focused on her breasts to take offense. When he continued to just stare, she shivered, the air cold enough to burn her overheated skin. "You can touch," she reminded him, needing his body heat, but more than that, just needing *him*. When he glanced at her face as if making sure it was okay, she nodded. "I already gave you permission, remember?"

"Wasn't sure if that covered…everything." His voice deepened on the last word, drawing it out in a way that immediately solved her issue. She wasn't cold anymore.

"Everything," she assured him. "You can touch me anywhere, anytime. Total access."

The sound he made was part purr and part growl and everything that was completely, addictively, wildly hot. Needing to be naked, Dahlia stripped down her long underwear bottoms, wiggling from side to side as she worked them off her butt and legs.

With an amused huff, she blew a loose strand of hair out of her eyes. "It's hard to be sexy undressing in a tent."

"Not for you," he countered in a growl so intense she had to believe he was telling the truth. "You're sexy no matter what you're doing."

That was so sweet she couldn't resist leaning over to kiss him once she'd extracted herself from her pants. "Thanks, Wins." She gave him a wicked smile. "Are you going to still think that if I leave my socks on?" She held up a foot and wiggled her toes at him.

He caught them in one big mitt. "Of course. Socks are definitely sexy."

"Silk stockings with lacy garters, maybe," she allowed. "But wool knee-highs? Really?"

"On you? Really." His growl was dead serious, and he was giving her that starving-lion look again—hungry and fierce and so focused on her that it was like nothing else existed.

Despite her distraction—*fine, obsession*—with Winston, the cold reminded her that she was naked except for those dubiously sexy socks, and she gave an abrupt shiver.

"Get back in bed," he ordered, and her eyes nearly rolled back in her head at how much she liked that bossy growl. She hurried to burrow into the sleeping bag, and he quickly joined her, zipping them both in together again. She cuddled close, since his body radiated heat like a furnace—plus she just liked to touch him. Their shared sleeping bag was becoming her favorite place in the world.

She'd loved being pressed up against him when they'd both been clothed, but naked was even better. Trailing her fingers over his furry chest, she flicked his nipple to make him grunt. Pulling a reaction from Mr. Stoic was fun, so the next time she touched his nipple, it was with her tongue. Instead of a quickly stifled grunt, she got an actual gasp from him. Dahlia grinned and then scored it gently with her teeth. *That* got a full-body jerk.

"Come up here," he rasped, hauling her up so that their lips were aligned. He immediately took over her mouth with his, nipping at her bottom lip in what she was pretty sure was retaliation. Since it felt really, *really* good, and he immediately moved on to stroking her tongue with his, she forgave him immediately.

She could've kissed him forever. They were quickly learning what they enjoyed, falling into a rhythm as if they'd been making out for years. Despite that, there was still a sharp edge of newness that ramped up all of her feelings with a shot of adrenaline and nerves, making everything bigger and better and just *more*.

He shifted his head back, and she made a sound of protest—at least until his lips moved to her neck. Tilting her head to the side, she gave him more room to explore, and explore he did—touching every inch with his lips and tongue and gentle teeth.

"You've got a thing for my neck." It was hard to speak, and she wasn't quite sure why she even attempted it. Probably because things were getting very intense and intimate and absolutely wonderful, and the unfamiliarity of those feelings was creating a wee bit of panic, since her brain was nothing but contrary and couldn't just relax and appreciate good things.

"Yeah." He didn't even hesitate to agree as he kissed her throat. "It's so soft and weirdly...*alive*."

"Weirdly?" Her panic eased as she ran her fingers through his hair, the conversation—as strange as it was—oddly soothing. "Why is it weird that I'm alive? Wouldn't it be weirder if I felt dead?"

His huff of amusement blew against the vulnerable skin of her throat. "I didn't expect you to feel *dead*. I expected..." This time, his exhale was still amused, but it had a touch of bewilderment, as well. "I don't know what I expected." He pressed his lips to a spot under her jaw that made her eyes roll back in her head. "I didn't expect to feel your pulse or a catch in your breath or your shiver when I find a good spot." He pulled back to meet her gaze with a concerned expression. "Unless you're shivering because you're cold?"

She felt her lips curl up on the ends in a purely unstoppable smile. "I'm not cold."

The banked fire in his eyes flared, and he kissed her mouth hard again. "Good."

This time, when he traced a line down her throat with his lips, he didn't stop there. With his hands on her waist, he shifted her up so he could reach her breasts. His mouth closed around her nipple, so hot and wet that her back arched, curving her body into the contact. He sucked and then pulled away, lightly scoring her with his teeth as he withdrew. She made an unhappy sound, and he grinned, looking so proud of himself that she almost laughed. She was too aroused to be amused, though, too frantic to have his mouth on her again. She tugged at his short hair, urging him back down to her chest, but he shifted her higher, instead.

Once he started working his way down her belly, Dahlia was perfectly fine with the switch, although her top half was exposed to the chilly air. She shivered convulsively from a mix of desire and cold, the difference between the heated blood roaring through her veins and the icy air touching her skin making her even more aroused. Winston, however, lifted his head and frowned.

Grabbing her abandoned sleeping bag, he covered her from her neck down with it, and then he dove underneath. Now that she couldn't see him except as a large lump beneath her improvised blanket, she didn't know where his mouth would touch down next, and she squirmed at the rush of lust this uncertainty caused. His hands clamped on her hips, attempting to hold her still, but his strong grip made her wiggle happily even more.

He ignored the way she was testing his grip, holding her steady as he shouldered his way between her legs. His bulk shoved her thighs wide, making her muscles ache with the stretch in a rather lovely way. His hand snaked out from under the blanket, feeling around next to the sleeping mat.

She eyed the wandering hand with amusement, even as she was annoyed it wasn't currently on her body. "What are you looking for?" she asked, surprised by how husky her voice was.

"Flashlight."

So he can see me. The thought sent a rush of heat run through her, making her point her toes and try to squeeze her thighs together. The feel of his muscular bulk between them, blocking her efforts, only ramped up her arousal even more. "You can just go by touch," she said, her voice going from husky to absolute sex kitten.

"I want to see what I'm doing." His blindly searching fingers found the flashlight and closed around it, drawing it under the sleeping bag with him. She froze, imagining him examining her, and then jumped as he lightly ran a finger along her center. "Beautiful."

She could almost feel the heat of his perusal, and it affected her just as much as his physical touch. She couldn't hold back a moan. It was impossible to stay still, especially when his exploring fingers found her bundle of nerves and stroked it lightly. "That's good," she rasped, belatedly remembering his request to tell him when he got it right. "Right there is...very, *very* good."

The air from his low chuckle brushed her wet skin, and she heated up another ten degrees when she realized how close his mouth was to her. Before she could even process that thought, he pressed an open-mouth kiss between her legs, and the tip of his tongue flicked over her clit.

She was pretty sure she levitated at that moment. "I call bull," she gasped as soon as she had the power to speak again. "There's no way this is your first time."

He chuckled again, his breath warming bits that were already on fire thanks to him. "I've done my research." He licked her again, making her pant. "And I'm a quick study."

"Yeah, you are," she said, although the words came out as more of a garbled moan. He'd apparently buckled down and gotten serious about his performance, and everything inside her was focused on the glorious things his mouth was doing between her legs. Forgetting her promise to coach, she dropped her head back, closed her eyes, and just *felt*.

Once he slid a finger inside her, then two, she felt her pleasure swell until she couldn't contain it anymore. He sucked her clit, and the sharp, intense pleasure bordering on pain shoved her over. Quicker than she'd ever reached her peak, her orgasm flooded her, and her thighs tried to crush him again as her muscles contracted. Her body fought against the waves of pleasure, overwhelmed by the intensity, but it was like trying to hold back an avalanche. She finally went limp, her brain filled with a bright-white stillness that was almost as impossibly good as the physical pleasure. It was utter, perfect peace.

The cold brought her back to reality, and she realized her sleeping bag had slipped to the side, leaving her partially exposed to the frigid air. Instead of pulling it over her again, she scooted down to join Winston in his again. He resisted at first, obviously wanting to stay where he was.

"Wins, I'm cold."

With a contrite grunt, he hauled her into the bag with him and zipped them in. She hid her triumphant smirk at the speed in which she'd gotten her way, but she must not have been quick enough, because he frowned disapprovingly at her. "I wanted to taste you some more."

Her breath caught at the raw sexiness of his words, but she didn't allow herself to be distracted. "Later you can taste me as much as you want." She had to swallow at the surge of desire that coursed through her just from imaging that. "Right now, I want you to feel as good as you made me feel."

His body jerked at that, and she didn't even try to hide her shark-like smile. "Okay," he said gruffly, the tension in his body and the rock hardness of the erection pressing against her thigh putting an exclamation point on that single word.

"I'll return the oral favor as soon as we're not in a sleeping bag," she promised, just to feel him jolt against her again. His overwhelming desire for her was a heady thing, and she took pleasure in every twitch and jerk of his aroused body, knowing that all of that was just for her. She kissed him, but she didn't allow herself to drop into her usual dreamy daze. Instead, she followed his example from earlier, leaving his mouth to trace little nipping kisses down the line of his throat.

She understood exactly what he'd been telling her earlier. With her lips on his pulse, she felt the fast but steady rhythm of his heart and the rise of his throat as he inhaled sharply. He felt so amazingly, wonderfully *alive*.

As much as she would've liked to explore all of his corners and crevices, she wanted him again, and that quick heartbeat told her that he was just as desperate for her. Stroking down his torso into the darkness of the sleeping bag, she found his erection—hot and so hard that it made her mouth water. A sound escaped him as she closed her fingers around his length, a groan and grunt with the smallest bit of sob thrown in, and she couldn't bring herself to torture him any longer. He'd been infinitely patient—not just with making sure that she found her pleasure first, but with his refusal for years and years not to find release with a stranger. She felt flattered and honored and the tiniest bit nervous that he trusted her enough to be at his most vulnerable.

Suddenly desperate to have him inside her, Dahlia rolled onto her back, tugging at him gently to ensure he followed. He didn't hesitate, shifting her beneath him in the burrito of the sleeping bag. "You sure you want this?" she asked, suddenly overwhelmed with the responsibility of being his first. What if he regretted his choice, regretted her?

She hadn't expected his low laugh, but that and the certainty in his "yes" convinced her fully. Instead of kissing him, she held his eyes as she smiled. He smiled back, the corners of his mouth curling into an expression so sweet that her heart started to pound. Wrapping her legs around him, she used them to urge him to close the distance, to join their bodies together.

Winston slid into her, driving in deeply as she watched his face. Feeling him fill her completely as she watched sheer bliss steal over his expression made everything seem that much more intense. It was almost as if she could actually feel what he did, experience the squeeze of her body around his even as she felt his erection stretch her.

"That's…" His voice deepened until it ground to a halt. "You're incredible." The hushed reverence of the words sent a stabbing pleasure so deep inside of her it almost felt painful. His forehead dropped to rest against hers as he took deep, unsteady breaths.

"You can move," she said. "I'm ready."

He shook his head the smallest bit, all he could manage with their foreheads touching. "You feel too good. If I move, it's going to be over."

She laughed, more because she was giddy and happy, and less because what he said was funny. "Then it's over." When he looked offended at her nonchalance, she laughed again. "The sooner it's over, the sooner we can do it all over again."

"Oh." The word was just a hard exhale as he shoved his hips against her, surging into her so deeply it felt as if he'd taken all the space in her body. Bracing himself on his forearms, he slid out of her and then drove inside her again, even more deeply that time. He gave a guttural groan as he held their hips tightly together. "I promised I'd tell you if something felt good," he managed to get out as he went still and stared into her eyes. "This…" He withdrew and then went deep once again. "Feels…" The word was simply a groan as he thrust again. "Good." Gasping out the last word, he began to hammer their hips together. If his movement was at all restrained by the sleeping bag, Dahlia couldn't tell. She clung to him with her legs and arms, holding that riveting gaze with everything inside her.

No wonder he was afraid to do this, she thought. Never had she felt so exposed, so vulnerable, all her worst and best parts laid open for Winston's viewing and possible judgment. It was terrible, sure, but it was also wonderful, the feel of him moving inside her amped to a thousand by that unhesitating, intent gaze of his.

Her second orgasm took her by surprise, sneaking in from the side while she was preoccupied with Winston and how gloriously naked he made her feel, urged on by the way he tossed his stoicism out the window at the first touch of his body against hers. She was caught up in his obvious enthusiasm when pleasure surged through her, tightening her body around him.

"Dahl," he gasped, but she wasn't able to respond, caught up in the mind-blanking swirl of her orgasm. Dimly, she registered that his thrusts had grown rough and uneven as he sped toward his own finish, and she forced her eyes not to sink closed in bliss in order to watch him reach his peak.

It was totally worth it. Winston looked almost startled as it hit, then his face twisted in what appeared to be pain, but she knew was ecstasy. A final aftershock of pleasure rippled through her at the sight of him, and knowing that *she* was the one who'd caused this life-altering experience was almost as incredible a sensation as her own orgasm had been.

When his muscles softened and he sagged on top of her, Dahlia was disappointed it was over. She held the image of how he'd looked in her mind, carefully locking the mental photo in place so she could pull it out whenever she needed. His heavy body pressed down on her, recalling her to the moment, and she had to admit that this—a sated Winston draped over her like a weighted blanket—was just as amazing a moment as the sight of his first partnered-sex orgasm.

Just as he was getting too heavy for comfort, he rolled to his side with a groan, taking her with him. They rested there, pressed together, until their hearts and breaths slowed almost enough to sleep.

That's when Dahlia remembered that she was supposed to be panicking, about Rose and about being in the mountains in a blizzard and about *Rose* being in the mountains in a blizzard and also about the terrifying fact that she liked the guy next to her much, much, *much* too much. "How was it?" she blurted out, needing to talk so that her thoughts would stop—or at least be drowned out by conversation.

He made a sound somewhat like a growl, but with a satisfied edge that turned it into a luxuriant purr. A shiver rippled through Dahlia, hunger starting to grow again, despite the fact that she'd just had two very nice orgasms. "I liked it."

"I could tell." Now she was the one purring. *We're quite the pair of sex kittens.* "Bet you wish you'd started doing this a long time ago." She tried to hide that the thought of not being his first made her sad.

"No," he said immediately, surprising her. Winston wasn't one to lie to save her feelings, so she knew he meant it.

"No?" she repeated, moving her face from the crook of his neck so she could meet his gaze. "Why not?"

He paused, his face pensive. "I like it with you. Doubt it would've been anywhere near as good with anyone else."

Tears burned behind her eyes even as she beamed at him. "I've told you before, Wins, but I'm going to say it again. You give the *best* compliments."

TWELVE

AFTER A SHORT NAP, DAHLIA woke to a ferocious hunger. From his heavy, not-quite-a-snore breathing, Winston was still sleeping, although how he managed it when her stomach was thundering like Zeus in a full-blown tantrum, she had no idea. She raised her head, listening between his breaths and her complaining stomach, and couldn't hear the wind. Since the storm had apparently subsided, she considered sneaking out of the shared sleeping bag and making the trek to their food alone, but the cold and possible wilderness dangers daunted her.

She waited an entire minute, but he stayed asleep and oblivious to her impatient squirming, so she decided to wake him up in a pleasant way. She kissed his neck as her hand crept down to find him already hard and ready to go. She grinned. The timing wasn't right for it to be morning wood—afternoon wood? Nap wood?

A sleepy groan from him interrupted her etymological thoughts, and she focused on stroking him as she licked his throat.

She felt his full-body startle as he came completely awake, and then he was the one who was kissing her. When he rolled them over so she was under him, one of his arms supporting his weight as the other roamed her body, her stomach grumbled unhappily.

Reluctantly, Dahlia broke their kiss. "Better eat something first, or we'll never leave this sleeping bag until they find our bones in twenty years."

"No," he said, moving to kiss along her jaw since she'd moved her mouth from his. "This is a popular campsite. They'll find our remains in the spring."

She laughed but still gave his shoulders a little shove. "Even so, I'd rather not become 'remains' just yet." Worry for Rose surged. Was her sister hurt? Hungry? Dahlia wouldn't let anything worse—like the possibility that Rose could be "remains"—even touch her mind, although it was getting harder and harder to shove those pessimistic thoughts away. Focusing on Winston helped, so she fixed him with her best pleading look and asked, "Feed me?"

He blew out an unsteady breath. "Fine, but you're going to have to let go of me first." His hips gave a small thrust, making her realize that she still gripped his erection.

"Oops." She forced her fingers to release him. "Sorry, little guy. We'll finish this up once we get back from the dining room."

"Little guy?" He frowned at her severely, which only heightened her amusement.

"Just relative to the rest of you." Since Winston seemed in no hurry to get to their food, she took the initiative of unzipping their sleeping bag.

"What's that mean?" Apparently, he was still caught up on the nickname. "Am I...*small*?"

She snorted. "Haven't you been in a locker room?"

"Yeah, but I don't look, and I definitely don't *compare*."

Cold air was creeping into their cozy nest now, so she forced herself to crawl onto the other sleeping mat. A hint of dizziness made her shake her head, reminding her of her need for food. "Hand me my stuff sacks and clothes, would you?" Although he obeyed, he gave her such a hangdog look that she relented. "You're a very respectable size." That just made him frown harder, and she found that she couldn't stand to be the cause of his unhappiness. "You're huge, okay? I said relatively, because your penis is not over six feet tall like you are."

His expression immediately shifted to smugness, which made her smile even as she shivered, yanking on her clothes.

"I forget how cold it is when you're not lying on top of me," she muttered. That seemed to please him even more, and she rolled her eyes as she yanked on her hiking shoes. It seemed that she was quickly developing an addiction to making Winston Dane happy, and that would be concerning if she wasn't hungry enough to make everything else seem inconsequential. She'd deal with her growing codependency later. For now, she tossed an empty stuff sack at the object of her growing obsession. "Get dressed. I desperately need a rehydrated meal in a pouch, and I need you to fend off any curious bears while I eat it." She tilted her head thoughtfully. "That's a sentence I'd never thought I'd say."

Once he got moving, he threw on his clothes much faster than she had. Apparently, dressing in a tent got easier with practice. Soon they were standing in the six inches of snow outside the tent. Even though the sky was still overcast, the new snow was bright and Dahlia had to squint, accustomed to the diffused light in the tent. Everything was framed in white like a Christmas card, making it even more dramatically beautiful. Snow weighed down the pine branches and capped the mountain peaks, giving the scene a quiet majesty.

Winston pointed toward the right side of the tent. "Go pee."

Tilting her head, she eyed him with more bewilderment than offense. "A hot, weird hermit who I just had tent sex with is ordering me to go pee in the snow. My life has gotten so strange."

When he just tipped his chin toward the side of the tent, she shrugged and trudged through the snow in that direction. The oddest part of the whole situation was that she didn't hate it. Well, the peeing in the snow thing wasn't *great*, but it could be worse. At least the ground next to the tent was cleaner and less malodorous than a porta-potty at a music festival.

As usual, he was done before she was and waiting at the front of the tent, squinting at the sky like he was angry with it.

"Something wrong, or is that just your resting bitch face?"

His right eyebrow expressed his disdain at the expression, apparently not realizing that he was just proving her point. "We could make it to the falls tonight if we leave immediately."

Why her stomach took a swooping, disappointed dive at that news was a mystery, since the whole point of their hiking and camping and peeing in the snow was to find Rose as soon as possible. Eyeing Winston's sturdy, broad body and scowling face under his beanie, she knew that it really wasn't much of a mystery. She wanted more time with him—more *naked* time, if possible. What she didn't want to think about—what she was doing her very best *not* to think about—was the simmering terror of what she might find once they reached the falls. What if Rose wasn't there? Or what if she was, but all that was left were her…remains. Shoving those thoughts away yet again, she cleared her throat so her voice wouldn't break, revealing her fear.

"Let's go then."

"Food first."

"But I thought we had to leave immediately to get there tonight?" Despite her words, she followed him toward where their food hung on the bear pole.

"We have time to eat." Even though Winston spoke in the same curt, surly tone he'd used since she'd first met him, their time in the tent together had changed things. Dahlia didn't know if her knowledge of how vulnerable he looked while naked and inside her changed how he sounded to her, or if his crusty exterior had actually softened. Either way, just looking at his wide back made her smile, and she hurried forward, wanting to grab his hand.

Before she could reach him, the light seemed to halo behind him as time slowed down. Her blood rushed through her ears too loudly, and the gray sky brightened to white.

"Winston," she said, her weak voice making her frown. "I feel strange."

A look of sheer terror filled his face as he moved toward her, and her last thought was that there must be a bear behind her.

She tried to turn her head to look, but the evergreens started to spin around her. Her knees went soft, refusing to keep her upright, right before the world turned black.

———

"Dahlia. *Dahlia.*"

Without opening her eyes, she smiled. It was wonderful to wake to the sound of Winston's gruff voice.

"There you are, sweetheart," he crooned, relief thick in his tone, almost hiding the panic. "Open your eyes now, Dahl."

It was harder than expected, but she forced her lids open, knowing that she'd do just about whatever Winston asked her. *I'm so gone on him.* Once she'd blinked away the blurriness, her smile widened at the sight of his scowling face. Distracted by Winston close-up, it took her a bit longer than it should have to realize she was lying on the ground. She started to sit up, but he didn't move out of the way, so she returned to her flat-on-her-back position. She didn't mind, since the movement made the scenery rotate around her. Also, although the ground under her was lumpy and really hard, her clothes kept her warm and dry, so lying down seemed the best option at the moment. Sending a mental thanks to the designer for the excellent waterproofing, Dahlia asked, "Did I trip?"

"Fainted." The strained lines of Winston's face didn't ease, so she lifted a hand to try to smooth the frown lines away. Although he pressed his face into her palm, he still looked more upset than she'd ever seen him. "I should've fed you last night."

She couldn't help the grin that spread across her face. "We did use up a lot of calories last night. How long was I out?"

"Just a few seconds." He moved back a little so he could help her sit. "Any dizziness?"

Her head spun the slightest bit, but she wasn't about to say anything and be pressed back down. Her lying on the ground like a fainting goat wasn't going to help them find Rose. "Nope. I'm good." Before he could find a reason to keep her on the ground longer, she scrambled to her feet.

"Wait," he grumped, standing with her and gripping both arms as if to hold her up. She didn't tell him, but she appreciated the support, since the quick movement had brought back a residual wave of dizziness. "I don't like your color."

She paused her efforts to brush snow off her backside. "What color am I?" she asked with interest. "Green?"

"Pale." He started patting her down, dusting her off as he ran his hands over her, like he was checking for broken bones or something.

"Wins." She caught his face between her hands so he'd meet her eyes. "I'm fine. My blood sugar must've gotten a little low, that's all."

The line between his eyebrows deepened. "I should've fed you."

"I'm fine," she repeated.

That didn't seem to help, since his scowl grew more ferocious. "You need to eat more."

"Good idea." Releasing his face, she tromped through the snow toward the bear pole that held all their food off the ground. Her legs wobbled a bit, but she ignored that. "I'll start now."

He easily caught up with her but remained a half step behind and to the side, as if he was ready to catch her the second she fainted again.

Giving him a bit of side-eye, even as she couldn't help but enjoy his solicitous attention, she said, "I'm really fine."

His only answer was a disbelieving grunt.

————

She only offered to help once and received such a blistering glare in response that she waited quietly for him to prepare their food after that…well, *relatively* quietly.

"Will we still have time to make it to the falls before dark tonight?" she asked between bites of beef stew, pretending like the thought of hiking in the dark wasn't completely freaking her out.

His right eyebrow jumped as he eyed her carefully. He'd been doing that every minute or so, as if checking to make sure she wasn't about to topple over. "We're not going tonight."

Relief and disappointment and guilt all surged inside her. "I can hike," she said when the disappointment and guilt won out over the relief of not having to walk on creepily silent trails in the dark, like she was an expendable character in a horror movie. "I'm eating, see?" She took another bite and chewed with emphasis.

"No."

"But—"

"Too many things could happen if you faint on the trail. What if you hit your head on a rock or fall down an incline or t—"

"I won't faint again," she interrupted his litany of possible fainting-while-hiking injuries.

"We'll leave early tomorrow," he promised, ignoring her interjection. "*If* you eat all of that and then all of your breakfast."

She studied him, about to protest that she wasn't five, and she didn't need to be coerced into eating her broccoli, but seeing his drawn face made her change her mind. Smothering the guilt and anxiety at the thought of Rose being in possible danger, she told herself to enjoy another night in the tent with Wins. There was no way he was letting her hike to the falls tonight. "Okay."

"We're not—" He broke off whatever he was about to say and blinked. "Okay?"

"Yep." She took another bite, chewed, and swallowed before continuing. "Although I'm perfectly able to hike tonight, you'd worry the whole time, and I don't want to do that to you."

His face, which had been a clenched sort of pale since she'd woken up from her faint, regained a little of its normal color. Cupping the back of her head, he pulled her in for a lingering kiss.

She was silent once he'd pulled away and resumed eating. "Well, now I'm a little disappointed," she finally said.

His fork froze in midair.

"I wish I'd picked the chicken and dumplings. It tasted pretty good." She winked at him before shoving more beef stew—which, really, was a close second—into her mouth.

He gave a crack of laughter as he forked up a bite and held it out to her. "Want some more?" he teased.

His flirty words made her insides give a hard twist even as

she leaned forward and opened her mouth to accept the proffered bite.

They shared the rest of their pouch meals that way, feeding
each other between kisses.

———

The next morning, it was Winston's turn to wake her with a
hand between her legs. She roused with a groan that was part
desire and part muscle soreness and part not wanting to be
awake yet. After all, morning meant that their sleeping-bag-sex
hiatus was over, and reality had to intrude once more.

Winston's fingers played with her, his chest pressed to her
back, and the next sound was more about arousal than the other,
not-so-fun things. "You're really good at that," she said, ending on
a gasp as a finger slid inside her. His smug, aroused expression—
her new favorite—made it impossible not to kiss him, so she did,
figuring morning breath didn't count while camping.

They'd spent the last part of the previous day and the entire
night together in the sleeping bag. Although Winston had
insisted they sleep the majority of the time, they'd also explored
each other, trying all the positions that their restricted space
allowed. Each time they'd finished, Dahlia had collapsed in sated
exhaustion and sworn that that was it. She was done with sex for
the night…and probably for the next few weeks as well. After a
short break, however, either she or Winston would start touching, and then the kissing began, and her arousal would roar to
life, stronger than ever. She'd never been insatiable before, and it
was a bit disconcerting.

The same thing happened now in the pale light of early morning, her desire ramping up so quickly, it was like Winston had installed an arousal button in her. All he needed to do was push the button, and she lit up like a whole box of fireworks. He didn't draw out the foreplay, but she was still more than ready when he slid into her from behind. His strokes were slow and deep, his fingers gentle as they strummed her clit, but her orgasm wasn't slow or gentle. Instead, it hit her like an oncoming train, leaving her limp and breathless in its wake.

He managed to hold off, even when her body gripped him convulsively, resuming his steady rhythm as soon as her muscles relaxed. The pleasure she felt was different then, comfortable and easy, buzzing through her until her entire body was warm with blissful peace. The build was slow, but when she finally tilted over the edge into her second, more drawn-out orgasm, it felt just as intense as the more frantic ones—*more* intense, even. This was new and scary due to that unfamiliarity, because it meant that her connection with Winston was different from anything she'd ever experienced before.

He held her to him as his thrusting finally sped up and gained a rough edge that she'd learned meant he was close. His arms around her tightened as he shuddered with pleasure behind her, and she felt a rush of gratitude that she could be the first person to give him this amazing experience, since what they had was a completely new thing for her too.

They lay pressed together for too short a time before he kissed the nape of her neck and reached for the sleeping bag zipper with a sigh. She groaned. Each time she had to leave their cozy bed, it was harder than the time before.

"How're you feeling?" he asked.

"Sore…sex-sore," she corrected when he sucked in a breath, probably to command her to rest for another day. "Excellently sex-sore. Otherwise perfectly fine."

"Good. Let's go find Rose then," he growled in her ear, and that got her moving.

They broke down camp quickly and were on the trail before the sun had completely made it over the mountain peaks to the east. Dahlia turned to give the spot where their tent had been a final look. "I never thought I'd be sad to leave a campsite, but here we are."

Instead of laughing, he gave her a sympathetic glance. "We'll come back."

She wondered if he meant on their way back from the falls or at some other time in the not-so-near future, which meant he was thinking long-term, which meant he didn't think of her as a quick hookup, which meant— She cut off her thoughts. *Why are you torturing yourself with this? He's right here. Just ask him. Then you'll know either way.* That was the problem, though. She didn't want to know if he was looking forward to the end of their trip and never seeing her again.

"Hey, Wins?"

He grunted.

"What are your thoughts on continuing to have sex in the future?"

He was looking straight ahead, so she only saw one corner of his mouth curl up into that irresistible smug expression. "Yes."

Although her question hadn't really called for a yes-or-no answer, she was encouraged. "With me?"

Now he glanced at her, and that right eyebrow was a tiny bit judgmental about her intelligence. "Of course."

She hesitated long enough that he glanced at her again, curiously this time.

"How long in the future are we talking? After we find Rose?" She knew she was probably being overly optimistic about both the sex-having and the sister-finding, but she needed to have hope about both of those goals.

He hesitated, looking uncertain for the first time that morning, but then his expression firmed and he even gave a tiny dip of his chin, like he was nodding to a silent question. "Okay. I'll visit you in LA."

"Yeah?" She smiled at him and tripped, only not falling on her face in the snow because Winston caught her arm and righted her, his movement so quick and effortless that she almost swallowed her tongue as heat surged through her. Clearing her throat, she gave herself a few seconds to regain her tattered composure. "I'd like that. You going to turn the traps off if I visit you at your hermit compound?"

"Maybe." Winston gave her a teasing glance before catching her hand and pulling her to a halt as he pointed through the trees at something. Her heart immediately started thumping, imagining all sorts of dangers he could be warning her about, but then something moved, catching her attention. The fawn-colored deer-like animal had white on its belly and in funny horizontal stripes across its throat. Black stubby antlers curved in slightly toward the top. The most striking part was that it couldn't have been more than three feet high, tops.

"Oh," she breathed, as quietly as she could. "That's the tiniest deer I've ever seen. It's like Bambi and Air Bud had a baby."

"Pronghorn," he rumbled. "If you think that buck is small, just wait until spring. The fawns are tiny."

They watched the pronghorn pick his way through the snow until he went deeper into the trees and they lost sight of him. Winston started walking again, towing her with him when she would've waited to see if the buck returned. Remembering their mission, she fell in next to him.

"That was extremely awesome." Her voice was still hushed, although inside she was positively giddy. Not only had seeing the pronghorn so close been exhilarating, but it also made her think that maybe she wouldn't hate visiting here. In fact, with Winston and close-up wildlife spottings and Winston and gorgeous scenery and Winston, who knew? She might even grow to love Howling Falls.

THIRTEEN

Walking felt amazing and terrible at the same time, waking all the aches caused by their sexathon, which hurt but also reminded Dahlia of all the lovely orgasms he'd given her. Even better than that was the mental image of Winston's face, his expression easy to read for once, telling her how he thought she was probably too incredible to be real. Even now, as their boots squeaked in the fresh snow, he was sneaking glances as if to make sure she hadn't disappeared back into his imagination where she'd originated. Just to show him that she was, in fact, real, and that his brain hadn't conjured her up, she did him the service of reaching over and pinching him.

Of course, the pinch was useless with all his layers, and his right eyebrow made a squiggly line. "What was that for?"

"Just so you knew that you weren't dreaming."

His eyes widened just for a split second, giving him away. "How did you…" He caught himself and stared straight ahead. "Never mind."

She laughed, the sound ringing out through the trees, and she saw Winston's smile fight to break through in response before he sternly smothered it. Reaching over, she grabbed his hand. Silence settled back over the snowy mountainside, and Dahlia's happy thoughts soured.

"What's wrong?" he asked, somehow managing to see her change of expression while not looking at her.

The idea of him monitoring her happiness through side-eye and sneaky glances made her oddly content, but then she remembered why she'd frowned in the first place. "Snow makes this place even quieter. In movies, snowy wilderness looks all peaceful and everything, but that's a lie. It's creepy-town." When Winston just gave an amused shake of his head, she realized it was up to her alone to figure out what could be done to fix the problem. An idea that she'd idly mentioned the first day of their hike popped into her brain. "This place needs a soundtrack."

"Isn't that what you're doing?" he asked. When she looked at him in question, he elaborated. "I haven't heard more than a few seconds of silence since I met you. You're providing the soundtrack."

She considered this before giving him a satisfied smile. "I am, aren't I? I'm the solution, the creepy-silence antidote."

"You're the solution to a lot of things," Winston said.

The implications struck her hard enough that she pressed her free hand to her chest, right above her heart. Her stomach dove and then lifted, a sensation she was becoming almost used to in the days since she'd met him. "And again," she said when she'd regained her ability to speak. He shot her a confused glance, and she beamed at him. "Another compliment that just about knocked me off my feet into the snow."

He still seemed a bit wary. "So that's…good?"

She smiled at the understatement. "Yeah. That's good."

His only response was a lift of his chin, and in the resulting quiet, a rumble reached her ears.

"What is that sound?" It could be a distant engine—maybe traffic from a nearby road or a plane overhead. She remembered the ATVs but quickly dismissed all three possibilities. The noise was more of a roar than an engine—well, a normal one, at least—would make.

The corner of Winston's lips turned up. "You get a break."

"A break?" Somehow, she didn't think he meant a hiking break, which she was fine with. When they stopped for water and a snack, she just got cold and her muscles stiffened up. She'd rather keep going.

"A talking break," Winston explained, although not really, since what he said just confused her. "A break from being the silence-killer."

The closer they got, the louder the roar, until a light bulb turned on in Dahlia's mind. "Oh! Howling Falls Falls! We're here!"

Although he rolled his eyes, Winston didn't complain about the additional falls in the name for once. Dahlia ran ahead, halfway convinced that Rose would be waiting for them and also just excited to experience the falls. It was the third-largest waterfall in Colorado, after all, plus they'd walked for days just to get here. This was their goal, and they'd almost arrived.

Winston sped up, staying close behind her as they rounded

a bend in the trail. It opened up to a carved-rock cavern. In the center, as if nature had sliced out big sections of rock intentionally to frame the natural wonder, was the falls. Although the day had warmed considerably, snow still clung to the rocks on either side of the water, adding to the impressive sight.

"Wow," she breathed, although the roar of the falls was loud enough to drown her out. "That's beautiful. And so tall." Neither word seemed strong enough to describe the dizzying height and slightly terrifying power of the waterfall, so she fell silent and just stared up at the natural marvel.

Winston moved around her and took her hand, leading the way closer to the pool at the bottom of the waterfall. Although they were still some distance away, a cold mist stung any exposed skin. She almost enjoyed the sharp bite, since it reminded her that she wasn't watching this on a screen. This was real and right in front of her. As with the moment watching the pronghorn, she suddenly understood why people ventured into the mountains, despite the dangers and discomfort and unpleasant silence. With the expectation—or even just the possibility—of getting a close-up look at something like this, she too would give up indoor plumbing and the ability to stand up straight in her temporary bedroom.

And this isn't the only perk of camping, her lusty brain commented. *Sleeping-bag sex is quite excellent.* She snuck a look at Winston's profile.

He leaned to put his mouth close to her ear. "Let's check the campsite," he shouted over the roar of the falling water as he tugged her toward a path leading away from the falls. She took a final glance over her shoulder, snapping a mental picture to store for later when she needed it, before focusing on checking the campsite for any sign of her sister.

If Rose had left anything behind, however, the heavy, wet snow hid it. Dahlia walked around the empty clearing three times before stopping to frown at a twisted bristlecone. Winston joined her, his scowl even more ferocious than hers. Despite her worry and disappointment, his cranky expression made her smile. "Why are you glaring at this poor tree?"

One of his shoulders twitched in a typically Winston-like shrug. "You started it. You tell me."

She gave his arm an affectionate squeeze. "Scowling in solidarity. I like it." Then her smile dropped away as she eyed the tree again. On first look, it was ugly—twisted and sparse—but there was a sort of ancient beauty to it too, and she felt bad that she'd directed her rage at the universe at its innocent, gnarled branches. "Just frustrated that trees can't talk, and that there isn't anyone else here to ask about Rose."

Winston's gaze moved from the tree to a spot just beyond it. Although his frown deepened, it was thoughtful. "No one's here *now*," he said, walking over to a wooden barricade meant to keep hikers off a closed trail. Dahlia followed. "But this is new, probably put up just a week or two ago."

Now that he'd mentioned it, she noticed the rough boards smelled of freshly cut lumber. Hope—which she'd thought had been beaten down so often it'd never rise again—bloomed in her chest. "So that means some Forest Service workers were here recently? Oh! Is this the drawn-in trail from Rose's map?" She pulled the folded paper from her pocket, trying not to get too excited by the possibility that there might've been a witness to see where Rose had gone, but it was hard to keep her expectations low. If Rose had been here when they were constructing the barrier, she would've chatted with them. Rose talked to *everybody*.

Winston glanced at the map and then the barricaded trail entrance. "Could be the same. It's going in the right direction." Despite his words, his brows lowered, the right one giving a suspicious twist as he glared at the barrier. "But this wasn't done by anyone from the Forest Service."

"Oh." She looked at the wooden blockade more closely, which did no good, since she had no idea what she was looking for. "How can you tell?"

"No sign." He straightened, his ferocious frown still in place. "And it's too late in the season. They don't service the trails in the winter."

"But why?" she asked, confused. "Who else besides the official guys would bother blocking a trail? Someone dragged tools and lumber up here and did all that work, and for what? Just to have their own private trail or something? It doesn't make sense."

"Exactly." He climbed over the barricade with an ease that Dahlia was glad the builders couldn't see, since they would've been demoralized that all their hard work was for naught. Once on the opposite side, he waved for her to join him.

She tucked the map back in her pocket and clambered over it with much less grace than he'd shown, feeling strangely guilty. "Since it's not an official barricade, we won't get arrested and put in unauthorized-trail jail, right?" she joked with an underlying sense of apprehension. It was ridiculous, she knew, but the barrier looked so solid and official.

Except for a bit of side-eye, he ignored her question and strode in his silent stealth-mode way along the trail. She followed, feeling more conspicuous with every crunch of her boots on the snow. She knew she needed to keep quiet since Winston had gone into hypervigilant mode, his gaze constantly scanning for danger, but questions were bouncing around her brain like popcorn.

Finally, she couldn't take it and whispered, "Do you think this unofficially closed trail is related to Rose's disappearance?"

His chin dropped slightly in a terse nod.

Chewing on that theory, she fell silent as she considered possible scenarios, the worst one being that Rose's body was dumped on this trail. Every time they rounded a bend, she held her breath, hoping they didn't make that grisly and heartbreaking discovery. Dahlia tried to push the possibility to the back of her mind, but it lurked there, shadowing all of her other thoughts.

If Winston hadn't told her that the barrier wasn't officially sanctioned, she would've been baffled as to the reason for its closure, since the trail was in great shape—wide and well-maintained. It somehow made the fact that it was blocked off even more ominous, and every minute that didn't reveal an avalanche or sinkhole or some other trail-blocking calamity drew Dahlia's muscles tighter.

As they hiked through the morning, Dahlia found herself relaxing a little. Tensing in expectation of something horrible around each bend of the trail was exhausting, and she returned to her usual mix of interest and unease that being in the wilderness brought out in her. The scenery was beautiful, as usual, the trees towering above her in a way that made her feel both small and part of something much bigger than herself. She was really getting to like the steadfast company of the mountains around them too. They felt like rock sentries, keeping guard over her and Winston.

"Should I not talk?" she finally whispered, not able to take the silence any longer.

Winston snorted. "You lasted forty-five minutes longer than I thought you would."

Since he'd spoken at a normal volume, Dahlia let out a relieved breath. "Oh, thank god. I was about to explode from all the words trapped inside of me. Talking's okay now?"

"Should be." Despite his reassurance, he was looking around, even more vigilant than usual. "If this *is* the trail marked on Rose's map, we still have several hours of hiking before we get to whatever the X is."

"Good." Dahlia paused. Now that she had permission to speak, all her roiling thoughts and worries and questions had melded together in a blob, and she couldn't pick just one thread to go with. Not once before in her entire life had she been at a loss for words, and it made her panic a little.

"Tell me about growing up with Rose," Winston said.

Dahlia stared at his profile in shocked delight. "Did you just start a conversation?"

His flush and flustered side-eye were flat-out adorable. "Just asked a question."

"It was more like an order," she corrected, grinning. Unable to help herself, she grabbed his arm and tugged him down so she could kiss his cheek. "Thank you."

Although she knew he tried to make his grunt sound surly, she could tell he was pleased.

"She lived with her mom, so I just got to see her on odd weekends until we were sent to the same boarding school, but we've always been tight. She let me practice makeovers on her, even after I accidentally turned her hair a pretty rancid green."

He huffed a laugh but then quickly sobered. "Boarding school? How old were you?"

"We were six."

"Six?" He looked nauseated.

"I didn't mind," she reassured him quickly. "I liked it better than being home. My nanny wasn't really the nurturing type, and at school I could hang out with Rose more often."

Although he looked even more perturbed by that, he thankfully changed the subject. "How'd you get into the makeover business?"

Relieved she didn't have to talk about her pathetic family life anymore, she said, "I've always known what I wanted to do, so while I got my BA in fabric and clothing design, I also took aesthetician courses—skin care, hair, makeup—and practiced on anyone who'd sit still long enough. Once I graduated, I made over a bunch of my boarding school friends, and it snowballed from there." She shot him an unsure glance. "I try not to be like the rest of my family—minus Rose—but I know it was thanks to those connections that I was able to build my career so quickly, and I feel guilty about that sometimes."

He stopped eyeing their surroundings to really look at her,

meeting her gaze with such complete focus that it took her breath away. "There's no shame in using the resources available to you if you do it in an ethical way. You deserve the success you built."

"I guess." His approval lit a warmth inside her, and she immediately felt a jolt of panic that he was starting to mean so much to her already. "Enough about me. You've never told me why you stopped teaching."

He grimaced silently, which just made her curiosity worse.

"You might as well tell me. We have *hours* of hiking left," she threatened sweetly. "Days even. You know I'll weasel it out of you eventually."

His scowl looked forced, as if he was trying not to smile. "You're a pest. Why do I like you?"

She beamed at him. "Because I'm amazing. Now spill."

He heaved an audible sigh. "Fine." He paused, but Dahlia resisted urging him on, and when he started speaking again, his voice was grim. "I used to teach a four-day training course for cops. A couple of weeks after taking my class, Officer Noah Barkley barricaded himself inside his house with his injured wife and two kids. After a three-hour standoff, the emergency response unit entered. Two responding cops were killed before Barkley shot himself. His wife died of her injuries. She went too long without medical care." He went silent, the muscle along his jaw working. "He used some of the techniques I taught him to extend the standoff and kill the ERU cops."

Dahlia dug for words, hoping desperately that they were the right ones. In the admittedly short time she'd known Winston, he'd never opened himself up like this, and the last thing she wanted was to make him feel worse. "You can't be responsible for what someone else does with the tools you give them."

"I was responsible." When she opened her mouth to protest, he continued. "At least partially. I couldn't keep teaching. I figured I'd move out here where I couldn't hurt anyone else and people would leave me alone." He gave her a meaningful look.

Despite her heart breaking for him, she gave a shaky laugh at that. "If you didn't want me bothering you, you should've built a more unclimbable wall."

———

Figuring that they'd both revealed enough emotional trauma for a while, Dahlia kept the conversation light after that, chattering about where she lived and bits about her daily life. He seemed entertained, although his gaze still scanned over the trees around them constantly.

"I think you'll like the walking trail by my house," she said, still not quite believing that she would get to take Winston home with her. "It's nothing as wild as this, of course, but it's pretty, with flowers and a lake—"

She broke off when he raised a hand, peering intently through the trees to their right. Her heart immediately started pounding, and silver sparkles danced across her vision before she realized she was holding her breath. She carefully inhaled and exhaled despite her fear. If she fainted a second time, Winston would wrap her in bubble wrap and carry her to safety. She strained her ears, trying to figure out why he'd stopped, but all she could hear was her frantic heartbeat.

After what felt like a million years, he started walking again, although his attention stayed on the trees bordering the right side of the path. He nudged her to go in front of him and to his left before picking up their hiking pace. Dahlia wanted desperately to ask what he was looking—or listening—for, imaging all sorts of dangers hiding in the shadows, but she didn't dare make a sound.

As she rounded a bushy pine, she glanced behind her and to the right. Nothing was there, although she immediately caught her toe on a rock. She regained her balance and avoided falling on her face, but she resolved to watch where she was stepping instead of searching for imaginary boogeymen behind them.

The trail surface flattened out, allowing her to raise her head to look at something besides her feet. She stopped abruptly. Ahead of them on the path, there was something huge and hairy and black. In the first frozen half second, her brain tried to tell her that it was a dog—a really, *really* big dog—but then she knew. It wasn't a dog.

It was a bear. A freaking, real-life *bear*.

Her body operated without thought, spinning around and bolting. She was only able to sprint three steps before she ran flat into what felt like a wall…if a wall had arms that wrapped securely around her. Winston grunted at the impact.

"Bear!" she managed to get out, although it was more a wheeze than an actual word. "Run!"

"Dahl," he said, quietly but firmly, and ridiculously calmly considering the situation. "Look."

She didn't want to look. She didn't want to see the enormous teeth that were about to envelop her head right before it was bitten off. Winston gave her a little squeeze, and the reminder that he was there gave her the courage to peek over her shoulder.

She stared, blinked, and then gave a semi-hysterical laugh.

"Is...it running away?" she asked, unable to believe she wasn't about to be eaten like a very fashionable protein bar. She blinked again, but she hadn't been mistaken. The round, furry bear butt was getting farther and farther away until it turned into the trees and disappeared completely.

Only then did Winston laugh. "You both saw each other, turned tail, and ran. You even had the same wide-eyed expression."

The mental picture played in her head, and it was comical enough to laugh at, although hers still had a bit of gasping panic to the sound. "Like a cartoon."

Giving her a final squeeze, he released her. "Next time, don't run from a bear," he advised, turning her by her shoulders.

"It wasn't really a conscious decision," she grumbled, taking one step forward before reconsidering and darting behind Winston. "You go first."

With an amused snort, he led the way.

———

The next half hour was nerve-racking.

Every sound, every dead leaf shivering in the breeze made her flinch. She couldn't bring herself to talk, instead walking as close to Winston as she could without actually being on top of him. His expression wasn't reassuring, his jaw tight as he scanned their surroundings with wary alertness.

A chittering sound broke the silence, making her flinch before she saw the fat squirrel flicking its tail at her chidingly. Her heart raced in the aftermath of the scare, and she reached over and clutched a handful of Winston's coat. His gaze dropped briefly to her clenched fist, but he didn't say anything.

"Sorry," she muttered softly, embarrassed by her literal clinginess, but not enough to let go.

He gave one of his twitchy shrugs and went back to scanning the trees on either side of them. The trail turned sharply, and Dahlia held her breath.

No bear no bear no bear no bear, she mentally chanted, as if she could prevent the existence of another carnivorous animal just through the force of positive thoughts. Once they rounded the turn, she got just a glimpse of the clearing in front of them—bear-free, thankfully—before Winston yanked her back into the cover of the trees.

She gave him a questioning look, his tenser-than-usual expression keeping her quiet.

Leaning so close that his lips brushed her ear, he spoke in a bare whisper. "That building shouldn't be here."

Her lips formed the word *oh,* although no sound emerged. She'd been so focused on the path, where any potential bears would be—and, more pragmatically, any rocks trying to trip her up—that she'd completely missed seeing the structure. Releasing her arm, Winston left the trail, making his way through the trees. She followed, her brain churning as the new information—a structure that shouldn't have existed in the middle of national forest land—changed her theories on what might've happened to Rose. She soon realized that she needed all her concentration to not crash through the underbrush like a drunken elephant. Focused intently on where she was placing her feet, she bumped into Winston when he stopped abruptly.

Reaching back, he steadied her with a hand on her hip while still staring ahead. Crouching, he slunk between two evergreens. Worried about losing him, she hurried to follow, staying low as he was doing, grateful for once for her short stature—less to hide from anyone watching.

He stopped behind a leafless shrub, taking off his backpack before dropping to his belly on the ground. With a mental groan, she followed suit, trying to ignore the cold snow pressing against her front. Peering through the thick mass of branches, she got her first glimpse of the building.

It wasn't much to look at—a single-level rectangle, obviously prefab. The front had a small office area with a door and a handful of windows, but the majority of the building was a windowless warehouse-type structure. The aluminum siding was dark brown, and the few windows were covered on the inside with dark material. The snow surrounding the building looked churned up and dirty, and two ATVs were parked near the only door she could see.

The breeze rustled tree branches around them and brought a nasty stench to her nose. She poked Winston in the arm and made a puke face when he looked at her. "How many cats do you think they have in there?" she whispered in a voice so low that she could barely hear herself.

Apparently, Winston managed to catch the question, since he shook his head and breathed into her ear, "Meth."

The method of delivering that single word was extremely hot, but she was brought back down to earth when what he said registered. Meth wasn't hot. "Lab?" she asked, squinting at the structure, trying to see inside the covered windows.

His chin dipped in a silent nod as he shifted, pulling a pair of binoculars from a side pocket of his pack before returning to his earlier position next to her. As he peered at the building through them, it was almost impossible for Dahlia to hold still. She eyed the binoculars, wanting more than anything to yank them away from him and take a turn peering at the place. She'd always been terrible at waiting.

As if he could feel her stare burning the left side of his face, he handed her the binoculars.

"Thank you!" she whispered, holding them up to her eyes. The building was suddenly very close to her, and she almost jumped before catching herself. She scanned across the exterior wall, paying more attention to each window. Halfway across, she saw a pile of blackened trash on the ground in front of the house and made a face. "Gross. What's that?"

"Burn pit," Winston whispered.

Her heart lurched. "For, like...bodies?"

He gave an almost soundless huff of amusement. "Trash, probably."

Irrational relief coursed through her, and she now allowed herself to look at the burn pit more closely. "Aren't those plastic bottles?" She knew it probably wasn't important, but she couldn't seem to skip over it yet. "They're burning plastic?" She wasn't sure why she expected meth makers to be more environmentally conscious, but she was still disappointed in their behavior, especially contrasting the grubby building and yard to the pristine wilderness surrounding them.

Winston's snort was soft but encapsulated all of the things she'd just been thinking about, so she let it go with just a nudge of her elbow against his side.

She finally moved off the burn pit and scanned to the last window, the only one that wasn't covered. "Bathroom?" she whispered, able to see the edge of a vanity and what looked like a grubby shower curtain.

His low grunt confirmed her guess.

"How are we going to see who's inside?" She didn't mention Rose yet, not wanting to count her chickens and set herself up for yet another disappointment if her sister wasn't in the building. "Should we sneak up close and try to find a crack in their sloppy curtains?"

This time, his grunt was a negative. "Look by the door and both front corners."

When she peered through the binoculars at the spots he'd mentioned, she saw what he was talking about. "Cameras." Her whisper was glum.

"We'll watch from here," he said, taking the binoculars back. "See if anyone comes out—or goes in. Once we have a rough head count, we can plan how to get inside."

She settled more comfortably, tugging her coat down where it had folded under her hip. "Next time we raid a meth lab to rescue Rose, let's bring two sets of binoculars."

He turned his head to give her a look, his right eyebrow

caught between amusement and distaste. "This better be the only time we raid a meth lab looking for your sister," he finally said, turning back to monitor the building.

"Agree." Her gaze returned to the burn pit, and her nose wrinkled. "Getting trapped in a meth lab once is understandable, but twice? She'd need to take a good, hard look at her life choices to see where she's going wrong."

They settled into a rhythm of watching the building, trading off the binoculars every five minutes or so, keeping an eye on the exposed bathroom window with an occasional glance at the door. "I thought the quiet was eerie before," she whispered as she offered Winston a drink from her water bottle. "I had no idea how creepy it could be. How young and dumb I was."

"That was this morning." He handed her the binoculars and accepted the water bottle.

"And now I'm half a day older and wiser."

His huff of a laugh was almost silent. He took a drink of water, and Dahlia couldn't look away from the muscles in his neck and jaw working as he swallowed. She finally managed to rip her fascinated gaze away and focus on the much-less-titillating building.

The minutes ticked away, each one stretching endlessly, until the front door swung open.

Dahlia was so startled that she almost made a triumphant noise. *Finally! Something's happening!* She gave Winston an elbow jab and handed him the binoculars. "Front door."

One guy stepped outside, then a second. They moved to stand next to the gross burn pit, the first one kicking a stray plastic pop bottle into the center. A third man joined them, and Dahlia squeezed Winston's arm—hard.

"I see," he grunted before handing the binoculars to her. "Recognize any of them?"

"Doubt I'd know them if you don't," she said, although she accepted the binoculars and peered closely at the three guys smoking by the burn pit. "You've lived here for years, and I just got here four days ago, and most of that time has been spent only with you." One of the men—the young dishwater blond— turned his head and seemed to look right at Dahlia. With a silent inhaled gasp, she jerked her head back automatically. Her heart thundered in her chest, but then the man looked away, flicking ashes into the burn pit with a bored expression.

He was the youngest and skinniest of the trio—probably early twenties, while the other two had at least a decade if not two on him. All three were white and rather pasty, as if they spent too much time in their lab rather than hiking. The biggest guy had short dark hair and beard scruff, while the redhead had a rather glorious mullet. He was wearing...*ack*. Dahlia clicked her tongue quietly against her teeth.

"What'd you see?" Winston asked, leaning his head closer as if to look through the binoculars with her.

"The ginger is wearing an acid-washed jean jacket with matching skinny jeans."

Winston was quiet for several seconds, and Dahlia fully understood why. She too was having trouble processing the reasoning behind such an unnecessary and upsetting decision.

"Where did he even *find* his clothes?" she wondered, unable to stop looking at him. "You can't just pick up such a hideous outfit anywhere, which means he made an effort to look like...*that*."

Winston sighed heavily. "Do you recognize any of them?" he asked again, managing to make his barely there whisper sound so long-suffering that she was impressed.

Even though she was already certain of her answer, she took another hard, magnified look at each man in turn. "No," she finally said before handing off the binoculars. "I've never seen any of them before."

Giving a grunt of acknowledgment, he ignored the proffered binoculars and pulled out his phone instead. Dahlia watched as he took several zoomed-in pictures of the three men, and then she turned back to her surveillance. The guys tossed their cigarette butts into the burn pit and headed back toward the door.

When Winston made a sound of annoyance, she looked over to see him powering down his phone. "No reception," he grumbled. "Can't even text."

She faced the building again, binoculars to her eyes, trying to keep her face placid as she absorbed the news. No cell reception meant that they couldn't call for backup. It was just up to the two of them to take down a meth lab and search it for Rose—or evidence that she'd been there. Dahlia was just grateful that she hadn't tried to go it alone.

"I'm so happy I blackmailed you into coming," she whispered.

His scowl lightened a little. "You didn't."

Rolling her eyes, she focused on the uncovered bathroom window. "You've already forgotten? It's only been a few days."

"You didn't blackmail me," he insisted. She was about to make an alternate-reality joke when he continued. "I wasn't about to let you wander around the mountain to probably die looking for your sister."

She shot him a quick side-eye glance. "So you weren't worried that thousands of Winston Dane fans would descend upon you, ruining your hermit-y peace?"

"No." Despite the quick denial, she caught the tiniest wince before he smoothed his expression. "They wouldn't have gotten past the fence."

"I think you underestimate your stans."

"Doesn't really matter." His gaze scanned the area. "It was just a bluff. You wouldn't have actually done it."

Although she disagreed with that, since she would've done pretty much anything to find Rose, she let it go. If he wanted to think she was a better person than she actually was, she wasn't about to stop him. It was a nice feeling, actually. Most people underestimated her, so having him think she was a shining beacon of morality was new and rather fun. Instead of contradicting him, she just gave a neutral *hmm* and left it at that.

Everything was quiet for a while. As she traded off turns with the binoculars, she processed what Winston had revealed. He'd given up days of his life to help her find her sister, putting himself in danger, all because he didn't want her to die. Dahlia had experienced enough of the mountains to know that she would've failed in her search if she'd been alone. She probably would've had enough sense to give up and return to Howling

Falls the town, but her stubbornness and determination to find Rose might've overwhelmed her survival instinct.

Reaching over, she gave the silent man next to her a pat.

"What's that for?" he asked quietly.

"Being a good guy." She kept her whisper even, although she was fairly bursting with feelings for him. Except for Rose, no one else in Dahlia's life—past or present—would've done what Winston had for her.

It was overwhelming and rather terrifying, and she was relieved when he stiffened and growled, "Movement in the bathroom. A woman." He handed her the binoculars. "Is that Rose?"

A rush of adrenaline hit her, making her hands tremble so hard that she fumbled, almost dropping the binoculars before she managed to hold them to her eyes. Her muscles seemed to turn to water as all her bottled-up fears rushed through her, all the frantic possibilities of what might've happened to her sister that Dahlia had forced herself not to even consider now rampaging inside her head. The magnified view of the bathroom came into focus, and Dahlia's breath caught in her chest.

There she was. Her sister. Upright and moving and not turned into the dreaded *remains* after all.

Rose was *alive*.

FOURTEEN

"Is that Rose?" Winston's repeated question broke Dahlia's paralysis.

"Yes," she choked out almost silently. "Yes!" Relief and joy swamped her. She dropped the binoculars and threw her arms around Winston's neck, hugging him as best she could from their awkward position. He didn't even have enough time to react before she released him and started to push herself up.

Winston grabbed the back of her coat, stopping her. "What are you doing?" he asked.

"Getting my sister." She tried to get up, but he held her still effortlessly.

"Settle down and think." Even though his words were so quiet as to be almost soundless, they still packed a punch, jolting her out of her instinctual need to run to her sister. She went still, listening to him even as her heartbeat thundered in her ears. "You can't help Rose if you get yourself shot. You run over there now and you'll give away the element of surprise—and you won't be able to even get inside that building."

"But what if she's hurt? She doesn't look good." Despite her objection, she dropped back to her belly and grabbed the binoculars again. Rose was leaning on the sink, her head dropped forward so that her blond hair—lank and dirty—hid her face. Defeat was in every line of her posture, and that just about killed Dahlia. Rose always bounced back from everything, somehow holding on to her cheery, kind disposition even when life repeatedly punched her in the face. Now she looked like she'd lost all ability or inclination to bounce, and seeing that made Dahlia want to hurt the people who did this to her sister even more.

Winston took the binoculars, but Dahlia resisted, not wanting to lose her first glimpse of Rose since all of this began. He won the tug-of-war, although she squished her head against his, which he tolerated surprisingly well. "She's alive, conscious, and even standing," he said. Even though Dahlia had seen that for herself, it was still a relief to hear him say it out loud in his steady, reassuring way. "She'll be fine while we come up with a plan."

Having her face squashed against his didn't allow her to see through the binoculars, but the heat of him warmed her. She also leaned her shoulder against his for the comfort as she seized on his words. "A plan. Yes." She pulled the binoculars to her eyes, and he didn't fight her. The bathroom door opened, and a man stood in the doorway. "There are at least four guys." She handed off the binoculars reluctantly, not wanting to let Rose out of her sight again, but knowing Winston should get a look at the new guy.

Winston accepted them with a small smile that acknowledged how hard it'd been for her to give them up before he peered at the building. "So at least four targets."

Despite everything, her mouth curled up at the word. "Target. I like that. Let's target them. Let's target them *hard*."

The corner of his mouth twitched as he set down the binoculars and started digging in his pack. "Hand me your bags— the fashiony ones."

Her eyebrows shot up even as she took her cosmetic and toiletry cases out of her backpack and handed them over. "Normally, I'd be all about creating a righteous vigilante look, but we don't really have time for a makeover."

He grinned as he pulled out her nail-polish remover, her big bottle of hand sanitizer, her eyeliner lighter, and—of all things—her dental floss. "No makeover."

"You look like you have a plan." It didn't matter that they were in a scary, dangerous situation. When Winston smiled wide enough to show his pretty white teeth, she followed suit. It was impossible not to return his smile.

"Just the bare bones," he said, still rummaging through her makeup bag. Normally, she would've lit into anyone making such a mess of her precious cosmetics, but this was for Rose. Nothing else mattered until her sister was safe. "I'm thinking we'll figure out the details as we go."

She was pretty sure her grin strongly resembled a shark's. "I'm *excellent* at improvising."

———

The hardest part was waiting.

Everything was set up, the plan in place, and Winston had even stopped grumbling about Dahlia taking some of the dangerous parts. Now, the sun was sitting halfway behind a mountain peak, and they just needed it to be dark.

"Eat," Winston ordered, shoving a bag of trail mix at her.

"Rude, but okay." She ate, even though her stomach churned in protest. If all went well, she'd be running later, so she needed to fuel up. This would be a really bad time to faint again. Once she'd managed to force down a few handfuls, she handed the bag back to Winston. He then shoved a water bottle at her and proceeded to watch her drink. "You too," she said when she handed back the water. He did, and then returned everything to his pack.

They settled back to wait again. Dahlia's heart was pounding, and she was more awake than she'd ever felt. Everything seemed to have extra-sharp corners, and the light was too bright, even though it was dusk. Winston, on the other hand, seemed to get calmer the closer they got to go time. Right now, he was completely still, the muscles in his face more relaxed than she'd ever seen them—well, except for before when she'd stroked his face. Or immediately after he'd orgasmed. She, on the other hand, felt twitchy, as if energy was going to burst out of her like a flash-bang grenade.

Finally, Winston soundlessly got to his feet. She popped up next to him, not as smoothly and definitely not as quietly. "Ready?" he whispered.

Her mouth was dry, even though she'd just drank half a

bottle of water, so she just nodded and picked up the broken branch at her feet. They crept right to the edge of the tree line. Pulling out the slingshot he'd fashioned from a forked stick and some rubber tubing, Winston fit a small stone in place, aimed, waited for the next noisy gust of wind, and then released.

Dahlia held her breath, but the only sound was a slight clatter as the rock hit aluminum siding. Before she could even feel disappointed by his miss, Winston released another rock. This time, there was the tinkle of breaking glass. The motion-sensor light was no more.

"Got it. Go."

Broken branch in her hands, she was already running toward the burn pit. Tossing the branch to the ground under the broken motion-sensor light, she peered at the mess in and around the blackened circle. She knew Winston would provide cover for her with his improvised slingshot and a pile of rocks they'd hunted down earlier, but she still felt completely exposed there in the yard.

Forcing herself to focus, she squinted at the scattered, half-burned items. The plastic bottles wouldn't work for their purposes—plus they had holes cut in them—but there were some glass beer bottles scattered around that would be perfect. It was hard to see in the near dark, so she crouched at the edge of the burn pit and felt around, enormously grateful for the protection of her gloves. Two bottles lay side by side, and she grabbed them both. The clank as the bottles in her left hand knocked together sounded hugely loud, but she continued searching the ground in her immediate vicinity for more bottles. She'd just seized a third when the dead bolt on the front door thumped open.

Clutching her three bottles, she ran for the trees. The door swung open, letting a rectangle of golden artificial light escape. She mentally prayed she wasn't detected and chased—at least not yet. She slowed before she reached the trees, not wanting to trip on the scrubby underbrush or a stray branch.

A hand closed over her upper arm, yanking her into the shadows between two evergreen trees. She swallowed an instinctual yelp as her thinking brain realized the grabber was Winston. He took the bottles from her and started filling them with hand sanitizer before tucking a strip of fabric in each neck to serve as a wick. Sucking in air, she tried to quiet her breathing as she alternated between watching Winston and the two guys examining the broken branch in the scattered glass next to the door.

"Wind must've blown this branch into it," the mullet-bearing ginger guy said, giving the maligned branch a kick. "Broke the light bulb." Dahlia gave Winston's arm a delighted squeeze. That was just the theory they'd hoped the guys would go with.

The other guy, the first blond they'd seen, frowned. "I don't know, Trapper. Seems suspicious." He muttered something inaudible as he peered into the darkness. Even though she knew he couldn't see them in the deep shadows of the trees, Dahlia still shrank back.

"Rick didn't see anyone break it, and he was watching the camera feed when the light went out," the ginger argued.

"Yeah, okay." Despite his words, the blond didn't sound convinced that the light was broken by an act of nature, and his gaze swept over the surrounding forest another time. "Better get a new bulb."

The two went back into the building, and Winston gave her a nudge. She ran for the door, flattening herself against the siding to the left of it, and he did the same on the right. Her breathing was coming quickly again, and she forced herself to take slow, deep inhales as she pulled a fist-sized rock out of her coat pocket. Between her panting breaths and thundering heart-beat, she couldn't hear anything else.

It felt like just a few seconds but also like an eternity before the door swung open again. The ginger was the first to step outside, and Winston hauled him to the side and popped him on the head with his own rock.

"What…?" The first blond rushed out next, lunging toward Winston and the redhead's sagging form.

Shoving the door closed, Dahlia hurled herself at the blond's back. She lifted her rock and whacked it against the side of his head. Although he swayed he didn't go down, and even started to turn toward her. She hurried to rock him in the head twice more, panic rising as she realized that it took more strength to knock a man unconscious than she'd thought.

He finally fell, toppling like a tree, and he hit the ground hard enough to make Dahlia feel a little bad for being the cause of any injuries he might've sustained. Winston, who must've trussed up the redhead while she was smacking the blond with her rock, immediately zip-tied his wrists and ankles before gagging the unconscious man.

Winston dragged them one at a time another ten feet away

from the door while Dahlia ran back to grab the three recycled beer bottles filled with hand sanitizer. She waited until he'd tied off the line of dental floss stretched across the doorway at shin height before handing the bottles off to Winston. He gave her a quick, hard kiss that made her brain spin, and then he turned her around manually and gave her a nudge. Shaking off her Winston-induced daze, she booked it over to the bathroom window. Panic was close, but she kept it walled up in her brain, concentrating on only the next step of their plan to keep her anxiety about what could happen at bay.

A quick peek showed that the bathroom was empty, although the door was ajar, so someone walking by would be able to see her if she stood directly in front of the window. Instead, she flattened herself to the siding next to it, trying to remember to breathe as she waited for her cue.

The crash of glass made her jump, even though she was expecting it. It was followed by shouts and a roar of flames, but she ignored what was happening on the other side of the building and concentrated on her part. She turned her face away and swung her rock at the bathroom window, breaking it. Most of the cheap glass fell out of the frame, but she was still cautious as she reached in to unlatch it. As she shoved it open, another chunk of glass was jarred loose, falling to the ground at her feet.

Headfirst, she shoved her upper half through the window, catching herself with her hands on the rough concrete floor, remembering the broken bits of glass too late. She scrambled the rest of the way inside, inelegantly pulling one leg through the window and then the other. Once she managed to get to her feet, her knees went a bit wobbly from fear and adrenaline, but she forced herself to straighten. Despite her glass-scattered landing, she didn't feel any pain in her hands, so she just brushed off her gloves and crossed the bathroom.

Shoving aside the dirty shower curtain that was so mildewed it looked disgusting even in the dim light, she started the shower and turned the knob all the way to the left. Steam almost immediately began drifting off the spray. A nasty-looking bath towel hung on a rack over the toilet, and she hung it from the curtain rod, covering the broken window. Grabbing the bottle of nail-polish remover from her pocket, she dumped it all on the floor. For a ridiculous second, she looked around the tiny room for a garbage can before just dropping the acetone bottle on the soaked floor. The smell burned her nose as she hurried to the door.

She peeked through the doorway, taking in the large open room that looked like a dirty, low-budget lab. Plastic bottles with tubing and filthy-looking coffee filters littered mismatched folding tables, and empty packaging and trash were everywhere. Two good-sized fires near the windows spread a haze of smoke through the space, and the older, dark-haired smoker from earlier was running toward the flames with a fire extinguisher. The younger guy in the red hoodie—the one who'd escorted Rose from the bathroom—darted to the exterior door.

This was her opportunity, but she couldn't resist pausing to watch the man yank open the door and rush through it. When she heard a yell and a crash, she grinned. *Dental-floss trip wire for the win.*

The dark-haired man jerked his head around to stare at the

door, but he didn't seem inclined to help his friend. Hoping the fire was enough of a distraction, Dahlia darted out of the bathroom—using a precious second to close the door quietly behind her—and across the space to the only other interior door in the building. Since there was no sign of Rose in the main warehouse area, she had to be behind that door.

Dahlia didn't allow herself to look at the man trying to put out the fires. She'd watched plenty of people get picked off in the first five minutes of horror movies, and she'd die of shame if she made the same stupid, fatal mistakes. It was harder than she thought, however, and she made a semi-hysterical mental promise to herself to give those doomed fictional characters more sympathy during future viewings.

The door was locked, and she yanked at it futilely, wishing that she'd grabbed Winston's lock-pick kit before realizing the deadlock was on the outside. Twisting it with fingers slick with sweat that had soaked through her gloves, she wrestled it open and slipped inside.

It wasn't until she'd pulled the door closed behind her that she thought to worry about another bad guy being with Rose. Her heartbeat raced only to settle immediately when her panicked gaze flew around the small room, and she confirmed that there was only one occupant, and she was tied to an ancient wooden chair.

"Rose," she breathed, dropping to her knees in front of her sister as she fished out the folding knife Winston had insisted she carry.

"Dahlia?" Rose blinked several times, either because the

acrid smoke was starting to seep under the door or because she couldn't believe what she was seeing. "Are you really here?"

Dahlia cut through the zip ties binding Rose's ankles to the chair legs, resisting the urge to hug her sister. "In the flesh. I can pinch you to prove it."

Rose's huff of laughter was a mishmash of relief, affection, and worry. "What are you doing here? Not that I'm not really excited to see you, because I am, but you shouldn't have come in here. These guys are dangerous. Why didn't you just call the cops and let them do the dirty work?"

"The cops didn't see the urgency of your 911 text, so I found someone to help me rescue you." She moved behind her sister to free her wrists from another thick zip tie. "And the guy I found is more dangerous than any of those meth-loving yahoos out there." Folding and pocketing her knife, she straightened, finding her knees wobblier now that she'd found Rose. The stakes were even higher. Rose was alive and appeared to be unharmed, and if Dahlia lost her in the last leg of the rescue, she'd never come back from that. Ignoring her own unsteadiness, she helped Rose stand. "You okay?"

"Okay enough to get out of here, but sore enough to be really pissed off."

"Good." Grabbing her sister's hand, she hurried to the door. As much as she wanted to hear exactly what happened to Rose, they had another, more urgent priority—getting away. "Channel that rage. Let's get out of here."

"Dahl?"

"Yeah?" She cracked open the door and peered out. The

dark-haired guy had emptied the fire extinguisher, and he threw it away from him with a roar of anger.

"Thanks for rescuing me."

"You're not rescued yet." Still, she couldn't resist sending a grin over her shoulder. "But you're welcome. I still owed you for being my model on *Cara and Corbin*."

Rose gave a choke of laughter. "That's right. You did."

Even though it wasn't a great time to run out into the warehouse, Dahlia knew it was only going to get worse if they waited. A burning meth lab was not a place they wanted to be. Taking a shaky breath, she shoved open the door the rest of the way and sprinted toward the bathroom door.

A shout immediately rang out, but Dahlia didn't let herself look. *You and Winston planned for this,* she told herself, trying to keep the panic at bay. She knew they were being chased, but she couldn't let that overtake her mind. She just needed to stick with the plan, step by step—literally and figuratively.

The bathroom door seemed to be a mile away, but she knew it took mere seconds for them to reach it. She fumbled with the knob, her gloved fingers slipping on the smooth metal, but she finally managed to turn it. With a sound of relief that was perilously close to a sob, she lurched into the bathroom, yanking her sister in behind her, and slammed the door.

She'd just pushed the button lock when a heavy body hit the other side of the door, making her jerk back away from it. *The plan, the plan*, she reminded herself, using the words as a calming mantra. Acetone fumes stung her eyes, carried in the steam that filled the tiny space.

"What's that smell?" Rose asked as Dahlia yanked the roll of duct tape and a small box of stick matches from her pocket.

"Nail-polish remover," Dahlia said breathlessly before ripping off a small piece of duct tape with her teeth.

"Uh...?"

Her fingers shook so much she dropped several matches before managing to adhere a line to the piece of duct tape. "Acetone," she continued her explanation. The banging on the other side of the door had gone silent, which should've been a good thing but wasn't, since Dahlia knew he was finding a tool to pop open the doorknob lock.

"You say that like it should mean something to me." Rose gave a shaky laugh.

Crouching down, Dahlia stuck the duct tape to the bottom corner of the door so that the heads of the matches rested against the rough concrete floor. "You should never use nail-polish remover in an unventilated room, especially with a candle or some other open flame."

"Why are you speeching at me like I'm one of your vlog watchers?" Rose asked in an attempt at teasing. The tremor in her voice gave away her fear, and Dahlia felt a fresh surge of anger toward Rose's captors.

Giving the duct tape a final rub to make sure it would hold, she pushed to her feet and rushed to the window, flipping back the towel to expose the opened window. "Its vapors are extremely flammable."

"Ohh," Rose said, as if she finally understood the plan. "I take it we're getting out?"

"Through the window," Dahlia confirmed, giving her sister a nudge. "Out you go."

Always game for something new, Rose launched herself through the open window, wiggling through much more gracefully than Dahlia had managed. Pushing down her sisterly competitiveness, she followed. Rose caught her arms when Dahlia was halfway through, attempting to help her maneuver her hips and legs through the opening. Unfortunately, she was getting in Dahlia's way rather than assisting her.

"Stop helping," she hissed, scraping her thighs against the bottom sill even through her multiple layers of clothes.

"Sorry," Rose muttered, immediately dropping Dahlia's front end onto the ground and giving her a face full of snow.

"Rose!" Dahlia's growl would've made Winston proud.

"Sorry," Rose said again, "but we need to hurry. There's a burning meth lab right here."

Her sister—although annoying—wasn't wrong, so Dahlia pulled her feet through the window and scrambled upright. Reaching into the bathroom, she twitched the towel back into place. "Run to the trees," she ordered her sister in a low voice. "I'm going to see if Winston needs help, and then we'll meet you there."

"Winston?" Rose repeated, although she didn't hesitate to turn toward the edge of the forest.

"You'll love him," Dahlia promised. She'd taken three running steps toward where she'd last seen Winston by the front door when, with a *whoosh* and blinding flash of light, flames filled the bathroom. She instinctively dove to the ground, covering her head, as a pained roar from their pursuer filled her ears. Despite knowing that it was worth everything to free Rose, a sick feeling twisted her stomach at the thought that she'd just immolated a person—or at least burned him. Not wanting to look but not able to *not* look, Dahlia moved back to the window, pinching a non-smoldering portion of the towel to pull it aside so she could see in the bathroom.

The worst of the fire had extinguished after the initial ignition, leaving only sluggish flames licking up the gross shower curtain, so she could see that their pursuer wasn't even close to being immolated. He was more…heavily singed. He didn't seem to appreciate his good fortune as he rolled on the floor, bellowing, a hand clutched over his eyes. Her guilt at hurting someone was overwhelmed by relief that he was incapacitated. From the look of him, he wouldn't be chasing anyone for a few minutes at least.

Turning away from the downed man, she quickly checked on Rose. Her sister was halfway to the tree line, running like the gazelle she was, so Dahlia moved on shaky legs toward the door. She found Winston removing the dental-floss trip wire, shoving the bundled string into his pocket.

Feeling a little dazed from all the events of the night, she blinked at him. "That's taking leave-no-trace camping to a whole other level."

His body jerked visibly, and he whirled around, reaching out and yanking her into his arms. Although she was startled by his quick movements, she immediately melted against his chest, absorbing his comfort and fighting the overwrought tears that ached to be released. "You okay?" he asked in a tone that was more of a command, which made her smile and also want to cry happy tears.

"Yeah," she answered when his hands moved over her more frantically and she realized her silence was making him panic. "I'm good. Rose too. She's waiting for us in the trees."

His arms tightened around her, leaving her breathless for just a moment before his hold eased. She stepped back reluctantly, not wanting to leave the comfort of his arms but knowing that standing outside a burning meth lab was not the time for cuddles. "Good. Let's go."

A growled cascade of muffled swearing drew her attention to the three bound men lined up next to the building. "What about these three?"

"We'll call the sheriff once we have cell reception." Wrapping his heavy arm over her shoulders, he guided her toward the trees.

"Probably the fire department too." She leaned into his side, feeling herself sag as her adrenaline started to wane. He just tucked her against him more tightly, and it was the most luxurious, wonderful thing she'd ever felt.

He grunted his agreement. "Good thing we've got some snow cover. That'll help prevent it from spreading to the trees."

"Should we be worried about the three baddies being too close to the burning building?" The way they were hog-tied, she didn't think they'd be able to move much. "And the guy in the bathroom? What if it explodes?"

"They knew the risk when they decided to make meth," he said flatly.

"True, but—" She broke off as a single headlight flashed. Twisting her head around, she watched in horror as an ATV flew around the last bend in the trail and hurtled toward them.

"Run," Winston ordered, but Dahlia was already in motion, heading for the trees. The cleared area around the building seemed endless, the concealment of the forest impossibly far away, but Winston's reassuring presence behind her gave her courage and incentive to run faster. She knew he was holding back in order to stay behind her, protecting her, just as she knew it'd be her fault if something happened to him because she was being a slowpoke. She pushed her legs to move faster, her eyes locked on the trees ahead.

A loud *crack* made her flinch. "Stop, or I'll shoot you in the back!"

Winston's back. She couldn't let that happen, so she jerked to a halt.

"No, Dahlia, run!" His voice was urgent and harsh with anguish.

Even though she'd like nothing better than to keep running away, it would be Winston's broad frame that would pay the price, and she'd grown shockingly attached to that particular back. She didn't want any new holes in him. He was perfect as he was.

With a groan of defeat, Winston turned to face the threat, shoving her behind him.

"You two!" The shooter snarled, and Dahlia, peering around the man-shaped blockade in front of her, recognized him. It was Fletcher, the guy from the gas station. "I should've known."

"*You* should've known," Dahlia spat out as she stepped to Winston's side, completely and thoroughly *done* with this guy. "*We* should've guessed that you're involved in this. I *knew* you were a gross perv. You gave Rose that map to lure her here!"

"Shut up, bitch!" He shifted to point the matte-black pistol in his hands at her. Although her heart pounded in fear for her life, relief washed through her that the gun wasn't aimed at Winston anymore. "You come sniffing around my town and now burn down my business? You're so dead."

He lifted the gun, cocking his head as he aimed, and Dahlia tried to shove Winston out of the way. All of this was her doing, and she wasn't about to let him get killed. Unfortunately, he was as solid and heavy as a boulder, and he didn't even budge except to push her behind him again.

"Winston, don't," she cried out, ducking around him to his other side, evading his grip. Her only thought was to put some space between them, to draw Fletcher's fire since she was the one he wanted dead anyway.

"No!" Winston reached for her, but it was too late. Fletcher had already shifted his aim to her now-unprotected chest. An unpleasant smile stretched over his face, the flames from the building casting him in an eerie, flickering light. He looked fully evil, ready to kill both of them as he lined up his sights and put his finger on the trigger.

He didn't see the tree branch before it crashed down on his head. He crumpled to the ground even as the gun roared and Winston grabbed her, yanking her against his chest.

"No. Shooting. My. Sister." Rose punctuated each swing

with another whack of the branch, even though it didn't look like Fletcher was conscious to hear her lecture. "And this is for luring me here with that messed-up trail map, you ransoming. Disgusting. Pig. Best place to see wildlife, my *ass*."

"Were you hit?" Dahlia asked Winston, feeling dazed at the close call.

"No. You?"

"I'm fine," she said, even though shock was making his face a bit blurry. "Rose, that's probably sufficient. You don't want to *kill* him."

"Yes, I do." *Whack!*

"Well, I don't want to visit you in prison, so please smack him one more time and then call it good."

With a final blow, Rose stopped swinging, although she held on to the branch and kept a suspicious eye on Fletcher's unmoving form.

"Thanks for the save, Rose." Dahlia tried to take a step toward her sister, but her leg didn't seem to be working. She started to fall, but Winston caught her. Apparently, her wobbly knees had finally given up the ghost, but that was okay, since he was swinging her up into his arms. "Who needs functioning knees when I have a wonderfully weird hermit to catch me?" Her voice sounded strange to her ears. "What's wrong with me?"

"You've been shot." The calmness in Winston's voice didn't fit with the panic in his eyes as he lowered her to the ground.

"Oh." She knew she should be more upset about that, but she was feeling rather floaty and couldn't seem to hold on to the proper emotions. "That's probably not good."

Rose appeared next to her, kneeling by her side and grabbing her hand as Winston frantically patted her down—looking for the bullet hole, Dahlia assumed. "I'm sorry I wasn't quicker," Rose said, her voice shaking. "I had to find the right branch. It had to be heavy enough to not just bounce off his head, but light enough that I could lift it. The first one I picked was rotten, and it fell apart when I picked it up, so—"

Dahlia squeezed her sister's hand, interrupting her tearful babble. "You did great. Who's watching to make sure Fletcher doesn't get away, though?"

Winston barely spared the man a glance as he moved his attention from her torso to her hips. "He's down for a while."

"Yeah, he is." Rose gave her a pathetic attempt at a smile. "Thanks to all the practice I got when I joined that softball league last year."

Dahlia frowned as she tried to focus her fuzzy mind on Rose's words. "You beat people during softball practice?"

From Winston's growl, he'd found the hole. This was confirmed by a tearing pain in her thigh as he pressed his hand against it. With a gasp, she arched up, and black spread over the edges of her vision.

"Okay, ow," she gasped when she could finally suck enough breath in to speak again.

"Sorry, baby," Winston said, although the pressure didn't lighten. He sounded so wrecked that she patted his arm with her free hand, needing to reassure him. "Just stay with me. You'll be okay."

"How badly is it bleeding?" Rose asked anxiously, leaning

over to get a better look. "Do you think it broke the bone? Do you have a first aid kit somewhere around here?"

"It's not broken, and I don't think the bullet hit the femoral artery." Although this seemed to Dahlia like it should be good news, his voice was grim. "Seems to have just passed through the meaty part of her thigh." He grabbed Rose's hand and pressed her palm down right on the spot that hurt the worst. Dahlia's vision grayed out again, but she fought to stay conscious, despite the pain. "Keep pressure here. Stay with me, Dahl. Look at me. No leaving me now."

Rose obeyed, using more pressure than Dahlia thought was entirely necessary. So much for sisterly compassion. "Good thing you have meaty thighs," Rose said, which was the very epitome of adding insult to injury, in Dahlia's eyes.

"Thigh gaps are out this year," Dahlia croaked, startled at how unfamiliar her voice sounded. "Why am I conscious if you're just going to be rude?"

"Stay with me," Winston ordered again as he stripped off his coat and shirt, not sounding at all amused by their sisterly exchange. "Your thighs are perfect."

Dahlia smiled, although she could feel her lips trembling. He was down to his bare skin from the waist up, which was a great motivation to keep her eyes open. From the way he was tearing his base layer into strips, he wasn't going to be redressing anytime soon. "Aww, thank you, Wins. I think you're perfect too. Isn't he beautiful, Rosie?"

"Stunning." Her sister's voice was flat, and she was focused on Dahlia's leg rather than Winston's bare chest, so Dahlia didn't feel like that was a well-considered compliment. She was start-ing to feel very tired, however, so she didn't have it in her to push the issue.

Winston tucked his coat around her torso with shaking hands. "Stay awake, Dahl. I need to tell you something."

"What?" She forced her heavy eyelids to stay open so she could meet his frantic gaze. He looked so scared, so unlike his usual impassive self, that she wanted to do whatever she could to reassure him.

"I'm moving to LA."

"You're going to move to LA?" She wondered if a side effect of bullet wounds was auditory hallucinations. "Why?"

He actually rolled his eyes at her. "To be with you."

Despite the pain and heavy exhaustion pulling at her, she smiled at him. "I'd like that." Her smile drooped a little. "But what if it doesn't work out between us?"

His eyebrow thought she was being ridiculous. "It will." There was a world of confidence packed into those two short words.

Dahlia wished she had an ounce of that surety. "What if you get bored with me?"

He actually gave a bark of laughter at that. "I won't."

He was demolishing her objections, sounding like the reasonable person in all of this, when he wasn't. Still, she scrambled to come up with another potential problem. "What if you hate LA?"

"Probably will." Despite his words, his shrug said it wouldn't matter. "It's warm there, at least. And you'll be there. That's all that matters."

Dahlia stared at his profile, marveling that she'd come to Colorado to find her sister and had somehow hooked a large, weird hermit and was now going to be taking him home with her. Excitement and contented happiness filled her. She tried to stop her growing enthusiasm for his patently ridiculous plan, but she couldn't. The positive emotions were too insidious, and they overwhelmed her brain before she could block them. "I don't have to live in LA full-time," she said before she realized what she was going to say. Apparently, Winston had jumped off the happy cliff, and she was going to hurl herself over after him. "We could be hermits here for part of the year and spend the other part in LA."

A smile curved his mouth again, more sweet than smug this time, and it instantly became her new *new* favorite expression. "Okay."

The sensible part of her brain screamed at her. *Why are you promising to live in the middle of mountainous nowhere for half the year? You'll hate it here!*

The remoteness didn't seem to matter at the moment. All she could focus on was that she and Winston were going to be together. That, and the fact that his fingers were *still* shaking.

"Put your c-coat back on," she scolded, having a hard time getting the words out right. "You'll get cold." She shivered—vicariously, she figured, since *she* wasn't the one who was half-naked in the snow.

Ignoring her order, he scowled ferociously and spoke to Rose instead. "Lift your hand."

The pressure released for a moment, to Dahlia's relief, but

then it returned as Winston bound up her wound, wrapping the improvised bandages around her thigh. He lifted her leg slightly, and pain blasted through her. Staring at Winston's furry, strong chest wasn't enough motivation to keep her eyes open anymore, and she allowed the creeping darkness to take over.

FIFTEEN

THE BLISSFUL, PAIN-FREE OBLIVION DIDN'T last long, to Dahlia's immense regret. The agony jabbed too sharply to let her stay unconscious, and she couldn't hold in a groan as her leg was jostled against something that seemed to be…growling?

Winston, her brain provided, and she relaxed despite the pain, even as she came awake enough to acknowledge that the rumbling sound was loud, even for him. With another reluctant groan, she forced her eyes to open, taking in the flames and smoke and ATV—the source of the growling sound, she realized—and the hard chest she was clutched against.

"Can you drive this?" Winston barked, making Dahlia jolt a little. She was pretty sure she was seconds away from passing out again, but if he needed her to drive, she supposed she could give it her best shot.

To her relief, however, Rose answered, "Yes, but I don't know how to get there, so you'll have to give me directions."

As Winston straddled the back of the ATV, Dahlia's leg was

jostled, and she clenched her teeth to keep from crying out. The pain cleared the last bits of fuzziness from her brain, however, and she was able to connect semi-coherent thoughts.

"I'm glad you put your coat on," she said in a croak. "Where're we going?"

To her surprise, Winston somehow managed to hear her over the rumble of the engine. Ignoring the first part of her comment, he just answered the second. "Ranger station."

"The one the nice ATV people told us about? Won't it be closed?" Despite the flickering light from the flames, it was obviously still nighttime, and she doubted forest rangers manned their posts twenty-four/seven like Walmart cashiers.

She was lifted slightly as he shrugged. "So we'll break in. It'll be warm, with medical supplies and radios."

"Maybe a snack too?" She giggled, which made her realize that she wasn't *quite* as coherent and clear-minded as she'd originally thought.

Winston didn't seem to mind as he squeezed her closer. "Don't worry. I'll feed you."

There seemed to be all sorts of underlying emotions in that simple promise, but she couldn't manage to parse them out. Rose straddled the seat in front of them, and the ATV jerked a little before rolling forward.

Dahlia tried to hold back her gasp, but Winston must've heard it—or felt it—since he growled, "Careful!"

"Sorry!" Rose called over her shoulder, sounding both contrite and panicky. "It's been a few years since I've gone ATVing. Which way?"

"See that trail at two o'clock? Take that."

The ATV jounced as it hit a hole, and in a sparkling flare of agony, Dahlia let go of consciousness again.

———

Dahlia came back to painful reality with a low groan, spending a minute with her eyes closed to orient herself. The ATV portion of the evening must've been over, since she was on a fairly soft surface that wasn't bouncing along a trail. Although she was grateful to be stationary, she missed the warmth of Winston's body and the secure grip of his arms around her. Her thigh was throbbing in a rather threatening way that made her very careful to not move or jostle it, but the blindingly sharp agony seemed to have faded. She opened her eyes to see a varnished pine ceiling with knobby peeled-log beams for just a second before Winston's face blocked her view.

She didn't mind in the least, and a smile spread over her face. "Hey."

One corner of his mouth twitched, but his right eyebrow was twisted in serious concern. "How do you feel?"

"My leg hurts." Despite that, she couldn't stop smiling.

"Dahl!" Rose gave an excited yip as she joined Winston in staring down at her. She tried to shoulder him out of the way, but Winston held his ground easily, and Rose gave up with a frustrated huff, leaning in the best she could with a man mountain in the way. "Quit going unconscious. You're freaking us out."

Dahlia gave an amused snort. "I'll do my best. I'd like to sit up, but I'm afraid my leg's going to make me regret it if I do."

"I'd give you a piece of leather to bite on," Rose offered with an appalling lack of sisterly empathy, "but everything I have on is synthetic." She glanced down at herself and made a face. "And filthy. I could go get you a stick?"

"Thanks," Dahlia said dryly. "But I think leather and/or stick-biting is just for digging bullets out without anesthesia or something." She felt a shock of horror and stared at them. "I don't need a bullet dug out of me, do I?"

"No. It passed through," Winston said in his flatly reassuring way.

Letting out a relieved breath, she reached toward him. "Help me sit up?"

"Not if you're going to pass out again."

"I won't." *Hopefully.* When he didn't move, she gave him begging eyes, keeping her arms extended. "Please? I'm already sick of that ceiling."

He held his ground for two and a half seconds before he folded. "Fine." Without giving her a chance to do any mental preparation, he caught her under the arms and gently hauled her up into a sitting position.

Black spots swirled across her vision, but she swallowed down the bile that'd risen in her throat and managed to stay conscious. "See?" she said proudly once those pesky splotches had cleared. "Told you I wouldn't pass out."

"How close were you?" Winston asked.

"Really close."

"Figured," Rose chimed in. "Your eyes did a super-creepy roll-up-into-your-head kind of thing."

Waving a hand to dismiss her sister's comment, she looked around what she assumed was the forest ranger office. It was really small and cute, with a visitor desk holding lots of pamphlets, glossy pine floor, and framed wildlife photos and maps on the walls. She was sitting on a tweedy couch that had seen plenty of use, but Dahlia very much appreciated it after several days of camping and the terrifying events of that night. "Rose."

"Yes?" Her sister cocked her head in that way she did, and Dahlia felt tears burn the backs of her eyes. Rose's wonderfully familiar Icelandic-yogurt princess face was dirty, and a fading bruise darkened the right side of her chin, but she still looked so healthy and not dead that Dahlia couldn't hold back the tears.

"Come hug me," she said on a sob, and her sister did, gingerly wrapping her arms around Dahlia so as not to jar her leg. Ignoring the potential for pain, Dahlia didn't bother to be careful, instead clutching her sister against her with all her strength.

Rose put up with it for a while, but then made a protesting sound. "Dahl, you're squashing me. I didn't survive the meth heads just to die of suffocation by sisterly love."

Giving her sister one final squeeze just to hear her squawk, a normal sound that proved Rose was just fine and very much not dead, Dahlia reluctantly released her. "Tell us everything then. Wait—what happened while I was passed out? Did you find a radio?"

"Yeah, just now," Winston said. "We got here a few minutes ago."

"Your hermit is a whiz at picking locks," Rose interjected.

"Right?" Dahlia loved that her sister appreciated Winston's skill as much as she did. "Isn't he amazing?"

Rose scrunched her nose. "I suppose?"

As if he hadn't even heard the interruption, Winston continued. "Sheriff's on the way to the lab. Smoke was spotted, so Fire was heading that way already. They'll stage close by until law enforcement clears the scene. Ambulance was in Rockton, about forty-five minutes away, but they're en route." He inspected the improvised bandage around her leg and seemed to be satisfied, since he stopped poking at her.

"Is it weird that I find the professional way you gave that update to be really hot?"

"Yes," Rose answered for him, while Winston didn't say a word, just stared at her with his most smoldering of smoldery gazes. "Did anyone hear me? I said yes. It is weird. Can we get back to talking about first responders and stop boning each other with your eyeballs?"

It was less her sister's complaints and more Dahlia's curiosity that allowed her to tear her gaze from Winston's. "Why didn't you take off my pants?"

"Because I'm here?" Rose said, throwing up her hands as if supplicating the gods to give her the patience to deal with her thirsty sister.

Dahlia gave her a flat look. "To treat my *bullet wound*," she clarified.

"Oh. Right."

"It'll hurt too much without pain meds," Winston explained, his slight amusement at their exchange fading as he focused on her bandage again. "And I didn't want it to start bleeding heavily again."

"Good idea." Now that he mentioned it, the thought of peeling off her pants made her whole body brace for the imagined pain. She was just fine waiting for the nice medics with the good drugs to arrive before any de-pants-ing happened. Her attention moved to her sister. She looked intact, but she'd been stuck in that meth lab for days. "Sure you're okay, Rose?"

"Yeah," Rose said as she settled on the floor next to Dahlia's hip, taking her hand and leaning against the couch. "The guys left me pretty much alone except for our first encounter when they tackled me." She gestured toward her bruise. "They didn't want to damage the merchandise."

"Merchandise?" Winston didn't sit but leaned against the visitor desk instead, crossing his arms over his chest in a way that made his biceps bulge distractingly. His gaze was positively murderous.

"Ransom," Rose explained.

Dahlia frowned. "I never got a ransom demand." Horror hit her, making her flinch. "I kept my phone off while we hiked to save the charge—and because we didn't have reception anyway. Did I miss their ransom demand? Did you almost die because I didn't get it?"

She dug her phone out of her zipped pocket and powered it up, relieved to see it was still functional and had enough of a charge to start, at least.

"Settle, Dahl." Rose patted the air with her free hand while giving her sister a reassuring squeeze with the other. "You weren't the target."

"I wasn't?" Now she was even more confused. "But no one else would pay it."

"Rude." Despite the word, Rose's tone was teasing. Only she would be relaxed enough to joke after being kidnapped and held in a meth lab. "True, but still rude. The guy at the gas station saw my name on my credit card. I could tell he recognized me. He figured he'd make some money by kidnapping me and sending a ransom demand to Dad. *They* didn't know they'd never see a dime. It was a bluff."

"A bluff." Dahlia was vacillating between terror and fury and relief, and it wasn't pleasant. "What about when they got sick of waiting for money that wasn't coming? What would they do to you then?"

Rose waved a hand, brushing off any concern about her potential death and dismemberment at the hands of angry meth dealers. "I just had to delay long enough for you to find me."

Dahlia blinked. "You knew I'd find you? *I* didn't even know I'd find you."

"Of course." There was no doubt in her sister's voice. "I sent you that 911 text. I knew you'd come rescue me."

Unable to find a response to that stupidly optimistic belief, Dahlia just threw up her hands. "You're ridiculous. I love you like a sister, but you're a complete doofus."

"I *am* your sister." Rose was laughing now. "And I love you too."

Her phone beeped with incoming texts, and she zeroed in on the one from their father.

Got ransom demand for Rose very amateur Im sure you can handle the situation

"Wow," Dahlia said. When Winston leaned closer, his eyebrow arched in question, she held her phone up so he could read the screen. He actually growled at the text.

"What?" Rose asked.

"Dad's text grammar and punctuation is really poor."

"He told you to deal with it?" Rose guessed flatly and without surprise.

"Yep." Dahlia wasn't about to hide their father's callousness from her sister.

"You weren't kidding," Winston said, giving her hand a gentle squeeze. "Your family—except for Rose—are objectively awful."

"Told you." With a grimace, she turned her phone off again and refocused on her sister. "How'd they grab you, anyway?"

Rose cleared her throat, shifting uncomfortably. "Yeah, so that wasn't my best moment. Creepy gas-station dude told me this trail led to a lake where tons of wildlife would come to drink. He said it was a local secret, so the hordes of tourists wouldn't drive them all away. Figured that's what the trailhead barricade was all about. I had to go see the animals, of course."

"Of course," Dahlia repeated, giving her sister a look.

Rose continued as if there'd been no interruption. "I followed it to a building that didn't belong, so I checked it out, tried to look in a few windows. The gas-station doink and his buddies must've spotted me in the security cameras. They chased me, and I managed to write that text before they finally tackled me. I slipped the phone into the doink's coat pocket while I struggled. They kept talking about how rich they were going to be once they got the ransom. Pretty sure I was their first and only kidnapping attempt."

"How'd you get your bruise?" Dahlia felt fury surging at the thought of anyone hurting Rose.

"Remember how I mentioned that they tackled me?" she asked, looking much too calm about the whole thing. It wasn't that Dahlia wanted her sister to be in hysterics, but she was feeling quite rageful and wanted some company in her vengeance-focused mode. "Whacked my chin on the ground when I went down."

"Ow. Poor Rosie." Dahlia squeezed her hand.

"Thanks." Tipping her head back against her sister's hip, Rose closed her eyes. "I feel like I could sleep for a week. This was the most unrelaxing vacation I've ever been on."

"Likewise," Dahlia said, but then had to elaborate for honesty's sake as she met Winston's intense gaze. "In a weird way, though—and I only say this because you're not dead, Rosie—this was the best vacation I've ever taken."

The corner of Winston's mouth quirked up, and she had further confirmation that what she'd just said was the truth.

"Yeah," she said quietly. "Totally worth a bullet hole in my leg."

SIXTEEN

A BUZZING SOUND MADE DAHLIA jump and then groan as her leg protested the quick movement. Although a lot better than it had been a week before, the injury still kept her stationary on Winston's amazing couch—that she'd quickly claimed as hers—as he brought her snacks and covered her in cozy throws like some kind of hot, surly, overly attentive butler.

"You okay?" he asked, his concerned gaze fixed on her.

"Yeah. What was that sound?" she asked, accustomed to him asking if she was okay at least a hundred and eighty times a day. "Did someone fall into one of your booby traps?"

"Front gate." He checked his smartwatch with a frown. "It's a Howling Falls Police SUV. You expecting them?"

"No." She craned her neck but was too far away to see his watch screen. "I haven't talked to anyone since the Forest Service office a week ago. Have you committed any crimes recently?"

He gave her an even look. "None that they know about."

She grinned at that. "You going to let them in?"

"I suppose," he grumbled, making her giggle again. She'd been a little worried that her connection with Winston had just been because of the intense situation and that they'd quickly start to annoy each other, but that hadn't been the case. She liked him more and more each day, and she was fully in love with his couch. "Stay here."

Before she could even lift her eyebrows at his high-handedness—and also his ridiculousness, because where was she going to go on her crutches?—he was gone. She put her book down on the coffee table reluctantly, since she'd been fully immersed before the interruption. For the past five days, since she'd been discharged from the hospital and Winston had bundled her into his home, she'd been working her way through the books he'd written, and it was fascinating reading. She would've found them entertaining even if she hadn't known Winston, but her favorite part was the bits of himself he'd left in each manuscript, a bread-crumb trail of insights into the mind of Winston Dane that she gathered up and held close to her heart. She was ridiculously infatuated, and it didn't help that he brought her ice cream and made a perfect grilled cheese sandwich that he cut into triangles for her.

Knowing personally how long it took to get from the main gate to the house, she gave in to temptation and picked up the book again, continuing to read about the adventures of the hapless Mr. Rupert Wattlethorpe until a woman's voice pulled her once more from her reading. Winston led the police officer inside, giving Dahlia the intent head-to-toe once-over he always did, even—like now—when it'd just been a few minutes since he'd last seen her. As usual, it gave her a warm feeling of security that he was checking to make sure that she was okay.

Pulling her attention away from Winston with some effort, Dahlia studied the cop, whose South Asian features looked familiar. "Oh!" she said as she made the connection. "Officer Bitts from the Yodel Tavern. With the gorgeous pores."

The cop dipped her chin in a nod. "That's right. How's the leg, Ms. Weathersby?"

"Dahlia, please." Being called Ms. Weathersby made her feel like she was back at school, being reprimanded by a disapproving principal after she conspired with the cheerleaders to alter their uniforms to something *much* more fashionable and flattering without first getting the permission from the higher-ups. "What can we do for you, Officer?"

Bitts looked a bit uncomfortable, which sparked Dahlia's curiosity, since the cop had seemed fairly unflappable the last time they'd met. "I just finished my shift and was in the area, so I thought I'd give you an update on the meth lab situation."

"Oh, good." Dahlia settled back against the arm of the couch, wishing for popcorn, since that would be the perfect accompaniment to listening to the conclusion of their adventure. "Rose was just asking me if I'd heard anything."

"She's back in California?" the officer asked, watching as Winston adjusted the throw over Dahlia's legs.

She thanked him, even though the blanket had seemed just fine to her before he'd messed with it. "Yeah, she went home. She decided she'd had enough of Howling Falls—the falls and the town—for a while."

"Understandable."

There was a pause that for some reason felt awkward, and Dahlia *hated* awkward pauses. It also ramped up her curiosity, because why would giving them an update on the case make Bitts so uneasy?

"Want to sit down?" she asked, gesturing toward a chair adjacent to the couch.

With a side glance at Winston, the cop settled on the edge of the seat, rubbing her knuckles with the opposite thumb. Winston took up a crossed-arm pose next to Dahlia's couch, which wasn't a surprise. Unless he was feeling extraordinarily comfortable, he wasn't a big one for sitting around other people. Or talking. Or doing anything but scowling, honestly.

It occurred to Dahlia what might be making Officer Bitts uncomfortable. "The guy's dead, isn't he? Or blinded? Oh man, I blinded someone." She immediately felt swamped by an unfamiliar medley of emotions. She'd been in the process of saving her sister, but she hadn't really explored other, less violent ways to get Rose out of the lab. Sure, the bathroom fire had given them a few extra moments to escape, but had that been worth someone's sight? Or life? Should she have gone back in and given him first aid?

"What guy?" Bitts asked after a pause.

Dahlia studied her, but she seemed honestly confused. "The last guy in the lab—the dark-haired one. He tried to follow us into the bathroom, so we turned it into a flamethrower."

"What did you turn into a flamethrower?"

"The room." As the cop continued to blink at her as if she

was struggling to follow the conversation, Dahlia tried to be more specific. "Some steam to carry the acetone fumes and matches taped to the door, and voilà—real-life firewall." Her bottom lip wanted to tremble, so she bit the corner of it. "Is he really injured then? He didn't seem too hurt when we ran away, but the building was, you know, on fire."

"Greg Jones?" the officer asked, and it made what Dahlia'd done even worse. Now her victim had a name. "No, he's still alive and has the use of his eyes. He had some first- and second-degree burns, but he'll recover."

"He's not blind or dead?" Relief rushed in, filling all the hollow spots that'd just opened at the thought that she was now a killer.

"Neither." Bitts looked amused, so Dahlia had to believe she wasn't lying. "He grabbed as much money and product as he could, which just meant we found all that on him when we stopped him before he even made it a mile."

"And Fletcher?"

"Concussed, but he should be fine. All five of them are being held in the county jail on an assortment of kidnapping, drug, attempted murder, and assault charges."

"Well, that's...good?" Dahlia frowned at the cop. "So if everything is as it should be, why are you so twitchy?"

Bitts frowned before she stood up to pace. Dahlia watched her cross the room twice before she came to a stop, faced Dahlia, and firmed up her jaw. "I came here to ask you about your business."

"My business?" Dahlia shot Winston a confused look,

but he just gave her the tiniest shrug and eyebrow lift. "What about it?"

"You're going to be staying here for a while, right?" Bitts asked abruptly.

Dahlia snuck another glance at Winston. Now she was the one who felt awkward. Except for the conversation immediately after she'd been shot, they hadn't really discussed how long she was going to stay or if he was serious about going back to LA with her. With the bullet hole in her leg, it'd just been assumed that she'd room with Winston for a while, and he seemed to be fully into having her there, but her injury had kept them from doing anything more than kissing and gentle cuddles, so she felt like they were in a sort of relationship limbo as she recovered. She realized that the cop was waiting for an answer, so she gave the only one she had. "Yes."

Her reward was a broad grin from Winston before he quickly shut it down, returning to his stoic scowl. She'd seen it, however, and it warmed her long after it'd disappeared.

"Okay. Good." Bitts took an audible breath. "I'd like to hire you."

"Hire…me? Or are you talking to him?" She pointed her thumb at Winston, who looked even more baffled than Dahlia did.

"You." Bitts seemed more at ease now that she'd gotten the words out, but Dahlia was still in the dark about what the officer wanted her to do for money. "I need a makeover."

Dahlia blinked at the cop for a full four and a quarter seconds before grinning and trying to swing her legs down so she could stand. Her injured leg immediately reminded her of why that would be a bad idea, and she sucked in a pained breath.

"What are you doing?" Winston scolded, hurrying to move her legs back onto the couch and tuck the throw around them again. "You're going to tear your stitches and start the bleeding again."

"Once," muttered Dahlia, although she submitted to his fussing and settled back against the arm of the couch. "I tore my stitches *one* time."

"Once is too many times." His scowl dug deep grooves between his eyebrows, and her annoyance slipped away like water through her fingers. "Why are you smiling?"

"Because I love you," she said easily, so confident that her words were true that she didn't even have any anxiety saying them.

Winston froze, turning into a statue as he stared at her with wide eyes.

Taking pity on him, she reached out and patted his immobile arm, giving herself a moment to admire the muscles under his sleeve. "We'll talk about this later. Right now, can you get me a notebook and pen?"

He made a strangled sound, and she had to bite back a laugh.

"Paper?" she urged. "Writing utensil?" When he still didn't move, she shifted like she was about to get up again.

"Don't!" He jerked out of his immobile state, one hand landing on her calf and the other on her hip. "I'll get them. You be still. Don't move."

"I won't," she promised, keeping her expression so serious

that she was afraid the affectionate laugh would burst from all her orifices. He was too sweet—and entirely predictable in his protective instincts. As soon as he was dispatched, she turned back to the officer—who had frozen in place, too, as if trying to become invisible through the power of sheer discomfort—with a grin. Her stomach was bubbling with excitement. As much as she'd loved her quiet week of healing and how little she'd regretted the time spent to find Rose, she'd missed her work. Now, a new challenge had literally walked in the front door, and she was more than ready for it. "Okay, Officer. Take a seat, and let's talk about you."

Warily, Bitts returned to her chair. Straightening her shoulders, she met Dahlia's gaze. "First of all, my name's Hayley."

"So tell me, Hayley…" Dahlia leaned as far forward as she could without overbalancing or jostling her leg. "How do you want to show yourself to the world?"

"Just…different from this." She waved a hand at herself, and Dahlia took in the starched uniform, the severely pulled back dark hair, the makeup-free face, and the sturdy boots. "I don't want to *just* be a cop."

"Oh yes," Dahlia said, her smile stretching even wider. "We're going to have fun."

Hayley gave her a tentative return smile. "I've been thinking about doing something like this for a while. You being in town gave me the push that I needed." She gave Dahlia a considering look. "There are a lot of people around here who could use your services, you know. Howling Falls isn't LA, but I think you'll be surprised at how well your business would do here."

Winston handed her a legal pad and a pen, and she thanked him even as her brain whirred. She hadn't considered working while she was living in Hermitville, just assumed that she'd treat her Colorado months as a vacation. Her previous years of working her tail off had built her a nice nest egg, and she would be fine if she only worked while she was in LA. It'd just been a week, however, and she was already twitching with impatience. She actually *liked* her job, so inactivity was more of a punishment than a reward. Winston had been a saint so far, but she figured even he had a limit for how many times he'd be her model. If Hayley was right about the mountains being an untapped market, her time in Colorado could be even better than she'd expected.

Putting the idea away to think about later, she focused on Hayley. "I'm glad you braved the booby traps to come."

The deputy's brows drew together. "Booby traps?"

Dahlia waved a hand and tried to make her laugh as airy as possible. "Nothing illegal or even shady. Just a joke between Winston and me. Let's talk about you, though. If your hair could be any color, what would you pick?"

"Black with peacock blue on the ends," Hayley said without hesitating, but then her eyes widened. "But my job…"

With great restraint, Dahlia kept her excited self still. She knew from past experience that bouncing on the couch made her leg hurt like someone was repeatedly stabbing her, and then Winston would pop back in like a genie to growl at her to sit still while he checked her bandage and then wrapped another throw around her. "Don't worry about that," she said with great satisfaction. "That's what French twists and buns are for. Did I mention how much fun this is going to be?"

After studying Dahlia's face, Hayley relaxed, settling back in her chair. "You did, and I'm starting to believe you."

———

Hayley left after an hour, but Dahlia continued adding notes and sketches until she realized her face was just a few inches away from the paper. Lifting her head, she saw that the sun was in the process of setting, and the room was gray with dusky light. Peering through the dimness, she smiled to see Winston leaning against the wall, his arms crossed as he studied her.

"Hi," she said, putting down the pad and pen so she could stretch.

Pushing off the wall, he turned on the lamp next to her and then scooped her off the couch. Careful of her leg, he seated himself on the sofa and lowered her onto his lap.

Dahlia leaned against him with a contented hum. "Hi," she said again, although this time it was more of a purr.

His chest rumbled with a chuckle as he gave her a welcoming squeeze.

"Did you hear that?" she asked.

"Which part? That Officer Bitts should wear jewel tones or that she has dramatic cheekbones?"

"Both are true, but I was talking about how she said the mountain folk around here are hungry for my services."

"Don't remember her saying it *exactly* like that." His tone was amused.

She poked him, but gently, since she knew he would win in a playful tussle. "I haven't really considered working while I'm here."

"Why not?"

She shrugged a little, playing with a button on his shirt. "Didn't think there'd be a market for what I do. I figured most people around here would be like you—hermit-y and happy in their flannels."

He grunted. "Even I liked it when you did all that." He made a circling motion around his face, which made her snicker.

"That's because you wanted me to touch you."

"Yeah," he agreed readily. "But I was impressed with the end result."

"Thanks." She rested her head on his chest, and her twirling thoughts quieted, contentment settling like a warm blanket over her. "You should market yourself as a meditation aid."

"You want me to rent out my lap?"

She frowned. "Never mind. Bad idea."

He chuckled again, and the vibration against her cheek made her smile. They sat in peaceful silence for a few minutes until Winston spoke. "I talked to an old buddy of mine, Jack, who moved to LA a few years ago."

She lifted her head. "Oh, good! You'll have friends then. I was kind of worried about you meeting people, since, you know, you tend toward hermit-y-ness."

He rolled his eyes. "That's not the point."

"Well, get to it then," she urged amiably. She couldn't seem to work up any true irritation with Winston. She either found him funny or adorable or incredibly sexy—most times all three.

"Jack said he could set up some training sessions for me if I wanted to teach. It'd be different students, though. Instead of military and law enforcement, I'd be teaching individuals how to protect themselves."

She studied his expression, trying to read it. "Do you want to teach?"

His shoulder twitched in one of his awkward shrugs, and she had her answer even before he admitted, "Yeah."

"Then you should do it." Overcome by a wave of tenderness for this man, she kissed his chin.

He smiled at that, one corner of his mouth rising as he hugged her more closely against him.

She hugged him back. "As much as I wish that tragedy with your student hadn't happened, I'm grateful you were here where I could find you."

Resting his chin on the top of her head, he let out an audible breath. "I am too. Scares me to think about never getting to meet you." His arms tightened, but this time she squeezed him just as hard. "I love you."

"I know." Releasing him, she gave a laugh and pretended it didn't tremble. "Who wouldn't love all this?" She waved down her body like she was presenting a prize on a game show. "You didn't have a chance."

"I didn't." Tipping up her chin, he kissed her thoroughly, only releasing her with a groan when her head was spinning.

"I love you too."

"I know."

She poked him even as she stared at his lips, wanting to kiss him again but knowing her leg wouldn't allow for anything more. The temptation was real. "You know because you're so lovable?"

"No," he said, his right eyebrow twisting in a scoffing way. "Because you told me so an hour ago."

She grinned at him, happiness building inside her until she felt like she was about to burst. "So, you're really going to teach in LA?"

"I'm thinking about it." He paused. "My publisher is hounding me for a fifteenth Wattlethorpe book too."

"Or you could just be my kept man. You have all sorts of options." Dahlia gave him another hug. "Just so you know, I'd be into you teaching. That way I'd get to play out a few of my professor fantasies."

His whole body jolted as his gaze grew hot.

Enjoying that intent stare, even though she knew it couldn't lead anywhere for at least another week, she traced a line down his shirtfront. "I'm dying to see you in one of your dapper waistcoats," she purred in her best sex-kitten voice.

"You're asking for trouble," he growled, pressing his face into her neck and teasingly nipping at her throat.

Her giggles faded into moans as she worked her fingers through his hair, scratching at his scalp in a way that made him groan deep in his chest. "I'm glad I picked your lock," she whispered, close to his ear.

He went still, his hot breath brushing her throat. "Me too," he said before capturing her lips again.

Dahlia smiled against his mouth even as her leg gave a painful twinge. Just as she'd suspected, Winston Dane was totally worth the pain of a bullet hole or two.

Enjoy this sneak peek of
THE SCENIC ROUTE
by Katie Ruggle, coming soon!

CHAPTER 1

FELICITY PAX INCREASED HER PACE, pulling ahead of the rest
of the group. Her sisters were reluctant runners, and she knew
they'd be happy to slow to a shuffling jog that was barely faster
than a walk once Felicity wasn't there to prod them on. Weaving
through the trees, she let her mind go blank, focusing only on
the way her thighs burned and her heart raced and the crisp air
filled her lungs.

Despite her trembling legs, straining lungs, and a rather ridiculous amount of sweat, Felicity smiled as she finally slowed to a
walk. As masochistic as it might be, there was nothing like a trail
run to settle her brain. The trees thinned as she reached her back-
yard, and Felicity was grateful for the gazillionth time that their
family's house sat right up against national forest land. Circling
to the front porch, she jogged up the steps and yanked open the
squeaky screen door as she pulled out her key. When she turned it
in the lock, however, the dead bolt was already disengaged.

Felicity went still for just a moment before sliding the key
out and turning the knob. It was too late to be sneaky, since the

screen door hinges had already announced her presence, but she still tried to be quiet as she pushed open the door and stepped cautiously inside.

Pulling out her phone, she quickly silenced it before tapping out a three-word text—front door unlocked—and sending it to her sisters.

The alarm didn't give its usual warning beep to let her know she had to enter the code before it started blaring. Instead, the control panel sat blank and eerily silent. The living room appeared empty, the early morning sunlight just starting to filter through the blinds on the east-facing window. She crept into the kitchen, relieved to see the family dog Warrant crouched— scared but safe—under the table. Soundlessly, she yanked open the door to the pantry, only to find it empty.

Upstairs then.

Felicity climbed the steps, knowing exactly where to place her feet to avoid the creaks from a lifetime of going up and down these stairs. As she reached the top, she heard the lightest of thuds to her left.

Mom's bedroom.

It wasn't really a surprise. That was the room the cops had focused on the hardest when they came with a search warrant looking for the priceless necklace Felicity's mother had suppos- edly stolen before she skipped bail and left her daughters to pick up the pieces. It made sense that any opportunistic thieves wanting to snatch the necklace would focus there as well.

Just yet another mess Jane Pax had left her four daughters to clean up.

Felicity moved down the hallway, trying to keep her steps as light as possible on the hardwood floor. She was grateful for her running shoes as she soundlessly approached the closed door of her mother's bedroom. Carefully, keeping her body flat against the wall in case someone were to shoot at her through the doorway, she turned the knob and cracked open the door.

No one was visible through the tiny opening, so she took a deep breath and shoved open the door, rushing inside to keep the element of surprise.

Instead of jumping on the intruder, however, she stopped abruptly and stared at the person digging through the small closet. All those searches, all that research, all those nights away from home, and nothing...until now.

"*Mom?*"

Jane jumped and spun around, her elbow making the plastic hangers rattle together. "Oh! Felicity, you startled me." Pressing a hand to her chest, she sent her daughter a chiding look. "Shouldn't you be out training your sisters instead of here trying to give me a heart attack?"

Even after almost twenty-two years of experience dealing with her mother's gaslighting, Felicity was still a little thrown by Jane's casual attitude. After a silent moment, however, a thousand questions pressed forward, making it almost impossible to speak. Felicity finally managed to ask, "Mom, where've you been?"

Jane waved a hand, brushing away the question. "Oh, here and there. Figured it was time to see some old friends." Tugging a phone from her back jeans pocket, she glanced at the screen and frowned at Felicity. "You usually train the other girls until seven. Have you been slacking off?"

Again, Felicity was struck speechless for a long moment at the sheer audacity of the woman in front of her. All the frustrating days on the road, all the sleepless nights in thin-walled motel rooms, all the dangerous and life-changing moments her sisters had experienced that she'd missed…all because of the selfishness and greed of the person who'd given birth to her and her sisters.

Something snapped inside her, and the last strands of guilt for hunting her own mother like she was just another skip slipped away. She reached for Jane's wrist, calm settling over her as she prepared to take the bail jumper in front of her down. Her mom was taller than she was, but Felicity was stronger, and she knew she could keep Jane contained until her sisters arrived to help.

Jane's well-developed sense of self-preservation must've kicked in, since she took a step back and yanked her arm out of reach. "Don't you dare put your hands on me, Felicity Florence Pax. I am your mother."

"You're a thief and a skip," Felicity stated grimly, moving to grab Jane again. "It's my job to bring you in—plus it's the only way to save our home." Bitterness surged through her at the reminder of yet another terrible thing her mother had done.

Her mom's gaze flicked over Felicity's shoulder. Stomach tightening with instinctual dread, she started to turn around when pain radiated from her temple and everything went black.

———

"Fifi! Open your eyes."

The command sounded like it came from far away.

"We're going to sit here eating Cheetos and Ben and Jerry's ice cream until you wake up." That was her sister Charlie's voice.

Annoyance gave her that extra push she needed to raise her weighted eyelids. The bright light felt like a laser cutting directly into her brain, and she squeezed her eyes closed again with a groan.

"I knew that would work." Charlie's voice was filled with satisfaction. "She'd come back from the dead to keep us from eating junk food."

"Thank you, baby Jesus," Molly said on a long exhale from directly above Felicity. "I'm really glad you didn't die on us."

Although Felicity agreed in theory that she was happy to be alive, her pounding head made her wish she'd at least stayed unconscious. She tried opening her eyes again, more slowly this time. The bright morning light still sent spikes through her brain, but the pain dulled as she adjusted. Once her head settled on a steady throb, she remembered the cause of her unconsciousness.

"Mom," she gasped, sitting up abruptly.

"Wait… What?"

"Mom was here? Our mom?"

"Of course our mom. What other mom would she be talking about? What happened, Fifi?"

Before she could answer, John and Henry—her sister Molly and Cara's partners, respectively—crowded into the room. "Rest of the house is clear," John said.

That meant her mom had slipped by them. "How long was I out?"

"Out?" Henry's eyebrows drew together in a frown. "You need medical?" He pulled his cell phone out as if he was preparing to call an ambulance.

"No!" By the way her smallest—and most tightly wound—sister Norah jumped, Felicity realized she'd gotten a little loud. "No ambulance. Thanks, though." When Henry, looking unconvinced, didn't put away his phone, Felicity shoved to her feet, determined to show just how fine she was. Her head hurt, but it definitely wasn't enough to warrant a 911 call since that would just bring the wolf-in-detective-clothes to their door.

As she stood, swaying slightly, Molly grabbed her arm to help her balance. "I'm not sure how long you were unconscious, although we just found you, and your text came through when we were about a mile away."

"You would've been proud of our sprint time," Charlie added.

Felicity offered her the best attempt at a smile she could dredge up at the moment. "You didn't see Mom or anyone else leaving the house?" Since four women and two oversized men blocked her exit, she waved everyone toward the door. "Let's go. We need to search for her and at least one of her friends, since someone knocked me over the head before I could tackle Mom. There wasn't a car out front—besides ours—which means they're on foot for at least a couple blocks."

As everyone moved out of the bedroom and toward the stairs, John asked, "What's the plan, Pax?"

Molly didn't even pause before she started rattling off orders. Despite her tension and aching head, Felicity had to smile. Her oldest sister loved having a plan. "Okay, Norah and Cara, you're holding down the fort here. Henry, you stick with them. I'm not thrilled that everyone and their mother—" She gave a humorless snort before rephrasing. "Too many people have bypassed that security system for comfort."

"Also," Felicity chimed in as she crossed the living room, heading toward the front door, "Mom was searching for something in her closet when I walked in on her. If it's important enough for her to risk coming here, she may wait for us to leave and then double back for it."

"We'll keep our guard up as we do a deep dive into Mom's closet," Cara said, stopping next to the couch. Henry was silent, but he took a protective half step closer to her. Norah, looking pale and tight around her eyes, gave a wordless nod.

Molly yanked open the door, looking at John over her shoulder. "Carmondy, you're with me in my car, checking the roads. Charlie and Felicity, you take the forest." She paused to give Felicity an assessing look over her shoulder, "You feeling up for this?"

"Yes." She put all her resolve into her answer. There was no way she was missing out on this search. Her throbbing head just gave her extra motivation.

Molly frowned but gave a small dip of her chin. "Stick close to each other." She and Carmondy headed toward the colorful Prius parked in the driveway.

"Let's take my car," John suggested, side-eyeing the Prius's painted pot leaves with *Weed on Wheels* in large pink bubble letters that decorated the passenger door. "It's less…conspicuous."

Molly barely hesitated before switching directions. "Fine. I really need to get that repainted. Freaking car thieves. Be careful, you two."

Already focused on the hunt, Felicity gave her sister a distracted wave as she picked up a jog toward the trees.

"Ready Fifi?" Charlie gave her a grin filled with anticipation.

"Beyond ready." Felicity didn't even complain about the hated nickname. All she cared about at the moment was finding Jane and finally finishing this endless search.

Before they reached the tree line, the hum of a garage door opener caught her attention. She stopped and turned to see her neighbor across the street, Mr. Villaneau, slowly back his white Cadillac SUV down their driveway and into the road. He paused just to shoot a glare out of his window at them before rolling forward. For some reason, this struck Felicity as oddly amusing, and she gave a huff of laughter as she entered the forest.

"Why do all our neighbors hate us?" Charlie asked whimsically. "We're all extremely likeable—well, except for Jane, I guess."

The reminder killed Felicity's amusement, and her smile fell away. "At least we're not invited to any of the neighborhood barbeques, so we don't have to come up with excuses to explain why we never go."

"True." They'd both dropped their voices as they started moving through the trees, and Felicity barely heard Charlie's response. The only sound was the occasional soft scuff of their trail-running shoes against the rocky path. Even the birds and small animals were quiet, as if everything in the forest was holding its breath.

It was too early in the fall for the trees to have dropped their leaves, and the underbrush was still heavy, which made it hard to see very far in any direction. Felicity kept her head swiveling, her gaze scanning the forest for any colors or movement that didn't belong. Her phone vibrated almost silently against her thigh, startling her. Still keeping her gaze up, she slid her phone from the pocket of her running pants and saw a text from Charlie.

Taking the trail fork toward Bear Creek

Felicity turned toward her sister and frowned, but Charlie was already mostly hidden by greenery. Felicity hated that they weren't in view of each other, but the fork was a narrow one, and the paths ran almost parallel for over a mile. The trees would block the visual, but they'd at least be able to hear each other if they yelled loud enough. Plus they *did* have their phones. Instead of protesting, she just responded OK and returned her cell to her pocket.

The woods felt different without her sister right next to her. Every rustle and snapping twig was ominous now. Her feet wanted to slow, but she made herself up her pace, forcing down her apprehension. This was probably pointless anyway, she figured, since her mom could be anywhere by now, and an entire national forest made a pretty big haystack to find that needle in.

A flash of orange up ahead and to the left caught her eye. She left the path and headed in that direction. Off the trail, she was forced to slow down so she didn't crash through the underbrush and tree branches like an elephant. Slipping around a scrawny aspen, she saw the orange again, bobbing along fifty feet in front of her.

Her adrenaline surged, making it hard to keep each step quiet and deliberate. She fished her phone out again and paused for a few seconds to tap out a message to Charlie.

Spotted someone, no ID yet, following

The orange patch was farther ahead now, and she upped her speed, giving up some of her stealth in order to narrow the gap between them. Closer now, she could see that the orange was actually a tuft of hair escaping a beanie. Although Jane was a redhead, it was too light to belong to her. Also, the person she was following was taller and thicker than Jane, and the way they walked was different, more lumbering than Jane's usual graceful stroll.

Mentally running through Jane's cohorts for a ginger, she winced as the obvious culprit came to mind. She quickly texted the name to Charlie.

Zach Fridley

Although he normally kept his carrot-red hair shaved close to his scalp, the shade of it matched, as did his body type. Of course it was Zach. He'd been up to his eyeballs in Jane's mess since the night she stole the necklace. It wasn't a surprise that he'd been involved in her latest break-in. In fact, he'd probably been the one to knock her over the head. Leave it to Zach-freaking-Fridley to attack her from behind like the cowardly man-slug he was.

Ignoring the multiple vibrations coming from her phone, which she assumed was Charlie demanding more details, Felicity put her cell away. With her gaze locked on Fridley's back, she unzipped the pocket on the inner part of her waistband and fished out her folded knife. Keeping it tucked in the top of her leggings for easy access, she upped her speed.

Once she was fifteen feet behind him, she dropped any attempt at keeping her footfalls quiet and started to sprint. Zach twisted around to look at her, his cold blue eyes annoyed, before bolting away. She gave chase, the thrill of the potential capture buzzing in her veins. Maybe she would've preferred finding her mom, but Zach Fridley had been a huge, felonious pain in their collective asses for as long as Felicity could remember. Bringing him in would be sweet, even more so because he was guaranteed to have several arrest warrants out on him. There might even be a bounty, a financial bonus to the bone deep satisfaction she'd feel.

Despite his long legs, Felicity was gaining on him. She ran in this forest every day while Zach was drinking at Dutch's or committing crimes. There was no way he could escape her now. His back was thirty feet away, then twenty-five, twenty... She dug for more speed, needing to close the gap between them before she'd be able to leap on him and tackle him to the ground.

As she rounded an evergreen in a full-out sprint, her toe caught on the edge of a rock, sending her flying. She immediately tucked her chin and transformed her fall into a graceful dive roll. Using the momentum of her fall, she rocketed to her feet, feeling just a tiny bit smug that her fall wouldn't cost her any time. Zach Fridley was still within her grasp.

Then a huge shape loomed right in front of her.

Going too fast to change course, she hit hard, bringing whatever it was down with her as she fell. Somewhere in the shocking blur of motion, she realized that the large thing she'd run into was a person. Muscle memory from thousands of training sessions kicked in, and she rolled clear of his grip once they hit the ground. Her freedom didn't last long, though. Before she could push up to her feet—or even sit up—he was straddling her hips, holding her down.

Ready to send him flying, she forced herself to pause and take stock. Ever since this person stepped into her path, she'd been reacting blindly, and she hated doing that. She gave Molly a hard time about loving her plans, but Felicity was almost as bad. She didn't like winging it. That was when people got hurt.

She looked—really looked—at the person straddling her hips for the first time, even as she palmed the knife she'd tucked into her waistband earlier. The guy was huge, and objectively hot. His rough-hewn features, shaggy black mop of hair, and liquid dark eyes somehow merged together into a whole look that was obnoxiously perfect in a messed up way. She also knew that he was a total stranger. If she'd ever gotten a glimpse of him before, she would've remembered. There was no forgetting that face.

He was staring back at her, his expression baffled, as if he hadn't been the one to bring her down and then sit on her. The reminder shifted her from information gathering mode back to full annoyance.

"What the heck?" It wasn't the most productive question she could've started with, but she still felt the shock of the sudden end to her foot chase. Her gaze snapped up, but of course there was no sign of Zach Fridley. The guy was nothing if not an opportunist, and he'd happily taken the opportunity to get far away from her. The knowledge that he'd slipped through her fingers again made her glare even harder at the guy who was *still* sitting on her. "What are you doing? Get off me!"

The stranger glanced down, as if surprised to see that he was, in fact, sitting on her. He stood and reached down to help her to her feet. Ignoring his outstretched hand, Felicity stood under her own power, brushing dirt and bits of twigs and other forest debris from her backside and legs.

She quickly gave up trying to get clean and turned to the still-silent giant in front of her. "What was...*that*?" She gestured toward the general direction that Zach was running in, indignation building as the shock abated a bit.

Instead of answering, he blinked at her, making her notice that his eyelashes were ridiculously long. Irritated with herself for focusing on such a random and not-important detail, she made an impatient gesture with the hand not holding her knife. Taking a breath, she concentrated on asking a simple, clear question.

"Why did you stop me?" Suspicion crowded in, making her narrow her eyes at him. "Are you working with Zach?" She almost added *and my mom*, but she swallowed the words before they made it out. No sense in giving the guy information that he might not know yet.

"Who's Zach?" The words rumbled out of his deep chest, the smooth bass of his voice twanging a muscle in her chest, kind of like when she walked into a club with the music turned up so loud she could feel it internally. Shaking off her strange reaction, she focused on his actual question.

She had to give it to him. The man had a good poker face. "Zach Fridley? The guy who got away, thanks to you?"

He was back to just frowning at her silently.

"If you don't know who Zach is, then why did you stop me from chasing him?" She held onto her patience with extreme effort as she looked him up and down. "And then sit on me?"

That got a reaction—just a slight twitch of discomfort, but at least he wasn't just watching her, stone-faced and silent. "You fell."

"Yes, and I got back up again." She narrowed her eyes at him. "How was knocking me down again supposed to help me?"

"I didn't mean to…" Trailing off, he switched gears abruptly. "I need to talk to you."

It was her turn to stare, thrown by how easily he'd dodged her accusation. "You need to talk to me?"

His chin dipped slightly in the smallest of nods.

"*You need to talk to me!*" Her voice went up to a higher pitch, but she couldn't stop it from happening. She'd almost had Zach Fridley literally in her grip, but this random guy decided to plant his mountain of a body in front of her because he wanted to talk to her. "If you need to talk to me, you come to my house or call my cell or even stalk me through the grocery store, but you don't tackle me in the middle of a chase!" Her voice grew louder toward the end, and she sucked in a breath, trying to regain her calm—or at least the outward appearance of calm.

Before he could respond, Charlie popped into view as she ducked under a hanging branch. "Where's Zach? Did you get him?"

"No." A fresh wave of aggravation rolled over her at the reminder. "I was really close, but then this random sat on me."

Charlie looked at the stranger and then back at Felicity. "What?"

"Yeah, he couldn't just stalk me like a normal person." With a final, longing glance in the direction Zach Fridley had run, Felicity huffed a frustrated sigh and forced herself to let go of her disappointment. "We may as well head back. Hopefully Molly and John had better luck finding...um, better luck." She almost mentioned their mom, but remembered at the last minute that letting this stranger know their mom was in the area—and that they were trying to hunt her down—was a bad idea. The fewer people who knew she had basically jumped bail, the better.

Chasing Zack had taken her off the trail, but Felicity had a general idea of where she was. Turning around, she started tromping back toward the house, taking a sour satisfaction in making all sorts of noise as she walked now that she didn't have to be stealthy.

"Wait," the stranger protested. "I still need to talk to you."

"Nope." Felicity didn't pause or even glance behind her, even though she felt Charlie's curious gaze on the back of her neck. "I don't talk to treasure hunters that ruin my takedowns and sit on me."

"I'm not a treasure hunter." From the closeness of his voice, the guy was following her.

"I don't talk to cops that skip-block me either."

"Not a cop." A hint of frustration leaked into his even tone, which lifted Felicity's spirits somewhat. At least she wasn't the only one annoyed. "I'm a private investigator."

Although she really wanted to continue ignoring him, that piqued her interest. She glanced at Charlie, who was being unusually quiet. Her sister was looking positively gleeful as her gaze bounced between the stranger and Felicity. Charlie always did love drama.

When the stranger didn't elaborate, Felicity couldn't stop herself from asking, "A PI? Who hired you?"

"Maxwell Insurance. They insured Simone Pichet's necklace."

Felicity's head dropped back as she groaned at the sky. "Great. Yet another person lurking and getting in our way."

Charlie finally broke her silence with a laugh. "You're so feisty right now, Fifi. I love it."

"I won't get in the way," the stranger said, sticking close to their heels. "Don't you want help prove your mom's innocence?"

Felicity met Charlie's incredulous gaze and almost laughed. "Why would we do that? She's guilty as sin."

"Fifi," Charlie muttered warningly, and Felicity rolled her lips between her teeth, regretting her words. In her defense, it had been a really rough day for her so far.

The PI seemed to roll with it though. "Don't you want help find the necklace then?"

What she could really use help with was finding her mom, but she couldn't say that. After all, they were pretending that Jane hadn't skipped bail, so they could hold onto their house for as long as possible. All they needed to do was make sure Jane made her first hearing in a couple of weeks. Unfortunately, that was proving to be harder than they'd first thought.

Realizing she hadn't answered him, she twisted her shoulders in an uncomfortable shrug. Finding the necklace would just bring the hordes of treasure hunters and cops down on their heads. They'd already had a slew of break-ins, despite their new security system. If there was even a hint that the necklace was in their possession, things would get a thousand times worse.

With a slight shudder, Felicity narrowed her eyes at the PI. "How about you do your investigation, and we'll stick to ours. If we find anything of interest to you, we'll text."

She broke through the tree line and strode across the yard, but the PI dogged her steps all the way to the porch. "Here." He thrust a card at her. "Let me know what you find out."

Knowing he'd probably camp out on the porch swing if she didn't at least play along, she accepted the card and then went inside, Charlie close behind. As the screen door slammed behind them, Felicity glanced back through the screen to see the PI still standing at the base of the steps, eyeing her thoughtfully.

Flustered for some reason, she tore her gaze away and closed the inner door a little too firmly.

ABOUT THE AUTHOR

A fan of anything that makes her feel like a badass, Katie Ruggle has trained in Krav Maga, boxing, and gymnastics; has lived in an off-grid, solar-and-wind-powered house in the Rocky Mountains; rides horses; trains her three dogs; and travels to warm places to scuba dive. She has received multiple Amazon Best Books of the Month and an Amazon Best Book of the Year. Katie now lives in Minnesota with her family.

Website: katieruggle.com
Instagram: @KatieRuggle
TikTok: @katieruggle